KW-554-171

A SHOP GIRL AT SEA

Bath, 1912. Amelia Wakefield loves working at Pennington's, Bath's finest department store. So when Miss Pennington sets her a task to sail on the *Titanic* and study the department stores of New York, she couldn't be more excited.

Frustrated with his life at home, Samuel Murphy longs for a few weeks of freedom and adventure. Meeting Amelia on board the *Titanic*, Samuel can't help wondering what painful history has made this beautiful woman so reserved. But he already has too many responsibilities for love.

Ruby Taylor has always kept her Pennington's co-workers at a distance. Making sure her little brother is safe has always been her priority. But when she accepts Victoria Lark's offer of sanctuary, more than one of Ruby's secrets is under threat of being revealed . . .

SPECIAL MESSAGE TO READERS

THE ULVERSCROFT FOUNDATION
(registered UK charity number 264873)
was established in 1972 to provide funds for research, diagnosis and treatment of eye diseases. Examples of major projects funded by the Ulverscroft Foundation are:-

- The Children's Eye Unit at Moorfelds Eye Hospital, London
- The Ulverscroft Children's Eye Unit at Great Ormond Street Hospital for Sick Children
- Funding research into eye diseases and treatment at the Department of Ophthalmology, University of Leicester
- The Ulverscroft Vision Research Group, Institute of Child Health
- Twin operating theatres at the Western Ophthalmic Hospital, London
- The Chair of Ophthalmology at the Royal Australian College of Ophthalmologists

You can help further the work of the Foundation by making a donation or leaving a legacy. Every contribution is gratefully received. If you would like to help support the Foundation or require further information, please contact:

THE ULVERSCROFT FOUNDATION
The Green, Bradgate Road, Anstey
Leicester LE7 7FU, England
Tel: (0116) 236 4325

website: www.ulverscroft-foundation.org.uk

74000985829X

RACHEL BRIMBLE

A SHOP GIRL AT SEA

Complete and Unabridged

MAGNA
Leicester

First published in Great Britain in 2020 by
Aria
an imprint of Head of Zeus Ltd
London

First Ulverscroft Edition
published 2021
by arrangement with
Head of Zeus
London

Copyright © 2020 by Rachel Brimble
All rights reserved

This is a work of fiction. All characters, organizations, and events portrayed in this novel are either products of the author's imagination or are used fictitiously.

A catalogue record for this book is available from the British Library.

ISBN 978–0–7505–4896–0

Published by
Ulverscroft Limited
Anstey, Leicestershire

Printed and bound in Great Britain by
TJ Books Ltd., Padstow, Cornwall

This book is printed on acid-free paper

HEREFORDSHIRE
LIBRARIES

With sadness in my heart, this book is dedicated to all those who lost their lives aboard the fated ship, *Titanic*. Also, to those who survived and went on to embrace their second chance, despite the trauma that undoubtedly haunted them forever. I hope I have shown sensitivity and respect in the writing of this book — it is meant as a heartfelt dedication to your memory.

As this latest book in the Pennington's series is about survival of every kind, I'd also like to dedicate *A Shop Girl At Sea* to my remarkable and entirely loved mum.

You inspire me every day, and although the last five years have been incredibly tough, you still manage to smile, laugh and listen to my worries with care and devotion.

I love you, always xx

1

City of Bath — March 1912

Amelia Wakefield darted her gaze from Elizabeth Pennington's secretary to Miss Pennington's closed office door. Her summons to the fifth floor could only mean she was in trouble. Why else would a mere assistant window dresser be called to Pennington's executive offices?

She searched her mind and conscience for any misdemeanour she might have unwittingly committed. Could she have arranged the dining set incorrectly in the west window? Selected the wrong country attire for the main window? She swallowed and glanced at Mrs Chadwick.

Please God, tell me I haven't inadvertently mistaken a piece of underwear for outerwear.

Elizabeth Pennington's door opened. 'Ah, Amelia.' She strode into the outer office. 'Thank you so much for waiting. Won't you come in?'

Amelia stood and ran her slightly clammy hand down the side of her long uniform skirt. 'Good afternoon, Miss Pennington.'

'Tea would be nice when you've a moment, please, Mrs Chadwick.'

Following Elizabeth into her office, Amelia failed abysmally in her attempt not to stare in awe around a room she had only been in twice before. As heiress of Bath's finest department store, Elizabeth's office was wonderfully opulent. The huge ornate desk stretched along a good portion of the back wall, the row of sash windows behind letting in the hazy March sunshine. A plush seating area was arranged on one side of the room, with four huge plinths in each corner holding vases filled to bursting with vibrant flowers.

'Take a seat, Amelia.' Elizabeth's green eyes were kind as she gestured towards one of the chairs in front of her desk. 'There's no need to look quite so afraid, you know.'

Amelia slowly lowered into the chair. 'I wasn't sure — '

'Why I asked you here?'

Amelia nodded.

'Then let me put you out of your misery.' Elizabeth pulled some papers towards her, on top of which lay a slim, embossed envelope. She folded her hands. 'As you know, I have been taking special care to ensure you are as proficient in the design department as Esther. Her baby is due any day now and I have no idea when, or if, she is likely to return after the baby is born. What I do know is that you have exceeded my expectations in every way.'

Amelia relaxed her shoulders a little and released her held breath. 'Oh, well, that's wonderful. Thank you.'

'You've not only been vigilant in your own work but have inspired everyone in the department. So much so that the improvement in their commitment and output is wholly noticeable. Therefore, as things are running so smoothly, I've decided we can spare you for a while.'

'Spare me?' Amelia's heart sank, her trembling returning. 'But I don't understand. If you are happy — '

The door opened and Mrs Chadwick entered carrying a tray laden with cups and saucers, and a china teapot. 'Shall I put this in the seating area, Miss Pennington?'

'Yes, please.' Elizabeth stood and picked up the papers and envelope before smiling at Amelia. 'Come, let's sit over here.'

Sickness churned in Amelia's stomach. Her job at Pennington's meant the world to her. It was her shining light in a life that had been filled with drudgery and service, abuse and, ultimately, rape. She had suffered a history that continued to haunt her, but Pennington's had given her hope — a reason to believe what had happened to her wouldn't always define her. If she were to lose her position here, would she find another job in retail? The mere thought of returning to domestic service . . . the hairs on her arms rose as she sat on the velvet-covered settee alongside Elizabeth.

The moment the door closed behind Mrs Chadwick, Elizabeth lifted the papers on her lap, her eyes shining as resplendently as her dark red hair. *How can she look so happy if she is about to sack me?*

Amelia swallowed. 'Am I to be dismissed, Miss Pennington?'

'Sorry?'

'You said you can spare me. I can only assume — '

'Oh, my dear girl. I am so sorry.' She squeezed Amelia's hand. 'Of course not. I apologise. I have clearly given you a fright and that was not my intention at all. You must know how invaluable you've become to the department? To Pennington's?'

'Well, I — '

'And that is why Mr Carter and I have come to the

conclusion, you can do more good for the store elsewhere.'

The excitement on her employer's face and the reference to her husband, Pennington's co-owner, completely contradicted Elizabeth's words. What on earth was happening?

'Elsewhere? I don't understand.'

Grinning, Elizabeth opened the envelope and held out its contents. 'Here. Read this and tell me what you think.'

Amelia slowly slipped the envelope from Elizabeth's fingers and dragged her gaze downwards. The words she read caused her heart to pick up speed. 'You want me to board the *Titanic*?' She stared at her name imprinted in gold. Second-class cabin. Departing 10th of April. 'But why? I couldn't possibly — '

'It's time for Pennington's to challenge America.' Elizabeth stood, her delight palpable as she opened her arms wide. 'We are the best in Bath, yes, but we are far from the best in the world. We need to know what the department stores in New York are doing. Compare their windows. Compare their staff and merchandise.' She laughed. 'Compare everything!'

Amelia's heart pounded.

'You have a wonderful eye. A wonderful instinct that I trust implicitly. You are young, beautiful, full of passion and keen to learn. I have every confidence you will soak up all there is to see and be inspired. You will then return to us and set about putting Pennington's on the world map. This is your chance to travel. To shine. What do you say?'

Any words stuck like pieces of glass in Amelia's throat. She had no idea what Elizabeth saw when she looked at her, but Amelia barely recognised the woman her employer had described. Any beauty she might hold attracted unwanted attention. Her age went against her so much that she often wished herself older. As for passion? For her work, maybe, but everything else inside of her was in a constant state of detachment.

She opened her mouth to say something, anything, when Elizabeth returned to the settee and picked up the teapot. 'Tea?'

Nausea coated Amelia's throat and she shook her head.

'I know you are the perfect person to do this,' Elizabeth continued as she filled a cup for herself. 'You will have an adventure, I promise you.'

'But to travel to America alone. I couldn't possibly — '

'Oh, you won't be alone. Mr Weir will be accompanying you.'

'Mr Weir?' Amelia's heart sank even lower. The head of the men's department was staid, strict, and if the man were to ever crack a smile, the rest of Pennington's would think him in the throes of some sort of spasm. 'But surely he would not want to accompany me? We work together reasonably well, but he and I are so very, entirely, different.'

'Which is exactly why Joseph selected him. My husband and I rely on our employees' eyes, ears and instincts as much as we do our own. Joseph believes this trip will open Mr Weir's mind to the ways of the world as much as it will yours to possibility. Mr Weir needs to be pulled into the new decade and quickly. He has been dragging his feet for far too long. As for you?' Elizabeth grinned. 'No pulling required. You will perfectly complement each other and ensure the success of this undertaking. Trust me.'

'But just the thought of boarding such a ship . . . I don't think I can.'

'Take a couple of days to think about it.' Elizabeth put down her cup and stood, her gaze gentle. 'I don't want to bully you into this, Amelia, I want you to embrace it. You will have a marvellous time, and what you learn will all be to Pennington's benefit.' She took Amelia's elbow as they walked to the door. 'Please, just think about it. You'll soon see you are the perfect person to see this special project through. Now, could you please send Mr Weir up to see me?'

Amelia nodded, her heart racing. *You are the perfect person . . .*

Nothing, absolutely nothing, could be further from the truth. She had never been the perfect person for anything. And never would be.

How could Elizabeth Pennington not see that? Not see Amelia for who she truly was?

2

No matter how hard he tried to be a better son and brother, the depth of Samuel Murphy's continual claustrophobia grew ever more suffocating. But now, he smiled, relishing that he would soon be away from his family's endless demands. In less than a month, he'd be free.

Even if only for a while.

The fact he wished himself absent from home didn't sit well in his heart or his conscience, but the clamour and proximity meant his mother's small terrace house resembled a prison rather than a home. Being solely financially and emotionally responsible for his mother's and sisters' welfare for over a decade had taken its toll, and now Samuel couldn't wait to be away.

Pushing himself out of his armchair, his smile dissolved as another argument between the women in his family erupted. He carefully placed his folded newspaper on the arm of the chair. 'If you can't stop bickering, then for God's sake take it out into the yard. My bloody head is splitting from the noise of you.'

His mother and two younger sisters stopped mid-quarrel. Their identical, bright blue eyes turned on him and Samuel crossed his arms, staring them down.

'Shut your mouth, Sam. We don't have to listen to you.'

'Because you're the *only* man in the house, that doesn't make you *the* man of the house.'

'Be quiet, the pair of you, and do as our Sam says.' His mother glared at her daughters, fingers splayed on ample hips. 'Go on. Outside.'

Samuel watched his sisters leave the room, still muttering and poking one another. 'Those two need to find some work while I'm away.' He faced his mother. 'Neither of them has kept a job for more than five minutes. I swear to God they purposely sabotage every opportunity they're given. There's plenty of work around if they would just show will — '

'They should be married, not working.' His mother's face was etched with tiredness as she walked to the small circular dining table in the corner of the room and began clearing away their dinner plates, remnants of cheese and breadcrumbs scattering the tablecloth. 'Never in my wildest dreams did I think I'd still have the pair of them unmarried and living under my roof at the age of twenty-three and twenty-one.'

Samuel swiped his hand over his face as he battled with how to break it to his mother that the reason neither Katherine nor Fiona were married might have a lot to do with how much she coddled her precious daughters. No man in Bath was good enough for them. Everything — from housework to shop work — was too demanding or demeaning.

After all, Samuel was there to look after them. It was his job to see them right.

He lifted the teapot from the table, snatched up a couple of napkins. 'Something has to change, Ma. I'm twenty-seven years old and wouldn't mind a life of my own. This job on the *Titanic* could be the start of something new for me. Something . . . '

His mother slowly lowered the plates to the table and turned, her eyes brimming with tears. 'Your job is to continue what your father would've done had he been here. How can you expect me and your sisters to do all that a man can? God knows, I wish I had a husband to look after us, but I don't. We are *women*, Sam. We're not designed for bringing in money and necessities. That's *your* job.' Her cheeks reddened. 'Your place is here, with us. You will go on that ship, earn your money and come home. These fantasies of a better life are just that. Life is hard and it's cruel.' She lifted the plates. 'And more fool you if you think differently.'

He fought the weakening in his heart. 'You think so, do you?'

'Your pa taught you all he knew. All he was happy with. But that's not good enough for you, is it? You always want more. Well, I'm sorry, Sam. This is it. This is your lot.'

'I've got plans, Ma. Plans to get out of Bath and see the world. Pa wouldn't have expected me to stay here for the rest of my life. He'd have expected me to have a family and life of my own by now.'

Sadness clouded her eyes and she sighed, 'Well, he's six feet under so your dreams and plans are nothing but a puff of wind.'

She swept from the room.

Cursing, Samuel put the teapot and napkins back on the table and made for the door. His mother missed her husband more than anything; the desperate despair and sadness that had enveloped her when he died had barely lessened in the many years he'd been gone. How in God's name was Samuel supposed to change the idle ways of his sisters? Make them feel the same responsibility and wish for more that he did?

He left the house and strode along the street towards town.

The evening was misty and damp, the March wind

penetrating his thin jacket. He clenched his back teeth and fought his frustration. He'd missed his father as much as his mother until his memories faded, only to be replaced by responsibility. Samuel remembered a man who idolised his son, taking him under his wing the moment Samuel left school at thirteen. Together, they had travelled back and forth from Bath to Southampton, Samuel working as a docker then a seaman. He'd followed in his father's footsteps, just as the old man had wanted.

When his father had been killed outright by a metal chain falling from such a height on the quayside that there had been no doubt in the witnesses' eyes that Jack Murphy had died instantly, he'd left behind a son determined to do his father proud.

Samuel breathed deep as the recollections of the grief, horror and fear after that fateful day rushed into his heart and mind. The raw emotions had wound through the rooms of their small house, seeped deep into the bricks and mortar. His mother had made it clear that it was now up to Samuel to work and provide.

So, he'd returned once again to Southampton.

He'd sailed.

He'd pulled rope and harness.

He'd travelled back and forth from his home in Bath to long stretches lodging near the Southampton docks.

Reaching his favourite local tavern, Samuel sat on a bench outside.

Staring blindly ahead, he imagined the scene that would greet him tomorrow when he arrived in Southampton. Boats gently bobbing from side to side, the dank smell of the water, the shouting and laughter filtering through the Platform Tavern's door as he and his fellow seamen toasted their upcoming voyage.

Samuel's heart swelled with anticipation and excitement. The *Titanic* was due to sail into Southampton from Ireland on the 3rd of April, just three short days away. His captain would arrive not long afterwards, and the crew would begin to learn more about the ship the press lauded as the most luxurious ever built. A floating hotel. Such a feat of engineering she was virtually unsinkable.

It was rumoured that over fourteen thousand men had helped build her, and soon Samuel would have his first glimpse and tour before they set sail on the 10th of April.

He smiled.

The *Titanic* represented days, possibly weeks, of freedom. His chance to say goodbye to his responsibilities, to culpability, to expectation from his family and finally live his own life. For a while, at least. He would send money home and live the days he was away as though they were his last. Lord only knew when such an opportunity would present itself again.

'Hey, Murphy. What are you doing sitting out here on your own?'

Samuel turned and greeted his friend and fellow seaman, Archie More. 'Just thinking about what the next few weeks hold for us.'

Archie grinned and lifted his half-filled glass in a toast. 'America, my friend.'

Samuel laughed. 'The ship will be like nothing we've ever seen before. They say the first-class decks are furnished better than a five-star hotel. God knows the types we're going to come in contact with.'

Archie snorted. 'You really think any of us will be

allowed near that lot? It will only be the stewards and such-like speaking to them.'

'Then I'll make myself known to the second-class passengers. How about that?'

Archie shrugged. 'Don't see the need myself. It's the experience and the chance to see the other side of the world that appeals to me. Not the people onboard.'

Samuel turned away and breathed deep, anticipation bubbling inside him. 'People are everything. It's who we meet, who we come to know and who we love that makes the world go around. I intend to get to know as many people as I can on this voyage. I want to know how the other half lives. I want to know what this world has to offer because, the one thing I'm sure of, there is more out there than Bath and Southampton.

3

In the back room of Pennington's men's department, Amelia stood at a table and met the eyes of her colleagues. George Weir, Mrs Woolden, the head of the ladies' department, and design department assistant, Ruby Taylor — each watched her with varying degrees of attention.

Tightly clenching her new window design, Amelia steadfastly ignored the derision in Mr Weir's eyes. It mattered so much to her that this design went ahead as she'd planned. Elizabeth had never before given her a free hand on the main window and this design was special — to celebrate the launch of the *Titanic*. It would almost certainly draw an infinite amount of attention. Especially considering how the store had been advertising its unveiling for the last month.

She cleared her throat. 'So, with just two weeks until the *Titanic* departs, it's time to start erecting the new window display. All the plans are in place and the merchandise selected, so I think it's safe to say we can have everything ready in two days' time.'

Mr Weir crossed his arms. 'I understand Miss Pennington would like an equal amount of space given to menswear, Miss Wakefield. I hope you have taken that into account . . . *this* time.'

'I have.' She fought to keep her smile in place, lest her nerves showed. 'I think you'll all be pleased with the design.'

Mrs Woolden smiled. 'I'm sure we will. Why don't we take a look, dear?'

Amelia glanced at Ruby who nodded, the younger girl's blue eyes unreadable. Although Ruby was a skilled seamstress, her often aloof manner meant she had few friends at Pennington's — something Amelia had tried, and failed, to help her rectify. There only seemed to be one person who had broken through Ruby's detachment and that was Victoria Lark who worked in Accessories.

Refusing to be party to the shop floor gossip circulating about the true nature of the two women's relationship, Amelia had neither uncovered its credence, nor cared to further speculate. To her mind, whatever went on between Ruby and Victoria was no one else's business.

Unrolling the design, Amelia smoothed it out on the table, taking some paperweights to secure the corners. 'I thought we could have an image of the ship on the backboard and then a selection of mannequins showing clothes suitable for first-class passengers, right through to third. From Accessories, we could make use of hats, shoes, parasols. From Jewellery, we could have the women wearing — '

'If I might interrupt . . .' Mr Weir peered over his half-rimmed spectacles at the design, his expression reminiscent of a bulldog chewing a wasp. 'For all Miss Pennington's insistence we are a store for everyone, I really can't believe she would want third-class passengers represented in our main window. Isn't such a notion profoundly insensitive? The *Titanic* is a ship of prestige, Miss Wakefield. Something of wonder and excitement. How would anyone travelling third class be able to afford the clothes you intend displaying?'

'That is exactly my point. We'll display clothes affordable to all.'

He arched an eyebrow, his brown eyes shadowed with annoyance. 'Isn't it myself and Mrs Woolden that Miss Pennington consults about the latest fashions? Who she relies on to know what will sell and to whom? Do you think she and Mr Carter wish to appeal to people likely to spend more, or less, money in the store?'

Amelia squared her shoulders, prepared for a fight even as Mrs Woolden and Ruby remained tight-lipped. 'I believe Miss Pennington and Mr Carter want Pennington's to be a place people feel encouraged, not defeated. By showing clothes and accessories affordable to every pocket, we are filling people's hearts and minds with possibility. That is what Pennington's stands for, is it not?'

'When Mr Pennington was here — '

'But he's not here, is he?' Amelia's heart raced at her own impertinence, but she refused to yield. 'Mr Pennington left the store to Miss Pennington and Mr Carter. They have run Pennington's for almost two years. The store is theirs now, and they have proven their innovative thinking many times over. I am willing to put my job on the line that Miss Pennington will agree with what I have in mind rather than go backwards, as you seem to want to do.'

'Hear, hear.' Mrs Woolden clapped her hands. 'I completely agree. Do open your mind a little, Mr Weir. Isn't the quest of your trip to New Year to gather information so that we might compete with America? To show that the British are equally as all-encompassing? Amelia's window is just the ticket to start things off in the right direction.'

Grateful for Mrs Woolden's support, Amelia's confidence grew and she looked at Ruby. 'Ruby? What do you think?'

Pushing a stray black curl from her cheek, Ruby leaned over the design sheet, her pretty brow furrowed. 'I agree with both Mr Weir *and* Mrs Woolden. Maybe it would be advisable to ensure first-class attire is given centre stage and the lesser classes positioned to the sides. We want people to know all can be included, but surely Pennington's would prefer the potential of higher ticketed sales?'

Surprised and pleased by Ruby's forthright response when she was usually so quiet, Amelia nodded, happy that Ruby seemed to be blooming under Pennington's employment as much as she had. 'I understand your thinking, but how about a compromise that will satisfy our clientele and Pennington's message of equal opportunity? We'll place first-class passengers in the centre but have second and third mingling together around them as though talking and enjoying one another's company. Why the need for obvious segregation?' Amelia held the gazes around the table before lifting her chin. 'I stand by my decision and would like to proceed accordingly. If any of you wish to consult Miss Pennington or Mr Carter before we start dressing the window, now is the time to do so.'

Amelia had no idea if her enforced bravado was convincing, but if she was to travel on the *Titanic* with Mr Weir, and then spend a further week with him in New York, it was imperative she exert her authority now. Lord only knew how the man would behave towards her when they were onboard. In his mid-thirties, he was tall and lean, and at least twelve or thirteen years her senior. His light brown hair was always immaculately combed, his Pennington's uniform spotless. Just looking at him made Amelia feel inept and unkempt, but Elizabeth's confidence in her had boosted Amelia's nerve.

She could not falter — not if this trip was to be the gateway to the liberty from the past she had craved her entire adult life.

'You have my vote to proceed with your design as it is, Miss Wakefield.' Mrs Woolden stood and gave a firm nod. 'I am confident I have selected garments suitable to *all* classes. Excuse me.'

Mrs Woolden strode from the room and Amelia looked to Mr Weir, her eyebrows raised.

He exhaled through flared nostrils and slowly stood. 'So be it. I will have someone in my department bring my selections to you this afternoon.'

Amelia crossed her arms. 'You won't voice your reservations to Mr Carter?'

'No. At least, not for the moment.'

'Thank you.'

'However, if I feel your display in any way demeans Pennington's, I will not be backwards in coming forwards when I next see him.'

Mr Weir marched from the room.

As soon as the partition curtain fell behind him, Amelia sighed. 'Well, I suppose winning the first battle is a step forward.'

Ruby stared at the design, a quiet sadness in her eyes, her shoulders slumped. Amelia frowned; a tangible melancholy seemed to surround her colleague that hadn't been there before.

Stepping closer, she moved to touch Ruby's shoulder before remembering the rebuff she'd received the last time she'd tried to offer the younger woman comfort.

The recent gossip came into Amelia's mind again.

Although it was not entirely impossible that Ruby was in love with Victoria Lark, the idea of people spreading malicious nonsense that could be founded on nothing was bound to be upsetting for those involved. Maybe Ruby had even heard the talk herself . . .

Amelia softened her voice. 'Is everything all right, Ruby?'

Ruby started and snapped her gaze to Amelia's. 'Of course.' She scowled. 'Why do people keep asking me such questions?'

'I just want you to know that if anything is bothering you, I am happy to listen. Mrs Lark isn't the only friend you need to have — '

'Mrs Lark?' Ruby's cheeks reddened. 'What does she have to do with anything?'

'Well, nothing, I'm sure. But if you — '

'I'm perfectly all right, thank you.'

Ruby stormed from the room and Amelia sighed.

As much as she would like Ruby to confide in her as Amelia had eventually ventured to do with Elizabeth, she wasn't strong enough to become entangled in the life of someone battling with obvious personal issues. She had more than enough pain in her own life to hide or mend.

4

Ruby sat in Pennington's staff dining room and morosely pushed at the remainder of her potatoes, blindly staring as they crumbled in a pool of gravy. Why did she have to be so horrible to everyone? Were her problems anyone else's? No, they were hers and hers alone. Every time she looked into Amelia Wakefield's eyes, Ruby saw her kindness, thought maybe she recognised Ruby's pain and could empathise.

Although, she couldn't imagine what could be happening, or had happened, in Amelia's life that was so bad. She excelled at everything she touched at Pennington's.

Ruby glanced at the wall clock and her heart sank. Just four more hours and it would be time to go home. A time when most people revelled in the idea of returning to their families, meeting friends or the prospect of an evening out.

For Ruby, going home meant only one thing.

Grief, violence and the demon drink.

Her fingers tightened around her fork until her knuckles ached, resentment and anger sweeping over her in a toxic wave. How was she ever to find an escape for her and her brother when they had nowhere to go? Nowhere to run. They were trapped in their mother's house like mongrels in a kennel.

'Do you mind if I join you, Ruby?'

Ruby raised her eyes and her heart swelled with love, her body with desire, just as it did every time Victoria Lark walked into a room. Ruby's fork clattered against her plate as she moved to stand. 'Of course.'

'Thank you.' Victoria smiled, her blue eyes dazzlingly bright, her gaze gentle. 'You looked so alone just now. I hoped I might cheer you up.'

Ruby swallowed and waved her hand dismissively. 'Oh, no. I'm absolutely fine.'

'Are you sure? Only —'

'I'm quite sure. In fact, I'm sorry, but I should be getting back. I —'

'Ruby, please. Will you spare me a moment?'

Victoria put her hand on Ruby's, and she felt such a surge of hopelessness that tears pricked hot behind her eyes.

'Ruby, I know you don't particularly enjoy your time at Pennington's, but I want to change that. Pennington's is such a wonderful place to work and if you spoke to others as you do me, I'm sure you would make friends in no time. There's no need for anyone to feel left out here.'

I could never speak to anyone as I speak to you. 'I don't feel left out.'

'I'm glad.' Victoria slid her hand from Ruby's and smiled. 'Because that makes it all the easier to invite you out with us tonight.'

'Out?' Ruby's heart thundered. 'Out, where?'

'Where else? The Cavendish.'

'The nightclub? I couldn't possibly.'

'Why not?' Victoria's gaze turned mischievous. 'I've been there lots of times and it's so much fun. So freeing. Everyone is dancing and drinking champagne, having a marvellous time. You'll love it.'

'But aren't you concerned about what people might say or think about you going to a place like that?'

'Why should I?'

'Well . . .' Ruby dropped her gaze, convinced people were talking about her singular tendency to talk to Victoria over anyone else. 'You are widowed, without a husband.' She looked up. 'Don't you consider what people might say about a woman being out alone after dark?'

'No, I do not.' Victoria's gaze darkened with angry determination. 'When Nicholas was killed, everything inside me changed. He was crushed to death by a tram. Can you imagine how it felt to be told my husband had been taken in such a way? How it felt to know he lay dying in the street while I was here working and in absolute ignorance?' Her jaw tightened, tears glistening in her eyes. 'I learned that day that life is short, and you should understand the same. Life is for living, Ruby. Not for worrying what others might think.'

'If only that were true.' The shame of her desires, the love she held for the woman in front of her brought a bitter taste to Ruby's mouth. 'People judge others all the time. Every day.'

'And what of it? It's up to you whether you listen or let what they say affect you.' Victoria's eyes lit with happiness once more, her smile wide. 'I insist you come tonight. What time do you finish?'

'Six.'

'Perfect. That will give you ample time to go home to change. Why don't we meet outside the store at eight and walk to the Cavendish together? There are a group of girls going from my department and they'd love to meet you properly.'

Ruby stilled as her mind filled with Pennington's most prevalent gossip monger, Hazel Price. The woman constantly watched Ruby, even more so whenever she was with Victoria. 'Which girls?'

'Oh, um, Clara, Nancy . . . is that a problem? Only — '

'No, it's fine.'

Victoria's smile dissolved. 'Am I wrong to pursue a friendship with you, Ruby? Would you prefer not to go out with me?'

I want to be with you more than you'll ever know. 'It's not that.' Ruby glanced around them, relieved that nobody seemed to be watching. 'I have nothing to wear to such a place. My clothes aren't as fancy as I'd like them to be.'

'Then you must borrow something of mine.' Victoria stood, her eyes shining. 'Come.'

'Where?'

'To my locker. I always keep a couple of frocks here in case the girls want to go somewhere straight from work.'

Victoria's gaze swept over Ruby from head to toe, so intensely, there was a slow pull deep inside Ruby's abdomen. She briefly closed her eyes, shame burning hot in her cheeks.

'Your figure isn't so different from mine. If we were to lay down together, I bet we'd fit like two pieces of a puzzle.' Victoria laughed and slipped her hand into Ruby's. 'Come. Let me show you my dresses. I'm sure you'll like one of them.'

Ruby allowed herself to be led from the dining room, the feel of Victoria's hand in hers absolutely torturous. Her skin was warm and as smooth as silk. She imagined what other parts of Victoria's body would feel like and forcibly pushed the thoughts far away where they couldn't cause her further pain.

They entered the staff room and Victoria walked to her locker and extracted two dresses.

She held them against Ruby. 'Hmm. With your beautiful dark hair and eyes, I think the lemon. It will bring out your colouring perfectly. What do you think? Or do you prefer the green?'

Ruby struggled not to tremble under their proximity. She could have leaned forward five or six inches and her mouth would be on Victoria's. She swallowed. 'The lemon is lovely.'

'Good, then it's settled.' Victoria pushed the dress into Ruby's hands. 'You wear that tonight and I will see you outside the store at eight o'clock sharp.' She grinned. 'See you later.'

Once Victoria had left the room, Ruby sank onto a bench and lifted the dress to her nose. She inhaled lavender and musk, Victoria and desire. What was she to do? There was no way of escaping her mother's clutches tonight for an assignation with the woman Ruby was in love with.

Why would she even want to when the torment of being beside Victoria would only escalate the pain of never being able to have her? Never holding or kissing her. Angrily, Ruby swiped at the tear that had dared to fall over her cheek and quickly hung the dress in her locker.

She closed her eyes and forced the rage inside her to calm.

One way or another, she would find a way to meet Victoria tonight. She would never disappoint her, let her down, or give her the slightest reason to turn away when Ruby so deeply cherished every moment with her.

Her mother could go to hell before Ruby allowed her to snuff out the singular light in her life.

5

Samuel slid onto a seat in the ballroom of the South Western Hotel, Southampton, just as the *Titanic*'s Chief Officer walked to the front of the room. The talking and laughter of the crew quieted as a wave of hush swept over the hundreds of men present.

The Chief Officer looked to be in his late thirties and bore a strong jaw and a stoic presence that indicated a man older than his years. A man of experience, confidence and wisdom. Excitement hummed through Samuel as he waited to hear what the crew could expect once they boarded the *Titanic*.

But, as the officer talked, the focus remained on the importance of the passengers, the care and attention senior officers, crew and staff were expected to bestow on them. How vital it was that the press response to this maiden voyage stretched beyond every expectation.

'The *Titanic* is the largest moving manmade object on Earth. It is White Star Line's intention that this voyage be an experience no passenger will ever regret or forget. The current schedule means we will arrive in New York on the evening of 17th of April and the Captain wants the crossing to feel like a week's holiday to the passengers, some of whom have paid thousands of pounds for the experience.'

Money. Of course, it was all about money.

Samuel looked along the row of men either side of him. Most seemed to be around his age, their weather-worn faces turned to the Chief Officer, hands tight around the hats they held, their faces sombre in concentration, confusion or disappointment. Sentiments that Samuel understood perfectly. He had expected a briefing on the mechanics of the ship, the individual responsibilities of the crew and procedures in case of an emergency. Yet, it seemed the eminence and press opinion of the *Titanic* was deemed most important.

When the talk had drawn to an end, Samuel brushed his hand down the front of his uniform jacket and stood, looking around for any familiar faces.

He spotted Archie as he neared the ballroom door and touched his elbow.

His friend turned, his eyes momentarily glazed in thought before he blinked, his face breaking with its usual quick smile. 'Murphy. What did you think?'

'Not a lot, if I'm honest. I can only presume we'll learn about the running of the ship when she arrives tomorrow. I suppose we still have a week to get our bearings.'

'Our bearings?' Archie shook his head. 'Seems to me all the powers to be are concerned with is making sure the uppity passengers are given the time of their lives. How the bloody hell do we know about what they're going to want or expect?'

'I have a feeling it isn't *all* the passengers they want to ensure a good time.'

'What do you mean?'

'I mean, all White Star are worried about is the aristocracy and the upper class. How are the poor buggers in steerage supposed to have a good time? I don't care if they're aboard the *Titanic* or a bloody tugboat, steerage is steerage.'

Archie frowned. 'Yeah but, apparently, even steerage on the *Titanic* is a cut above.'

'I'll believe it when I see it.'

'*If* you see it.' Archie glanced at his wristwatch. 'What are you doing now? Fancy joining me in town? There's bound to be a woman to catch your eye for the night.'

They walked outside and made their way towards the quayside. 'Don't start that nonsense again, Archie, for God's sake.'

'What? I'm in love with my Nancy, but you're young and free. Why not enjoy yourself before we sail out?'

'Because that kind of life isn't for me. You know that.' Samuel stopped and stared out across the quay, imagining how New York would look the first time she appeared on the horizon. 'I might not have a lot, but what I do have is loyalty, and the next time I'm with a woman she's going to have the whole of me, not bits and pieces. The future is bright, Archie . . . New places. New people. New countries and new experiences. That's all it's going to be for me from now on. Who knows? I might even stay in America at the end of this voyage.'

Archie followed Samuel's gaze across the water. 'Yeah? And what about your ma?'

A horrible knot of guilt formed in Samuel's gut. 'Are my family supposed to be what anchors me to Bath forever?' He glared. 'I'm cutting the rope. On the 10th of April, my life becomes my own before I drown under the weight of other people's.'

Turning away, he marched along the dockside towards town and Archie's hurried footsteps followed before his friend slung his arm around Samuel's shoulders. 'Hey, take a breath, will you? You deserve a bit of adventure and I'm glad to be serving beside you on this trip. You're a good bloke, Sam and I want you to be happy. Mark my words, once we're aboard, we'll be told everything we need to know and then it will be onwards and upwards.'

Samuel tried to relax a little of the tension in his shoulders, grateful to be away from the subject of his family. 'I assume no one, including the senior officers, are entirely sure what's what until they get onboard. The man who designed the ship — Bruce Ismay, I think his name is — and Captain Smith are due to arrive in the next few days. Once they've looked the ship over, it will be our turn.'

Archie shielded his eyes as he looked to the sky. 'Well, if the weather stays as fine as it is today, we'll be away right on schedule.' He grinned. 'We'll soon be out in the Atlantic feeling like kings. Sod the first-class toffs, my friend, once we're on the ship of dreams, we'll be no different to anyone else.'

Samuel smiled, keeping further thoughts about his aspirations to himself. What did it matter that his mother and Archie couldn't imagine what he could? All that mattered was that Samuel didn't have a single doubt that the *Titanic* was the vehicle, the machine, he'd been waiting for to finally set him free.

6

'Are you quite sure you have everything you need?' Mrs Woolden glanced at Amelia. 'I don't want Miss Pennington thinking I've sent you off to New York without you looking your best. The last thing she will want is to have your appearance reflect badly on Pennington's.'

Amelia smiled in an attempt to mask her unease about the upcoming trip and all that was expected of her. 'I will be wearing finer clothes than I ever have before. The hats Miss Pennington has loaned me are priced at more than I earn in a month. I shall feel like a queen. You've been wonderful, Mrs Woolden. I just hope that I bring back all the information Miss Pennington would like.'

'Of course, you will. Your eye for design and innovation is only second to your predecessor's and I have every confidence you will do equally as good a job as Esther would have, if she'd been in your shoes.'

'I'm not sure Mr Evans would agree.'

'Mr Evans? What does Mr Weir's deputy have to do with anything?' Mrs Woolden frowned. 'Has he been bothering you?'

Amelia turned her attention to the dress in front of her. 'Not bothering me as such. He just makes me a little uncomfortable.'

'Well, pay him no mind. The man has a chip on his shoulder the size of St Pauls. As for Mr Weir, he is quite amiable away from the store. Now . . . ' Mrs Woolden held out a hat box and a pair of kid gloves.

'Here. These should be the last of what you need.'

Amelia took the hat and gloves, still concerned about Mr Evans. He was Mr Weir's second in command, and she had no doubt that Mr Evans had been whispering words into Mr Weir's ear about her. The man seemed to watch her from every corner of the store. She would be glad to be out of his way for a while, even if she would miss the store terribly. Pennington's had become her haven. Her refuge. And now she was to embark on a journey most never would. How she would fare without the safety of the store to protect her she had no idea, but she had to find the inner strength to embrace all this trip had to offer.

She pulled back her shoulders. 'Right, I'd better set off for the night. I will see you when I get back.'

Mrs Woolden softly smiled, her gaze tender as she grasped Amelia's hand and squeezed. 'You are a lovely young woman. Don't ever let anyone tell you differently, do you understand?' She feigned a glare. 'Including Mr Weir *or* Mr Evans.'

Amelia nodded.

'Good. Trust me, underneath Mr Weir's harsh exterior is a man who will ensure you are safe and well while under his care. Enjoy yourself. This is a wonderful opportunity.' She inhaled a shaky breath. 'Now, off you go.'

Touched by Mrs Woolden's obvious emotion, Amelia left the ladies' department and wandered slowly along the long, carpeted landing to the grand staircase. She stood at the top step and stared down into the atrium.

Pennington's was a store like no other.

Despite the hour being near closing, people continued to mill around, moving from one illuminated counter to the next. The women's eyes were wide, their smiles stretching the breadth of their faces as they gasped and squealed in delight at jewellery, silk scarves, gloves and scent. Everything could be touched or sampled. Everything a possibility. Everything in hand's reach.

But it wasn't just the merchandise that Pennington's laid out for a person to believe could be theirs. The displays were so artfully executed, they projected a silent promise that no matter how fanciful a person's dreams, anything was possible.

And it was that feeling Amelia drew deep inside her heart where no one could see or steal it. She had to believe that her shame would not forever taint the woman she could have been had she never been attacked when she was in service. Had to believe that trusting in good people, and working hard, led to success and happiness. That one day she would have someone to love, maybe even a family of her own.

Blinking back tears, Amelia slowly descended the stairs, imprinting every inch of Pennington's glory on her mind. It seemed impossible that New York's department stores could be in any way better, but her employers had both voiced fears that Pennington's shine would tarnish for Amelia once she'd visited America.

The notion seemed utterly ridiculous.

She surveyed the sparkling glass counters and tempting merchandise, the huge glass dome overhead, the famous mahogany staircase that stretched to four floors and, finally, the gilded front doors.

Her heart and life lay in Pennington's.

Yet tomorrow, she would board the train to Southampton for an overnight stay before she and Mr Weir stepped onto the *Titanic* for the very first time.

Fighting her growing trepidation, Amelia walked outside and down the stone steps into the street. Darkness had fallen along with a fine drizzle that had entirely dampened her hat and the shoulders of her coat by the time she'd caught the tram to take her to her lodgings.

She was looking forward to sharing a last meal with her landlady and the two girls she boarded with. The last thing she wanted was for Mrs Cambridge, Elsa or Martha to think she was getting ideas above her station. Amelia's mind wandered back to her escape from the house where she'd been a maid and her heart turned heavy.

If it hadn't been for Mrs Cambridge passing on Pulteney Bridge that night, Amelia had no doubt she would have gone through with her plan to throw herself into the river's churning waters. Fate had stepped in and Mrs Cambridge had taken her back to her boarding house, offering Amelia room and board for next to nothing until she was on her feet again.

Something the kind landlady had also done for Amelia's housemates.

The New York trip was exciting, and Elsa and Martha were full of questions and exhilaration but, no matter how hard she tried, Amelia couldn't rid herself of the feeling that, sooner or later, she would be revealed as a fraud. A victim. A woman who'd been violated. Dirty and used.

What if being in such close proximity with Mr Weir meant he would look at her a little more closely and see her for what she was? Exposed her secrets to the whole of Pennington's upon their return? The man had the eye of a hawk and the ears of a bat and there was very little that escaped his notice.

If she made a slip or spoke a careless word, Mr Weir would discover she was tainted. Her body molested and her virginity stolen. What would he think of her then? He already looked at her as though waiting for her reality to be revealed. If it was, he would hold her entire future in his hands, both personally and professionally.

The tram jolted and Amelia blinked from her reverie, sitting a little straighter in her seat. Staring through the window at the passing shopfronts and pedestrians, she fought to get her self-pitying thoughts under control. Her imagination was running wild. Deep inside, she knew her secret was unlikely to be discovered. Yet, sometimes, she longed to confide in Elizabeth and Esther, Elsa or Martha, four women who had come to mean so much to her, but fear of their rejection ensured Amelia's silence — and loneliness.

Trapped. Caught. Gagged.

The strain was merciless.

Hastily brushing at her eyes, she lifted her chin.

She was going to America. She must take this chance to grab a whole new world by the scruff of the neck and wring every last opportunity out of it. Make herself invaluable to Pennington's. Make herself matter. And the only way to do that was to be braver than she'd ever been before.

7

Having rolled and pinned her hair, Ruby critically assessed herself in her bedroom mirror. She'd lightly applied some powder and a soft pink rouge to her cheeks. Small paste diamond earrings, given to her by her grandmother before she died, glittered at her ears and her hands were a little smoother from a sparse application of some cream.

She stood a little taller. She could almost pass for attractive, if it wasn't for the permanent frown lines between her brows. Even when she purposefully forced a smile, she only looked pained. Her shoulders slumped. Victoria's lemon dress showed off Ruby's black hair, but it did nothing to alleviate the nervousness in her eyes.

How was she to prevent Victoria from sensing her lack of self-confidence? If she failed to convey a self-assured woman who knew her own mind and feelings, her dreams of having a relationship with Victoria would never come true . . . not that there was even the smallest chance of that happening, of course.

A bang and smash of china downstairs jolted Ruby from her contemplation and she quickly yanked opening her bedroom door and made for the stairs. Every nerve in her body stretched tight as she hurried towards her mother's screaming and cursing in the kitchen.

If she's laid as much as a finger on Tommy, I'll wring her bloody neck.

Ruby shoved open the kitchen door. 'What's going

on?' Her eyes darted to Tommy who stood in the corner of the room, part of a broken bowl in his bleeding hand. 'Oh, Tommy, are you all right?'

Hurrying to the sink, Ruby snatched up a cloth and ran it under the tap.

'Oh, that's right,' her mother snapped. 'Look after him, why don't you? Who cares less about me or the bowl that won't get replaced?'

Ruby bent down in front of her brother and carefully took the broken china from his hand and pressed the cloth to the cut on his palm, her back turned to her mother. 'It's donkey's years old, Ma. Don't fuss.'

'Fuss? Who the bloody hell are you to tell me not to fuss . . . and what in God's name are you wearing?'

Heat immediately warmed Ruby's cheeks and she briefly closed her eyes before focusing on Tommy. 'A dress.'

'That's not a dress I've seen in this house. Who gave it to you? Got yourself a fancy man, have you? Well, we don't need dresses from him, we need cash. Lots of cash if you want to keep living in this house.'

'A friend lent it to me. I haven't got a fancy man and have no need of one.'

'Is that right?' Her mother gripped Ruby's shoulder and roughly pulled her to her feet. 'Take it off. You're going nowhere dressed in someone else's castoffs.'

Ruby's blood pulsed in her ears as she shrugged out of her mother's grasp and led Tommy gently across the room. 'Let's put a bandage on that and in the morning, you'll be as right as rain.'

'I'm talking to you, my girl. Don't you dare turn your back on me.'

Ruby fought to hold her temper as she took some bandage from the sideboard and wrapped Tommy's hand. 'I'm going out with some friends from work. I won't be home late, and I'll bring you back a bottle.' She stood and pressed a kiss to Tommy's cheek. 'There you go. Now up to bed and get your pyjamas on. There's a good boy.'

Tommy threw a hasty, fearful look at their mother before hurrying from the room as quickly as his eight-year-old legs would carry him.

Ruby took a deep breath and faced her mother.

Her mother's eyes burned with malice. 'You're going nowhere.'

'You can't stop me.' Ruby battled to keep her voice level even though she knew what was coming. What *always* came. 'I'm old enough and ugly enough to do as I please, aren't I?'

'Oh, you're ugly enough all right, but until you're out of this house and taking that good-for-nothing half-brother with you, you ain't old enough. Now, take off that dress and get upstairs out of my sight.'

'No.'

Her mother was across the room before Ruby had drawn her next breath. Talons gripped Ruby's hair and pulled, her scalp burning. She grabbed her mother's meaty wrists and fought back with everything she had, already knowing her plans for the evening were over. Her mother stepped back and slapped Ruby hard across the face, sending her reeling across the room.

She slammed into the dresser and instinctively picked up the knife laying there. Trembling, her face and head stinging, she thrust it towards her mother. 'Take a step back, Ma. Right now. I mean it, or so help me God . . . '

'Don't you dare raise a knife, your fist, or anything

else to me, my girl. You are my daughter and — '

'Your daughter?' Ruby smiled wryly. 'You aren't a mother to me or Tommy. What mother stands by and continues to yell at her son while he's bleeding? What mother grabs her daughter's hair, slaps and punches her?'

Her mother's cheeks darkened as she stepped closer, her eyes blazing with fury. 'Get yourself up those stairs, take off that dress and the whore muck on your face before I wallop you into next week. Go. Go on!'

Ruby tightened her grip on the knife, her body trembling. Hatred burned through her like poison, overtaking the happiness provoked by the anticipation of spending the evening with Victoria. *What the hell am I doing? Mooning over a widowed woman who prefers men? Why am I even considering leaving Tommy with our cow of a mother tonight so I can nurse a pipe-dream?*

Defeated, Ruby lowered the knife and purposefully laid it on the dresser. Her mother had already destroyed Ruby's minimal self-esteem, convinced her that her life would never get better. She would not make her a murderer, too. Taking a deep breath, she brushed past her mother who whipped out her hand like the jaws of a snake and clamped Ruby's wrist.

Leaning in, her mother's breath whispered over Ruby's lashes. 'Your only reason for living is to do my bidding, girl. Get that into that stupid head of yours. You cook, clean, go to work and bring home your wages. That's it. Going out, putting on clothes that look ridiculous on you and pretending you have a life outside of these four walls is never going to happen. Do you understand? Never.'

She shoved Ruby towards the door, and she stumbled backwards. 'I wouldn't leave our Tommy with you tonight for anything, but know this, if you ever lay a hand on him while I'm alive, I'll kill you.'

Her mother laughed. 'I'd like to see you try.'

'It's a promise, Ma. I mean it.'

Ruby walked from the kitchen and mounted the creaky staircase before she gently knocked on her brother's bedroom door. Walking into the darkened room, a spear of moonlight spilled across Tommy's still form as he lay in bed. His dried tears shone silver on his thin cheeks, his overly long hair like rats' tails on the grey-white pillowcase.

'I love you, Tommy.'

'I love you, too.'

Ruby folded her arms, too afraid to hold him, lest she fall apart. 'Our lives won't always be like this. I'll find a way to get us out of here.'

'I know you will.'

'Do you?'

'Yes.'

Swallowing against the lump in her throat, Ruby's eyes burned as she sat on the bed and brushed the hair from Tommy's brow. She pressed a kiss to his temple. 'Ma didn't believe I'd get the job at Pennington's and she didn't believe I'd pay rent on this place for the last five months, but I've done both. I will see us all right, Tommy. It's just going to take some time. Maybe a lot of time, but we'll get there in the end.'

He nodded and snuggled deeper under the blankets, his eyes softly closing.

Ruby watched him until the flickering beneath his eyelids stilled and his breathing softened. Once she was sure he was asleep, she left the room, gently closing the door behind her.

She stared down the narrow stairwell towards the open parlour door where she could see her mother's roughened hands on the arms of her threadbare chair. She hummed a tune, the clink of her beer bottle keeping time as she tapped it against the glinting steel of the knife Ruby had left in the kitchen.

8

Amelia stared around the dining room of the South Western hotel in wonderment. Completed in 1872, the hotel was as beautiful inside as it was outside. The majestic, redbrick building, with its exquisite white-framed windows, doors and pillared main entrance was resplendent. She and Mr Weir had checked in five hours earlier and she still hadn't managed to stop staring or fully close her gaping mouth.

'Really, Miss Wakefield,' Mr Weir admonished as he lifted his water glass, his overly oiled hair glinting under the lights. 'You might not have been in so luxurious a hotel before, but there is no need to act quite so stupefied. At least try to stop your mouth from dropping open over every little thing. Working at Pennington's has surely exposed you to how some people are able to live.'

'I can't help it. It's like watching a play at the theatre. Or imagining how people look at a weekend retreat on a huge estate. The hotel, the furnishings, the people, the clothes . . . everything is marvellous.'

A rare smile curved Mr Weir's lips and he smoothed the lapel of his grey suit. 'Well, the hotel is only our home for a single night, and tomorrow you will have more wondrous sights to stare at agog.'

Amelia returned his smile, pleased with his thawing formality. The man actually looked as though he might come to enjoy this trip on a personal level as well as professional. His stiffness seemed to be abating, his gaze not quite so hardened above the rims of his spectacles. So much so, she suspected he might secretly be equally as enthralled with their surroundings and upcoming trip.

She reached for her water. 'So, we board at half past nine tomorrow?'

'We do. We will breakfast at half past seven. That will give us time to eat and an hour or so to collect our things before we head outside to join the queue ready to board. I have no doubt it will be complete madness at the quayside. The first-class passengers will get the superior treatment, whereas we'll be bundled along with everyone else. So, unless we want to be swallowed up by the crowds, we must prepare to leave the hotel as early as possible.' A waiter approached with their meals, another behind him holding an opened bottle of wine. As the food was placed on the table and the wine poured, Amelia sneaked another look around the cream and pale blue dining room.

The tables were clothed in white, the crockery simply patterned with sprigs of red roses and leaves, the cutlery of the highest quality silver. Chandeliers and glass wall sconces sparkled and shone above the diners as they talked and laughed, the atmosphere one of subdued, yet palpable excitement.

Amelia could hardly believe she was here, sitting among such wealthy people and gazing at such wonderful clothes, hats, shoes and jewellery. Her eagerness to reach New York was reaching ridiculous heights with every new guest who entered the room.

Passengers had been arriving in their dozens all afternoon and now, as they congregated for dinner, she couldn't resist studying them more closely. American accents mixed with upper-class British as men and women conversed, laughed and joked. Talk of the impending voyage and the ship's passengers abounded, but it was the overwhelming sense of anticipation that ebbed and flowed through the occupants, regardless of their clearly established privilege, that captivated Amelia.

It had been so generous of Elizabeth to pay for her and Mr Weir to stay here for the night — not to mention the selection of outfits they had been loaned. Even as Amelia watched people who would quite obviously be first class, judging by the glint and shine of diamonds, rubies, emeralds and sapphires all around the room, she didn't feel the need to hide away.

'Amelia? Do you intend joining me in eating?'

She jumped and smiled. 'Of course.'

'Why don't we talk about the stores we will be visiting once we arrive in New York? Mr Carter and Miss Pennington have named Lord & Taylor, Bloomingdale's and RH Macy's as our primary interests. After we have exhausted all we can learn at these establishments, it is for us to decide how we further our investigations.'

Amelia cut into her potatoes. 'I would love to take some time to walk through the streets and observe people as they go about their daily lives. I think it's important we see if there are any particular fashions or accessories that Pennington's knows nothing about. I'm sure there will be just as many curious things on the streets as in the stores.'

Mr Weir's expression morphed into its usual disapproval. 'I do not believe the purpose of this trip is to introduce curiosities to Pennington's, but rather to ensure we are keeping up with the latest fashions.'

'But surely it's our duty to inform Miss Pennington and Mr Carter about the unusual things we see? We wouldn't have completed what we are being sent to New York to do unless we venture further and delve deeper into the American way of life.'

Annoyance darkened his gaze. 'It is I who have been put in charge of this assignment, not you. You will do well to remember that once we board the ship. I am your chaperone and intend taking the role seriously.'

Disappointment shrouded her and Amelia looked to her plate. What she wouldn't give to escape Mr Weir's beady eyes for a while. To move around the *Titanic* and see how people behaved and interacted. To spend time wandering New York's streets with her imagination running amok.

There had to be a way she could do both.

'Ahh, there is one of the ship's most famous passengers. The American millionaire, JJ Astor.'

Amelia immediately followed Mr Weir's gaze to a smartly dressed man she guessed to be in his mid-forties, his dark hair oiled into a severe centre parting, his moustache prominent, but neatly trimmed. 'Is that really him?'

'Yes, an astute businessman, property investor and builder. I very much doubt we'll catch another glimpse of him once we are away.'

Amelia slid her gaze around the room, pondering who was who and what their lives were like. She had no idea who was exceedingly rich or merely wealthy, but during this trip she would be the ultimate student and learn all that she could.

And not just about the moneyed either.

Whatever Mr Weir's opinion about their employers' wish to focus on Pennington's more expensive merchandise, she didn't believe it to be true. Elizabeth would expect Amelia to return to Bath with knowledge across the classes. Information that could be used to instigate change, improvement and innovation to make Pennington's Britain's flagship retailer.

'I suspect we will see plenty to show us how the other half lives.' Mr Weir sipped his wine. 'You know, I often wonder how different my own life could have been had I made alternative choices.'

Unsure how to respond to such a surprising change of subject, Amelia swallowed. 'Oh?'

He flashed a stiff smile. 'Many deem me to have always been married to my vocation and whereas that is not strictly true, I cannot deny my loyalty will forever remain with Mr Pennington and his store.'

Annoyed, Amelia focused on her meal. Would he ever forget Elizabeth's father once ran Pennington's? From what she'd heard, he had been as dated in his opinions about the store as he was about women and class. She had absolutely no desire to discuss Mr Pennington now or any other time throughout this trip.

'Mr Pennington was a wonder and had a mind for retail that I feel would rival Mr Astor's were they in the same industry.' Mr Weir glanced in Mr Astor's direction. 'Yes, money is one thing, Miss Wakefield, but class is quite another.'

Amelia drove her knife deep into her meat, surreptitiously watching Mr Weir from beneath her lashes. Maybe there was a chance he might occasionally relax during this trip, but whatever Mr Weir's changing demeanour, she would remain on her guard. She had so much she wished no one to discover and mistaking Mr Weir's amiability for friendship would be very foolhardy indeed.

9

As Samuel took his designated position at the top of the *Titanic*'s second-class gangplank, a strong certainty came over him that his life was about to change forever. Thank God he'd been taken on by White Star as a casual worker during the current coal strike. He stared up at the ship. He and Archie were lucky to be on this voyage and earning a wage when so many other workers scratched around for a living. Too many liners lay idle without coal to fuel them, but not the *Titanic*. It seemed she would be untouched forever.

The enormous vessel rose from the water like an apparition. Her four gigantic funnels almost seemed to touch the sky, her decks so high, the boarding passengers below looked like ants disappearing, one by one, into an enormous iron anthill.

Samuel had boarded at dawn, his boots thumping over steel and iron, rivets pushing into the soles of his boots as he'd moved his grip along the railings, marvelling at everything he saw and heard. Noise and steam had surrounded him, people shouting, calling orders, all peppered with intermittent cries of urgent attention or euphoria.

The explanation of procedures and expectations the crew had received felt minimal and, despite not feeling particularly more well-informed than he'd been at the hotel presentation, Samuel's fascinations with the luxury, décor and mechanics inside and outside of the ship had eased his anxiety.

Some of the crew had been directly involved in the

emergency procedures and word passed around that the lifeboats would only be needed in the unlikely event of a 'man overboard'. Two sailors were expected to row each boat, if needed.

The prospect was so improbable it was almost laughable.

The ship was said to be unbreakable, unsinkable, and now that Samuel stood on its decks, he believed it entirely true. The boat was everything and more that the press had led the public to believe. It was, indeed, *Titanic*.

He glanced at Archie beside him. His friend stared down at the people rushing back and forth on the quayside, a mile-wide smile on his handsome face.

Excitement and expectation streamed through the air on a tangible wave and Samuel breathed deep as he clapped his hand to Archie's shoulder. 'I feel like a king. Just standing here like this makes me happier than I've been in my whole life.'

'It's unbelievable.' Archie shook his head. 'Now we're aboard, nothing feels real. Are we really here?'

'Oh, we're here, my friend. There's no doubt about that.'

He and Archie, along with tens of other crew members, had been assigned the responsibility of helping passengers board and directing them inside the ship. Once there, they would be greeted by the stewards responsible for getting them safely to their designated cabins.

'I'm not surprised we ended up looking after second class,' Archie said, peering further over the railing. 'I suspect the senior officers will be in charge of first. They say some of the richest people in Britain and America will be taking this journey. The mind boggles just thinking about what being that wealthy means.'

'It means nothing is out of their reach. They will want and demand everything they fancy. Yet, the fact is, they are taking advantage of the opportunity of a lifetime, just like us. After all, why would anyone who can afford to be on this voyage, not be?'

'Whereas we're the lucky bastards being paid for the privilege.'

Samuel laughed. 'Exactly.' A long, shrill whistle sounded along the deck and Samuel gripped Archie's elbow. 'That's our call. It must be nearing ten o'clock. Look . . . ' He pointed along the quayside. 'Here they come.'

Men, women and children surged onto the dock, their faces raised in wonderment as they strained to see the very top of the famous ship.

Archie walked to the other side of the gangplank and flashed Samuel a wink as he adjusted his hat and straightened his collar, pride oozing from his every pore.

Samuel looked at the sky and the same gratification washed through him. There had been breaks of sunshine through the cloud since dawn and the dry weather looked set to continue. A cool north-westerly wind gave a bit of a chill to the air but nothing unexpected for April. They should set sail in two hours without any problems.

The next hour passed in a blur as Samuel helped passengers aboard, he and Archie directing them left and right along the deck dependent on their cabin numbers. Bouts of sympathy flashed inside him when he considered what a maze the *Titanic* was inside and how people would struggle to navigate the corridors. He still wasn't entirely sure how to get back to his own cabin, let alone find anything else. Then he envied that these people would be able to relax and enjoy all the ship had to offer from food, to wine, to music and entertainment.

'Excuse me, young man. Might I have your attention?'

Samuel turned and met the steely gaze of the tall, lean man in front of him, his chin raised in a haughty manner. He dipped his head. 'Yes, sir. Do you have your ticket?'

The man bristled as though the question was inappropriate. Without moving his study from Samuel, he barked, 'Miss Wakefield, our tickets, please.'

Samuel glanced to the side and immediately stood a little taller, barely resisting the urge to brush the front of his jacket and puff out his chest. *Wow* . . . 'Thank you, Miss . . . Mrs . . . '

She smiled, showing beautiful white teeth, her caramel eyes shining in the sunlight. 'Miss Amelia Wakefield. How do you do?'

Samuel touched the brim of his hat. 'Very well. Welcome aboard, Miss Wakefield.' He dropped his gaze to the second ticket he'd been given. 'And to you, Mr Weir, sir.'

'Thank you.' Weir glanced along the deck. 'Now, if you'd like to point us in the right direction.'

'Yes, sir. You and Miss Wakefield are along the way there. Use the third entrance and a steward will be there to accompany you to your cabins.'

'Much obliged to you. Good day.'

Samuel looked at Miss Wakefield as she studied the windows and railings around her, her eyes wide with wonder and her smile heartstoppingly beautiful.

'Um . . . Miss Wakefield. I believe Mr Weir is

expecting you to follow him.'

'Hmm?' She blinked. 'Oh. Yes, of course. Thank you.'

'Not at all.' He grinned. 'It was entirely my pleasure.'

Her cheeks blushed a pretty pink before she smiled again and rushed along the deck after her chaperone, her dark hair swaying beneath the brim of her hat and her green skirt floating around her ankles.

Samuel barely heard the family that approached him next.

10

Ruby knelt on the floor in Pennington's main window, pins pinched between her lips, as she lifted the hem of a mannequin's skirt. The nervous energy surrounding her was palpable, made all the more intense by Elizabeth Pennington walking among her workers inspecting their labours.

They had half an hour before the window's curtain was lifted and Pennington's *Titanic* window was revealed to the masses of people walking back and forth along Milsom Street.

Even by Ruby's self-deprecating standards, she had to admit she'd excelled herself. The window design was by far Amelia's best so far and Ruby and the rest of the team had done their utmost to ensure it shone.

'Now, ladies, as Miss Wakefield won't be with us for the next three weeks, please don't hesitate to ask if you should need my help.' Elizabeth smiled as she stood at Ruby's elbow. 'That said, Miss Wakefield's design was very clearly drawn, and you have executed it to perfection. You have all proven just how well you are able to work without your supervisor here to help things along. You have all made me immensely proud.'

Ruby inserted a final pin and rose to her feet. They did indeed have a lot to be proud of. Elizabeth's concepts and how she liked Pennington's to be ran were high and, with this window, they had excelled.

'Now then . . . ' Elizabeth looked at her wristwatch. 'Let's make sure any last bits and pieces are cleared away before you make your way outside. I don't want you to miss the inevitable cheers and exclamations when the curtain is pulled back.'

With a final glance over the display, Elizabeth left the window leaving the rest of them to follow and Ruby quickly returned her pins and tape to their box. Giving a final tug to a couple of jacket lapels and adjusting a mannequin's hand, Ruby gave a furtive glance at her colleagues, steadfastly refusing to return their smiles. It didn't matter how much she would have liked to have joined in with the celebrations, she could not afford the luxury of friendship while she lived with her mother.

Already aware that Elizabeth had been studying her for longer than usual this morning, the last thing Ruby wanted was to rouse additional curiosity. No matter how hard she'd tried to disguise the cut on her cheek from her mother's ring, the livid red mark remained obvious. Humiliation burned inside of her as she left the window, silently praying that no one asked her how she had come to hurt herself.

A stiff upper lip at work was possible as long as no one showed her sympathy.

She was already worried about seeing Victoria. Her questions were inevitable considering Ruby hadn't arrived for their evening out. The mark on her face would ensure Victoria wanting answers. Ruby inhaled a shaky breath. She would come undone if Victoria were to sympathise with her or, God forbid, she should touch her fingers to Ruby's skin.

She quickly glanced at her watch and realised it was almost time for the big reveal. She hurried towards the staff exit and through the alleyway to the front of the store. Crowds had already gathered thanks to Mr Carter's tantalising advertisements about the new window in yesterday's papers. The excitement about the *Titanic*'s maiden voyage had reached fever pitch and Mr Carter had ensured Pennington's was also at the very top of people's imaginations.

Finding a spot at the back of the crowd, Ruby peered over the shoulders of the people in front of her, but even on her tiptoes, she couldn't see the entirety of the window.

'Miss Taylor, come and stand with me.' Elizabeth appeared beside Ruby, her gaze warm. 'As someone who has worked exceptionally hard on this project, you deserve a front-row seat.'

Before she could object, Elizabeth had gripped Ruby's elbow and propelled her through the crowd to stand at the front.

'You know, Ruby, you have been a marvel in Amelia's absence. It hasn't escaped my notice that you have been at the store from early to late almost every day this week. Your hard work is much appreciated.'

'Thank you.'

'Of course, I don't like my staff to be overworked, but it's impossible the window would have been finished to such a high standard had you not shown such commitment.' Elizabeth's smile wavered as her gaze wandered to Ruby's cheek for a brief second before she returned her focus to the window. 'I know Amelia is fond of you so if you have need to talk to me while she is away, my door is always open.'

Ruby swallowed. 'Yes, Miss Pennington.'

Amelia had told Elizabeth she was fond of her? Her supervisor might have offered the hand of friendship now and then, but Ruby wouldn't have said Amelia particularly pressed the idea of them becoming closer. In fact, it seemed Amelia had her own reasons for keeping things professional. The only obvious aspect about Amelia was that she had ambitions to excel at Pennington's — clearly something Elizabeth recognised, having sent her on a scouting expedition to America.

Whereas Ruby's ambitions lay in getting her and Tommy out of their home and somewhere safe. That, and the strength to accept her love for Victoria would never come to anything and she was best advised to keep it hidden.

If her secret desires were ever made known to her employers, she'd undoubtedly lose her position on top of everything else she struggled with. Her savings were nowhere near enough to start making escape plans, but she and Tommy would bide their time. One day, they would be free.

Mr Carter looked at his wife and winked before they strode to the front of the window and faced the crowd.

Elizabeth smiled, her voice raised and clear. 'Good morning, one and all. It gives Mr Carter and me such pleasure to see so many of you here and eager to witness the unveiling of Pennington's latest window. I am proud to announce that we have two of our employees aboard the *Titanic* and ready to set sail to America, as we speak.'

There was a rush of whispered conversation and intakes of breath among the crowd before Miss Pennington continued.

'They will soon be on their way across the Atlantic to check up on our friends in American retail so that we might garner and share new ideas in fashion, homeware, silks and satins. Pennington's prides itself on innovation and bringing you the very best the world has to offer.' She looked at her watch, exchanged a glance with Mr Carter and then opened her arms. 'It is exactly midday, the *Titanic* is leaving port, ladies and gentlemen. I give you Pennington's newest window.'

The curtains drew back and the cheer that rose from the crowd was so loud, Ruby could not stem her laughter or avoid putting her hands over her ears.

The window looked outstanding.

A mammoth image of the great ship was spread across the backboard behind eight supremely dressed mannequins, donning everything from the finest to the most affordable in Pennington's jewellery, fashion and accessories. Colour flashed from every corner, jewels glistened, and the hats almost moved under the imagined sway of their feathers, flowers and adornments.

The crowd surged forward and soon fingers pointed in every direction as more and more wonderment was discovered and admired.

'Well, Ruby, I really hope you're proud of yourself.' Elizabeth smiled, before walking away towards the store's entrance.

Ruby stared after her and crossed her arms, hugging herself. She couldn't be sure, but maybe, just maybe, the knotting in her stomach was pride. A feeling that had never, ever visited her before and it felt wonderful.

Truly, truly wonderful.

11

Amelia closed her cabin door behind the steward, walked to the middle of the room and stopped, entirely stunned by her surroundings.

Although the room was not particularly big, there was a decent-sized bed, a mahogany wardrobe, a chest of drawers and a small writing desk with a chair, beautifully upholstered in ivory damask. A woven rug sat atop the linoleum floor and the most darling washstand and mirror completed the interior perfectly.

The room was as grand as she'd dared to imagine, and even though there was a second bunk and she'd have someone joining her, the fact she was here was still beyond her belief. What she would give to possess a camera so she could share pictures with Elsa and Martha upon her return. They wouldn't believe their eyes any more than she could!

She danced a jig and laughed aloud, before slapping her hand over her mouth and collapsing backwards onto one of the beds.

How was it possible she was here? Already she had seen so many people, so many faces, clothes and hats. She had heard accents originating from every part of the globe and met the most exemplary, welcoming staff she'd ever encountered.

If this was a mere glimpse into second class, she couldn't imagine the luxuries in first. She had to find a way to visit every deck of the ship. From bottom to top, she wanted to see it all.

Pushing up from the bed, Amelia picked up her

suitcase, vanity and hatbox, and hauled her luggage to the bed. Extracting her dresses, she carefully hung them in the wardrobe, contemplating again how generous Elizabeth had been in making her presentable for the trip. She carefully arranged her hats on the wardrobe shelf, her shoes at the bottom, before setting out her limited jewellery, brushes and comb by the small sink and mirror.

Satisfied and happy, she left her cabin to reunite with Mr Weir as he'd requested once she had unpacked.

She tentatively knocked on his cabin door, which was just across the corridor from her own.

'Ah, Amelia. I trust your room is to your satisfaction?'

'Oh, yes. It's wonderful.'

'Good. These rooms are . . . indeed, adequate. Have you met the person with whom you'll be sharing?'

'Not yet. Have you?'

'No, but the gentleman is most definitely already aboard. His belongings are well and truly in situ.' He gave a disapproving sniff. 'All over the place.'

Amelia bit back her smile.

'Now, I think we should take a walk and find somewhere to have some light refreshment. I understand luncheon will be served once we set sail.'

Mr Weir closed his door and Amelia walked beside him, barely able to contain her laughter that he thought his cabin merely *adequate*. She didn't doubt for a moment he was as overjoyed as she with their accommodation . . . if not the untidiness of his travelling companion.

They walked out onto the deck and looked to the quayside below. People continued to board, the first-class passengers now arriving in earnest. Amelia stared, once more entranced. The latest and most fashionable cars, carriages and luggage lined the dock as finely dressed men, women and children alighted their vehicles and stared up at the ship.

A rainbow of colours lined the gangplank. Huge, richly adorned hats interspersed with flat caps and bowlers. Class divides and reasons for boarding the ship were illustrated by the slow plod of immigrants, the happy saunter of those embarking on an adventure or the tilted chins and proud gait of the privileged. Voices filled the air and Amelia's heart raced as she breathed deep, wanting to inhale every aspect.

'Well, it's a wonder the ship will stay afloat,' Mr Weir murmured. 'There is enough furniture, pianos, food and Lord only knows what already aboard and now they're hoisting on motor vehicles. It's said nearly two thousand passengers and crew will be travelling. Not to mention the number of tonnes the ship must weigh.'

'It's a sight to behold.' Amelia sighed, her cheeks aching from the breadth of her smile. 'I doubt we will see anything like this ever again.'

'Indeed. I wouldn't have thought Mr Carter and Miss Pennington would consider a second investigative trip of this scale. Come, let us find a drink. I have a taste for some lemonade.'

Surprised once again, Amelia followed Mr Weir. To think he might enjoy a glass of lemonade amused her. She couldn't have imagined him to drink anything other than tea or the finest cognac. His layers were being revealed one after the other and she hoped it boded well that he might lessen his careful watch over her the longer they sailed.

They wandered into a glassed room serving drinks,

the weak sunshine filtering through the many windows, sparkling on every chandelier, mirror and drinking glass. The space was, as everything else, exquisite.

They weaved through the tables and chairs and Amelia glanced around, her happiness slowly faltering. One gentleman after another looked her way, their appraisal of her clear in their staring eyes and quirking lips. Unwanted vulnerability rose and she steadfastly kept her gaze on Mr Weir's back.

The penetrating study she received lingered on her skin like a brand, sending her reeling back to the shame and degradation that haunted her. Her mind filled with how she'd naively believed her past master's kindness towards her came without condition. How she'd thought he respected her and considered her a valuable member of his household, her work appreciated and needed.

Nothing could have been further from the truth.

Tears burned and her hands trembled as vile memories tormented her. Leering eyes, lingering touches . . .

'Ah, this table will do nicely.' Mr Weir smiled. 'We have a view of the deck and the horizon.'

He held out her chair and Amelia gratefully sat, her hands tightly clenched around her purse, her eyes lowered.

Although Mr Weir continued to talk, his words sounded far away as Amelia's pulse thundered. She wanted to leave. Get off the ship. Tell Elizabeth she was incapable of taking this trip . . . this opportunity.

Once they each had a glass of lemonade, Mr Weir sipped his drink and sat back in his chair. His grave expression and the sternness in his eyes immediately dashed Amelia's hopes of him lessening his watch over her throughout the voyage. She picked up her glass, the liquid trembling in her shaky grip. Was it not the reality that men everywhere could change their personalities and intentions on a whim?

'Now, Miss Wakefield, your full attention, please. We have much to discuss.'

She met Mr Weir's gaze as her defences rose. How had she even begun to think she could shed who she really was during this voyage? It was ingrained in her skin, scarred inside her heart. It did not matter how far she travelled, she was Amelia Wakefield.

A woman violated.

12

Samuel stared across the water as the *Titanic* sailed from port and into the English Channel, headed for Cherbourg, where they would pick up more passengers before repeating the same in Ireland.

Then, at last, they would set sail for America.

Pride swelled inside him as he worked alongside his fellow crew members, carrying out their superior's commands, the relative relaxation of seeing the second-class passengers aboard now fading as the job of getting the ship safely out to sea took precedence.

Whatever this voyage might mean to others, for Samuel it meant liberty. A chance to stretch his skills, his experience and dreams. Guilt threatened as the satisfaction he'd felt at saying goodbye to his mother and sisters a few days ago echoed in his conscience. It niggled that he'd volunteered — pursued — this chance with such passion when his motives lay more in the escape than money. Yet, the need to have some time for himself, no matter for how short or long that might be, burned hotter than ever.

He wanted to breathe. Pretend it was only himself he had to look out for.

Even for a while.

His mother's shock after his father died had given way to depression and then a neediness that hadn't been there when her husband lived. She'd leaned on Samuel emotionally, mentally and financially until it had got to the stage that he woke each day with a clawing suffocation hanging over him. Now, he was escaping, and although it felt necessary to his own wellbeing, he feared the affect his absence might have on his mother.

'Officer Murphy. A word, if I may?'

Samuel blinked and stepped back from the controls to face his senior officer. 'Yes, sir.'

'Your shifts at the helm will be split between time on the ship's decks. The same applies to every seaman of your rank. As well as your role as part of the sailing crew, you are also commanded to spend time looking after the second-class passengers and making their time aboard as entertaining and interesting as possible.'

Entertaining? What in God's name . . . Samuel straightened his shoulders. 'Sorry, sir. What exactly — '

'It is White Star's wish that the *Titanic* not only provide the fastest and most luxurious voyage to New York the world has ever seen, but also the most memorable. Passengers are to be given the chance to speak to us. To learn as much as they wish about the mechanics of the ship, seamanship or anything else they might want to know.'

Annoyed that he was to be entertainment, Samuel looked past the officer. 'I understand, sir.'

'Your face says differently, Murphy.' The officer's gaze bored into Samuel's. 'Serving on this ship is an opportunity you don't want to waste. If you prove your capabilities on this voyage, you will undoubtedly be invited to sail on the *Titanic* again. I assume that's something you aspire to? I oversaw your appointment; Murphy and I won't be happy if I am proven wrong in selecting you among the hundreds of sailors from Southampton who applied.'

'Yes, sir.' Samuel cleared his throat and buried his misplaced pride. 'I will not let you down.'

'Good.' The officer gave a firm nod. 'Then you are dismissed until 1900 hours upon which time you will return to the control room. In the meantime, you are to report to the second-class decks and play host to the passengers. Dismissed.'

The officer walked away, and Samuel lowered his salute. As much as he'd enjoyed welcoming the passengers aboard, the thought of bowing and scraping didn't sit well at all. Would he have anything in common with these people? Even the second-class passengers seemed to have a pretty penny or two, judging by their dress and manner.

He should be grateful he hadn't been commandeered to first-class. God only knew how he would manage to keep up with their demands if the thought of entertaining second-class irked.

Striding from the control room, Samuel walked along the winding corridors. The higher he rose through the decks, the more the clanking and banging in the working underbelly of the ship gave way to an increased volume of laughter, conversation, clinking glasses and music.

Samuel emerged onto the Boat Deck which was also one of the second-class promenades. It seemed as good a place as any to tip his cap and engage in some conversation. Fighting to silence the internal voice in his head telling him he was expected to behave like a puppet in a theatre, Samuel drew back his shoulders, pulled on his most amiable expression and stepped to his task.

The late afternoon sun drifted towards the horizon, purple-grey clouds stretching across the sky like lengths of gauze. Passengers had taken to the deckchairs and loungers, woollen blankets placed over their knees and hat brims shielding their eyes.

Wherever Samuel looked, happy faces and friendly nods came his way which he returned, the tension in his shoulders relaxing. Maybe this wouldn't be such a bad assignment, after all.

He strolled further, stopping to speak with an elderly couple, learning that they were sailing to New York to celebrate their ruby wedding anniversary. The more people he spoke to, the clearer it became that New York had been in the minds of many wedded couples for honeymoons, anniversaries or birthday celebrations.

Then there were the families sailing away from England in pursuit of a better life.

He only had to look into the eyes of the people he spoke with to know if it was for happy or desperate reasons they were onboard.

Glancing towards the deck's railing, Samuel stopped, his eye caught by the caramel hair of the woman who had captured his attention that morning.

What was her name? Ann? Audrey? Amy . . . Amelia. Amelia Wakefield.

Samuel smiled, pleased she stood alone and, at least momentarily, unchaperoned.

He looked around, searching for the older gentleman she'd boarded with but Weir was nowhere to be seen.

Clearing his throat, Samuel approached her. 'It's a beautiful afternoon, Miss Wakefield.'

She jumped, her dark eyes startled and then wary as she pulled her hands from the railing and stepped back, opening the space between them.

Confused by her clear unease and lack of smile when she'd seemed so happy just a few hours before,

Samuel also stepped back and raised his hands in a gesture of no harm. 'Excuse me, I'm sorry if I scared you.'

'Scared me?' Her cheeks reddened. 'You did no such thing. I was distracted, that's all.' She looked pointedly past him as though purposefully avoiding his gaze. 'And yes, it is a beautiful afternoon.'

Samuel stared at her, discomfited by her obvious nervousness. 'I hope the delay at Southampton hasn't spoilt your excitement, Miss?'

'Not at all. I thought how the crew handled the near collision with the other ship when we departed was remarkable.'

'Yes. Ironically, the other ship is called the *New York*. It somehow came loose of its ropes.'

'I see. Well, it was most admirably navigated.'

She turned to the sea and Samuel followed her gaze. 'My name is Officer Samuel Murphy, Miss. At your service. If there's anything I can do — '

'There isn't, but it's nice to meet you, Officer Murphy.'

Samuel stared into her dark eyes as her gaze lingered on his, his curiosity about this beautiful woman escalating. 'Well, I hope you might have need to call on me during the voyage sometime. I understand I'll be walking these decks almost as much as I'll be helping to sail the ship.'

She stared at him a moment longer before turning and glaring out over the water, an aura of unmistakable hostility enveloping her.

He cleared his throat. 'Pardon me for asking, Miss Wakefield . . . '

She pinned him with her glare, her cheeks mottled.

'But are you quite all right?'

'Of course.' She straightened her shoulders. 'Why wouldn't I be?'

Torn between offering her some words of comfort or leaving her alone, Samuel hesitated. Neither option seemed appropriate. 'Might I walk you back inside? It will get chilly once the sun goes down.'

'I'm fine where I am, thank you.' She turned back to the water. 'Good afternoon, officer.'

He stared at her turned back, slowly gliding his gaze over her hair, the curve of her neck, down to her elegant hands gripping the railing. Although astoundingly beautiful, an indescribable sadness also surrounded her. No, not sadness. Tension. Like she had been waiting for him to pounce.

Samuel walked along the deck but couldn't resist another look over his shoulder at Amelia Wakefield. It pained him to leave a woman in distress, but he wasn't on the street, in a shop or at a dance. He was serving on the greatest ship in the world and Miss Wakefield was a paying passenger.

Space had to be enforced.

Self-control implemented and instinctive gestures restrained.

Yet still, he risked another look, but this time she'd gone.

13

Ruby stood back from the mannequin she was dressing and eyed it critically. Something wasn't quite right. Frustrated, she removed the pale pink sash before carefully lifting off the hat. She placed both on the chair beside her, put her hands on her hips and studied the range of headwear on display in Pennington's ladies' department. Maybe the ivory dress would look better accessorised with blue. Or maybe green. Or lemon.

She briefly closed her eyes, not wanting to consider anything lemon and have it remind her of Victoria and the loan of her beautiful dress on the night that never happened.

Selecting a pale green hat, decorated with dark green ribbon, leaves and ivory-coloured flowers, she returned to the mannequin, positioned the hat and stood back a second time. Much better.

Humming happily, she selected a dark green sash.

As she turned, the sight of Tommy under the hand of one of Pennington's security watchman made her freeze, the sash falling like a feather through her fingers.

The watchman raised his eyebrows. 'He says he belongs to you.'

'Um, yes, he does.' Ruby hurried forward. What on earth was Tommy doing here? 'He's my brother.'

'I see. Well, brother or not, it's not good for Pennington's reputation to have him roaming around, touching whatever he fancies without a care in the world. I'd assumed him a thief from the way he's been wandering around for the last half an hour.'

'I apologise.' Ruby eased Tommy from the watchman's grasp and steered him behind her. 'I'll look after him from here.'

'I don't think Mr Carter would be happy with me just leaving him — '

'If Mr Carter would like to speak to me about it, you know where I am.' She pulled back her shoulders, her insides churning despite her bravado. 'If there's nothing else . . . '

The watchman narrowed his eyes at her and then Tommy, before turning and walking out of the department.

Ruby released her held breath and gripped Tommy's arm, marching him into the back room and dropping the curtain. 'What are you doing here? You can't just come into the store looking for me. Does Ma know you're here?' She threw a hurried look towards the curtain. 'Oh, God, don't tell me she's here, too?'

'No, she's at home.'

'Then why — '

'Because she's drinking with some fancy man, that's why.' He snatched his arm from her grasp and marched to the settee, sinking heavily onto it. 'I'm not staying there while they're smooching and kissing. It's disgusting.'

Revulsion clenched Ruby's stomach. 'Well, who is he? Did you get a look at him? Someone new? One we've seen before?'

'No, he's new and dressed a bit better than the others, I suppose. But still, they're drinking and she's flirting and it's disgusting.'

'Ma didn't see you?'

‘No, I let myself in the house as quiet as a mouse after school because I didn’t know what state she’d be in. Then I heard laughing in the parlour. So, I sneaked my head around the door and there they were, all over each other on the settee.’

‘It’s enough to turn my stomach.’ Ruby grimaced, trying to think of the best place to put Tommy until her shift finished. There was no way she’d send him home alone now she knew her mother to have company. ‘Right then, you’d better wait in the staff dining room.’ She glanced at the wall clock. ‘I’ve an hour until I finish so I’ll get you a cup of tea, a pencil and some paper. You draw me one of your lovely pictures. All right?’

Tommy’s eyes lit with relief. ‘I can wait here for you?’

‘Yes.’ She winked and ruffled his hair, before walking to a bureau where the paper and pencils were kept. ‘Let’s go, and you’d better pray we don’t bump into Mrs Woolden or Miss Pennington. Or Mr Carter, for that matter.’

Ruby peered around the curtain. Mrs Woolden was nowhere to be seen and the shop girls were all busy with customers. Confident they wouldn’t ask questions, even though she knew there was every chance someone might mention Tommy being here to Mrs Woolden upon her return, Ruby gripped Tommy’s wrist and propelled him through the department and onto the second-floor landing.

The store was heaving with customers and Ruby was grateful for the cover they provided as she hurried Tommy along, heedless to his occasional exclamations about the strength of her grip or the multitude of wonders that caught his eye. At last, they entered the back staircase leading to the staff dining room and Ruby breathed a little easier.

She might not have friends at Pennington's, but she didn't have enemies either. Fingers crossed, no one would take umbrage with Tommy waiting for her and mention it to their supervisor.

They walked down the stairs and upon sight of the woman coming up the stairs, Ruby inwardly cursed. Fine, so there were enemies and there was Hazel Price.

Hazel's thin lips curved into a slow smile, her contemptuous gaze fixed on Tommy. 'Well, well, what do we have here, Miss Taylor? Your beau?'

'Of course not. Tommy's my brother. Now, if you'll excuse us . . . ' Ruby moved to step past her.

'Hello, Tommy.' Hazel offered Tommy her hand, her brown eyes gleaming with curiosity. 'I'm Miss Price. Nice to meet you.'

Tommy glanced nervously at Ruby and she nodded her permission. If they demonstrated some manners, maybe Hazel would leave them be. Tommy shook her hand before shoving his own back into his trouser pocket.

She lifted her eyebrows. 'So, where are you taking him?'

'He's going to wait in the dining room until I've finished my shift.'

'Oh, dear, Miss Taylor. Do you really think it's a good idea to be sneaking around with your family when you should be working? I'd say Miss Pennington wouldn't really think that the ticket.'

Ruby's cheeks warmed. 'Then pretend you haven't seen me, and Miss Pennington won't be any the wiser, will she?'

'Are you asking me to keep a secret?' Hazel smirked.

'Well, I suppose I can keep *another* of your secrets, if that's what you want. Nice to meet you, Tommy.'

'What do you mean another secret?' Ruby swallowed and purposefully squared her shoulders, keeping her gaze steady with Hazel's. 'You don't know anything about me.'

'Oh, but I do, Miss Taylor. I know plenty.'

Sickness unfurled in Ruby's stomach as Hazel wriggled her fingers in a semblance of a wave and ascended the stairs, her quiet laughter grating on Ruby's stretched nerves. *What could Hazel mean? Does she know Ma is a drunk? That we live on the bread line and if it wasn't for my wages we'd be on the streets?*

She glanced at Tommy and he looked back at her with wide, worried eyes. She quickly forced a smile. 'Come on. Let's get you settled, shall we?'

They entered the staff dining room and Ruby pushed Hazel to the back of her mind, glad that there were only a few people present on their tea breaks. She led Tommy to a table in the far corner where he'd hopefully stay out of trouble and go relatively unnoticed.

'Now, keep yourself to yourself and if anyone talks to you, be polite and tell them you're waiting for me. With any luck, that will be enough, and no one will feel inclined to cause either of us further aggravation.'

'I'll be good, Ruby. I promise.'

She kissed his cheek before heading for the door, her mind reeling with what Hazel could possibly know. Ruby briefly closed her eyes. She had more secrets than most. Some more shaming than others.

And to people like Hazel Price, that knowledge would be an endless source of entertainment.

14

Amelia reached for her water glass as she surreptitiously watched her fellow dinner companions. The table of twelve was split equally between British and American couples. The style of their clothes were somewhat different, but she hadn't noticed anything in particular to keep in mind for her return to Pennington's. At least, not yet.

'So, Mr Weir, what is it you do?' The husband of the American couple beside her had a booming voice.

Mr Weir laid down his knife and fork. 'I work as the head of the men's department at Pennington's in Bath. Perhaps you know of it?'

'Pennington's? No, I can't say I do.'

'Well, I certainly do,' his wife exclaimed. 'I understand the store compares quite admirably with Selfridges and Fortnum and Mason.'

Amelia smiled into her glass. A compliment like that would feed Mr Weir's pride until summer.

'It does indeed, madam,' he beamed. 'Miss Wakefield has been our head window dresser for a number of weeks now and we both take great pride in working there.'

'Ooh, a window dresser. How exciting. Do you find your work interesting, Miss Wakefield?'

Amelia set down her glass. 'Very much so. I have learned so much and hope to continue working at Pennington's for many years to come.'

The woman raised her eyebrows. 'Don't you wish to marry, my dear?'

'Maybe. One day. But, for now, my work more than sustains me. Have you been to London? Is that from where you are travelling?'

The husband sat back in his chair. 'It is, indeed. London's a great city. Not on the scale of New York, of course, but good enough.'

'You're from New York?'

His wife smiled. 'Yes, we are. I do apologise, we haven't even introduced ourselves. My name is Winifred Carlton and this is my husband, Marshall. We love to travel, and London has been on our list for quite a while. Although, I am looking forward to going home. We've been away for six weeks.'

'Six weeks? How wonderful.' Amelia sat forward in her seat, her interest piqued. 'Can I ask, how did you find the department stores in London compare to those in New York?'

'Oh, it's very difficult to state the differences. The London stores are better in some areas and New York's in others.'

'I would love for you to explain what you mean, Mrs Carlton. I want to soak up as much as I can about America's department stores and the American way of life while I'm there. For example, what do people like to do in the evenings? Are the social classes quite so apparent as they are in England? Do you find — '

Mr Weir coughed. 'Miss Wakefield, you are asking an awful lot of questions.'

'We don't mind in the slightest.' Mrs Carlton laughed and reached for her wine. 'Your questions are most interesting. I can only assume your trip to New York is more business than pleasure?'

'It is.' Amelia glanced at Mr Weir before addressing the woman again. 'Would you mind sharing in what way London stores do things better than New York and vice versa? You see, Pennington's strives for innovation, and it seems to me America leads the way in that area.'

'It certainly does.' Mr Carlton beamed. 'And I'd wager there is no one better than my wife for you to discuss the merits and flaws of shopping with.' He turned to Mr Weir. 'What do you say to joining me in the library for a brandy while the ladies talk?' He stood and held out his arm towards the dining room door. 'Any talk of shopping and I make a speedy departure, lest I never recover from Mrs Carlton's enthusiasm with my wallet.'

Mr Weir looked at Amelia and then Mr and Mrs Carlton, indecision in his eyes. Amelia bit back her smile. It would be torture for him to leave her to lead the conversation as far as Pennington's was concerned, but there was no way she'd forgo this opportunity. The more she could learn before they arrived in America, the better. All information would prove useful, no matter how small.

At last, Mr Weir stood. 'I trust you know where the library is, Miss Wakefield?'

'I do, but I think I'll head back to my cabin once Mrs Carlton and I have finished talking. I'm really quite tired.'

'I should really escort you.'

'Not at all.' Amelia held his gaze, her tone firm in her determination that she begin to enforce some time alone. 'I am perfectly all right to return to my room unchaperoned. Shall we meet at nine for breakfast?'

He pursed his lips before he gave a firm nod. 'As you wish. Good evening to you, Mrs Carlton.'

'And to you, Mr Weir. Good night.'

Satisfaction and opportunity unfurled inside her as Amelia faced Mrs Carlton. 'So, you were about to tell me about New York's strengths and weaknesses?'

Coffee was served and an hour had passed before Amelia bid Mrs Carlton good night. Her mind reeled with the new and interesting information she'd learned. Hurrying from the dining room, she walked along the maze of corridors towards her cabin, desperate to make a note of everything Mrs Carlton had divulged.

As she emerged onto one of the decks, she noticed Officer Murphy talking to two attractive young women and an older woman Amelia assumed to be their mother. The younger women stared at Officer Murphy with stars dancing in their eyes, blushing and giggling while their mother looked on with pride.

Amelia looked at Officer Murphy from the corner of her eye as she passed. The man smiled and laughed, clearly basking in such unashamed female attention.

Considering the manner in which he'd spoken to her earlier, the way his bright blue gaze had so openly bored into hers, it seemed Officer Murphy had a blatant capacity for flirtation.

She was not surprised in the slightest. His character had been laid bare for her when he'd approached her and suggested she might call on him for his help. Clearly the man thought himself irresistible to every female aboard. Well, he'd soon learn she was most likely more different than any woman he'd ever met.

There would be no fawning and flirting from her . . . no matter what charms he might decide to direct her way.

Forcing her eyes forward, Amelia walked on.

Once she'd safely reached her room, she opened

the door and stopped. 'Oh, hello.'

A woman in her late twenties turned from the chest of drawers where she was arranging her undergarments. She pushed her blonde hair from her eyes and smiled, her startling blue eyes friendly. 'Good evening.' She offered her hand. 'It's nice to meet you. I'm Catherine . . . Catherine Hill.'

Amelia took her hand, immediately relaxed by Catherine's gentle amiability. 'Amelia Wakefield. Have you enough space? I can easily move some of my things around.'

'Oh, I'm perfectly fine, thank you.' Catherine walked to the desk and put down the novels she carried. 'I'm glad to see a friendly face. It's more terrifying than I thought travelling alone.'

'You're travelling alone? My goodness.'

'I'm a widow, you see. I'm travelling to New York to stay with my aunt and uncle who have a farm in Ohio. They've assured me that I will be welcome around the farm and house. They run a very successful dairy and want me to help them.'

'That sounds wonderful. I'm dreadfully sorry you have lost your husband.'

'Thank you.' Catherine turned towards her open suitcase, closed it and stored it under her bed. 'I'm just going to have a little walk before I turn in. Would you like to join me?'

'Would you mind if I said no this time? I'm exhausted and just want to climb into bed. But you are more than welcome to join me and Mr Weir for breakfast tomorrow, if you'd like?'

'Mr Weir?'

'My colleague. We're travelling to America to study the department stores there. We work at Pennington's in Bath.'

Catherine's eyes widened. 'Goodness. I've heard of Pennington's, but never been there. I'm from Devon. I'd love to tag along for breakfast, if you don't mind. Thank you, Amelia.'

Catherine left the cabin and quietly closed the door.

Amelia quickly undressed. As she would be without dressing help, Mrs Woolden had been mindful in the Pennington's outfits she'd selected for Amelia to take with her and, so far, she hadn't had too much difficulty with clasps, buttons and laces. Relieved to be in her nightgown, Amelia wandered to the porthole and looked out into the darkness. The sky was spangled with stars and a half-moon shone amid a wispy covering of clouds.

The longer she stared, the more a horrible sense of foreboding stole over her and Amelia shivered. Nothing seemed to move, nothing made a sound. It suddenly felt as though she was floating out here alone on the vast ocean. Even the corridor was absent of people coming and going. No laughter rang, no voices spoke.

She briefly closed her eyes, willing her nonsensical apprehension into submission.

Her feelings were little more than fear of the unknown. Her internal anxieties poking and prodding to the surface. Opening her eyes, she tightened the belt of her robe, inhaled a determined breath and sat at the small writing desk. She pulled her notebook towards her, pen poised and feverishly set to work.

The information Mrs Carlton had given her poured onto the page, and Amelia's excitement for what adventures lay ahead grew. Everything she saw, heard, tasted and smelled would be noted in this book. She would absorb every conversation, every piece of clothing, every accessory and piece of jewellery. Times were changing and Miss Pennington had given her the opportunity to be at the forefront of that transition.

She would not waste a single moment. This trip was her chance to live. To experience. To challenge convention.

And she would embrace every second of it.

Her past would undoubtedly drift farther behind her, the closer she sailed to the place once called the New World. For the next three weeks, this voyage and America would be *her* new world. And, tomorrow, with or without Mr Weir, she would find a way to spend some time in first class. She wanted to report everything to Miss Pennington.

Absolutely everything.

15

Samuel glanced at the clock in the control room and stretched the kinks from his neck and shoulders. He was halfway through his ten-hour shift and would soon be released to grab his evening meal. After that, he was expected to spend another four hours doing his duty throughout second class.

Spending time with the passengers was proving to be unexpectedly enjoyable. Talking with so many different people, from so many different places, was interesting. Maybe even a little inspiring. He'd spoken to men chasing their fortunes, women wanting to make a difference for their gender and children who believed America to be a land of magic and mystery.

The last forty-eight hours had put a fire in his belly for change and adventure; if his dream of staying in America turned out to be impossible, then at least he was starting to believe he would return to Bath a different man than the one who'd left.

How that man would show himself, he wasn't yet sure. All he knew was he could not go on any longer being so caged in by his family. Trapped and anchored in a role he could stand no more.

His father's face appeared in his mind's eye and Samuel looked out across the ocean.

Am I a disappointment, Pa? It's only for you I'm working as I am. Looking after Ma and the girls. But I'm not sure I can go on as I have. Not anymore.

Shaking off his melancholy, Samuel straightened his shoulders. He was working a grand job on a grand ship and he'd be sending money home as his dad would have wanted. Whatever else he might get up to while he travelled was no one's business.

They had made their final stop in Ireland the day before and were already making good time on the three-thousand-mile trip to New York. The captain was happy with the crew and the crew happy with the captain. The atmosphere in the control room was relaxed, the comradery tangible.

He had a lot to be grateful for.

'Hey, Sam.'

Archie walked across the room with a tall, broad man who looked to be in his early twenties. 'Have you met Harold? He's working with me.' Archie grinned. 'Harold Buckley meet my good friend, Samuel Murphy.'

Samuel shook Harold's hand. 'Nice to meet you.'

Although beset with a slightly pockmarked face and a shock of bright orange hair sticking out in all directions from beneath his hat, Harold's eyes were kind enough, his smile friendly.

Archie nudged in between them and laid out a newspaper. 'Have a look at this.'

Samuel peered at a large black and white photograph of a construction site, the headline *A Work In Progress but Progress Indeed*. 'What am I looking at?'

'Tell him, Harold.'

'That's the new Grand Central Station in New York. They have hundreds of men building, laying track, constructing all kinds of amenities and Lord only knows what else. They reckon it's going to be a train station like no other. A sight to behold when it's finished.'

Samuel frowned. 'And why should this interest me?'

Archie raised his eyebrows. 'That's all you've got to say?'

'What else should I say? I don't know the first thing about railways. I can't be impressed by something I know nothing about.'

'Blimey, Sam, you're half blind sometimes, do you know that?' Archie shook his head and nudged Harold again. 'Tell him.'

Unsure if he wanted to know where Archie was going with this, Samuel crossed his arms. He and Archie had been friends for ten years despite their different personalities. Archie was impulsive, a risk-taker, a man who didn't consider tomorrow until the sunlight broke through his bedroom window each morning. Samuel, on the other hand, had responsibilities that curbed any impulsiveness, swamped any risks and ensured he planned for his tomorrows. Whatever had lit Archie's eyes like lanterns, Samuel was under no delusion he would most likely blow their flames out pretty quickly.

He faced Harold. 'Go on then. Tell me what hare-brained idea Archie's dragged you into.'

The other man shook his head, his gaze serious. 'No hare-brained idea. Grand Central are calling out for workers. They aim to open the station as early as next year and want as many hands to the pump as possible.'

Samuel looked from Harold to Archie's beaming face and back again, as his suspicion about where this was going grew. 'And?'

'For the love of God.' Archie glared at Samuel. 'Can't you see what's right in front of you?'

Harold puffed out his chest and grinned. 'I, for one, won't be coming back to Southampton. I'm staying in America to work on the station and make my fortune.'

'Ah, I see.' Samuel faced Archie. 'And you're telling me this because I might have mentioned about staying there myself.'

'Exactly.' Archie nudged Samuel's shoulder. 'This is your chance. You'd get a job there, no problem. You should do it. Stay in America.'

Samuel's gut knotted with possibility and he looked at the station photograph again. For all his words and bravado, never returning home still didn't sit well in his conscience. He might have hopes and dreams but could he ever really abandon his family? Abandon his promise to his father? His mother was fragile at the best of times and to desert her could result in her falling ever deeper into depression or worse.

He shook his head, regret coiling inside of him. 'I've got responsibilities. You know that, Archie.'

'That doesn't mean you have to stay right in the thick of them. This is your chance, Sam. I just want you to bloody well take it.' Archie slapped his hand to Samuel's shoulder, staring hard into his eyes. 'You don't have a woman waiting for you at home. No kids. And no set-in-stone reason to go back. Harold is a seaman, a sailor, same as you. Except he's taking his life in his hands and living it. He wants more than he has right now, Sam. Sound familiar?'

Samuel's heart picked up speed, excuses and reasons to stop Archie on his optimistic path battling on his tongue. Cowardice to do what he really wanted in his life caught in his throat so painfully, Samuel found it hard to swallow. Maybe he should've kept his mouth shut about what dreams he had; how much he sometimes resented the role that had been dropped on him from a great height. His friend never failed to want the best for him, but Archie was a man without commitment or ties to anything other than what *he* wanted. A man who would never know, God willing, what it was to have a family that became his duty to care for, not by love or marriage, but by death.

'Look . . . ' Archie sighed. 'We have a few days before we reach America, just think about it. You're not happy, my friend and I don't want you carrying on as you have.' He smiled. 'Rightly or wrongly, I care about you. This could be your way out. I know it.'

Claustrophobia stole through Sam igniting a simmering irritation. Was he just a mug everyone thought they could order around? Tell him what he could and should be doing? He had enough of that at home. If Archie thought he could start acting like his damn mother while they were aboard this ship, he had better think again.

He shrugged Archie's hand off his shoulder. 'I might not have a woman or kids, but I *have* got a family. Bloody hell, Archie, don't you think I would've got out before now if I could? I shouldn't have said anything to you.'

'You haven't said anything to me you haven't been saying to yourself. And, for your information, I don't think you would've got out before now because when has such an opportunity come your way before?' Archie crossed his arms. 'There's no reason you can't stay on in America. Find work at the railway. With your mechanical expertise, they'd take you on, no questions asked. There's nothing to stop you sending money home and, in return, you get a life. One of your own making, where *you* make the decisions. *You* get to have some fun instead of your sisters. Isn't that what you're hankering? Imagine not having to answer to the women in your life, Sam. Christ.'

Samuel stared at his friend and then at Harold, who shrugged and picked up the newspaper before walking away, one hand raised in surrender.

Samuel faced Archie. 'Why did you say all that in front of a bloke I don't even know?'

'Because Harold isn't thinking about what he hasn't got, he's thinking about what he wants, that's why. My life is in Bath, Sam. I've got a woman I love who I fully intend to ask to marry me when I get back. I don't want out, you do. We're working for White Star on a casual basis. If you don't want to be on the *Titanic* on the return trip, you don't have to be. That's all I'm saying.'

Archie squeezed Samuel's shoulder before heading across to the other side of the control room. Samuel stared after him, his mind reeling and his heart beating fast. Not return home? Just send word with his latest pay packet that he wasn't coming back?

The idea was little more than a pipe dream.

Yet, as he looked out over the ocean, the sun sparkling on its surface, the sky meeting the sea, America suddenly felt like the promised land it always claimed to be.

Archie was right.

There wasn't anything stopping Samuel from staying in New York now that he'd finally broken free. His mother couldn't keep him in England through words of guilt and responsibility because, in his heart and mind, he was already gone.

Everywhere he looked on deck, people's faces were alight with happiness and excitement. As though everyone else had something to look forward to during and after this trip. Was there any reason why he couldn't have that, too?

16

Ruby slid some eggs onto Tommy's plate and then her own, before laying the crockery on the kitchen table, its surface forever sticky no matter how much she scrubbed it. She glanced at her mother who, of course, had been served first and now happily shovelled the food Ruby had prepared into her mouth.

Repulsed, Ruby sat down next to her brother and forced a smile as she picked up her fork. 'How was school today, Tommy? Did your teacher like the sums I helped you with?'

'He said — '

'No talk about school at the table,' their mother snapped, speckles of food spraying out of her mouth. 'You'll put me off my dinner.'

Hatred burned like a hot coal in the centre of Ruby's chest as she glared at her mother's bowed head. She sent up a silent prayer for the means to take her and Tommy away from this godforsaken house. To find somewhere for them to live where the windows didn't rattle in the winter, and paper didn't peel from the walls in the summer. Somewhere with a garden, no matter how small, rather than a concrete yard that stank of rubbish and rot. A place where Tommy might speak freely about the school he loved, and the dreams he shared with Ruby whenever she spent a few precious moments alone with him each night.

'Why are you so quiet, girl? More scheming going on in that head of yours, I'll bet.'

Ruby raised her eyes to her mother's. 'Haven't

anything to say. There seems little point if you don't even want to hear about your son's schooling.'

'Whatever you two have to say bores me senseless.'

Ruby speared some potato as the need to rile her mother grew. Provoking her temper might be a senseless thing to do, but Ruby's need to vent, to rant and rave, bubbled dangerously. 'Well, what about you, Ma? How was your day?'

'How do you think it was? I spent most of it cleaning the bloody house while you pissed away your day at that place you call work. You, my girl, wouldn't know hard work if it upped and slapped you in the face.'

'I work hard. You know I do.' Ruby looked at the dirty tea towels hanging from the cupboard door handles, the soup pot still unwashed on the counter from two days past and the pile of paper and ashes in the grate that had been there since yesterday. Resentment burned. 'And, for your information, Miss Pennington has been so complimentary about my work on the *Titanic* window, I might have the confidence to try for a higher position someday soon.'

'She was *complimentary*, was she?' Her mother squeaked the word in spiteful, upper-class mimicry. 'Look at Miss Fancy Pants using her big words. You have a screw loose if you think that high and mighty trollop thinks any more of you than I do.'

Ruby gripped her knife and fork tighter. 'Wouldn't you welcome me bringing home more money?'

'Anything you bring home will be an improvement on what you're earning. I have a mind to go to Pennington's and accuse *Miss* Pennington of child labour. It's criminal what they pay you. Not enough to feed me, let alone you two.'

'I don't want you setting foot near Pennington's.'

Ruby glared as she fought to keep hold of her brewing temper. 'Not ever.'

Time stood still. Even the ticking of the wall clock seemed to stop. The only sound Ruby heard was her heartbeat pulsing in her ears. Her mother's eyes bulged in their sockets, her mouth twisting into a tight line.

Adrenalin washed through Ruby and she braced, ready for whatever came next. With her eyes still locked on her mother's, she said, 'Tommy, go upstairs.'

The legs of his chair scraped across the tiled floor as he scrambled from the table and raced from the room. His feet thundered up the stairs, followed by the slam of his bedroom door and the scuffle of a chair being moved across the floor. Ruby prayed he'd properly lodged it under the door handle as she'd taught him.

Slowly, her mother put down her cutlery and wiped her sleeve across her mouth.

Ruby tensed, half praying her mother's next assault would be verbal, rather than physical. The other half prayed for the physical because, by God, Ruby was in the mood for a fight. The day had been hellish avoiding Hazel Price as she slid sly looks her way, giggling and talking with a group of shop girls known for their bitching. She was more convinced than ever that Hazel had seen into Ruby's heart and knew of her true feelings for Victoria. Well, Hazel Price was just another person to add to the list of those out to cause her trouble and Ruby would handle her as well as she handled her mother.

'Are you telling me what to do, Ruby Taylor?' Her mother's voice was dangerously low. 'Because if you are, you're making a terrible mistake.'

'I'm not telling you what to do, Ma. I'm stating a fact.' Ruby purposefully put down her knife and fork and reached for her water, pleased that the liquid remained steady. 'I want you to stay well away from Pennington's.'

'And if I don't?'

Ruby tightened her jaw, protectiveness over the life she was fighting so hard to create for herself and Tommy threatening to erupt in an almighty explosion. 'Then we will have no choice but to leave this house and never come back.'

'We?'

'Me and Tommy.'

'Ha, you think that sop will follow you out of here? I don't think so.'

'He will, Ma. I wouldn't leave him here alone with you unless I was carried out in a box.'

'Don't tempt me.'

'I know you'd like nothing more than to see the back of your children, but just bear in mind, if I go, I take my earnings with me.'

'And you think that matters to me?'

'I do. Especially if the sex you give to the waste of space men that come through here runs out.'

'Why, you . . . ' Her mother's cheeks reddened as she leapt from her chair. It clattered against the floor as she rounded the table, her hands outstretched towards Ruby. 'I'll rip your bloody face off.'

Ruby was on her feet, but she didn't move fast enough, and her mother grabbed a handful of her hair. Pain screamed through her scalp as Ruby gritted her teeth, pushing her nails deep into her mother's wrists. She dug in as hard as she could until her mother cursed and released her enough that Ruby could spin away from her.

She put up her fists. 'Has it really come to this, Ma?

Us fighting like a pair of boxers? My God, what is wrong with you? Can't you see what you're doing to Tom — '

'There's nothing wrong with me, my girl. No mother worth her salt would put up with her daughter telling her what she can or can't do. Where she can or can't go. You think I even want to step foot in Pennington's? No, I bloody don't. But that doesn't mean I won't, if you tell me I can't.'

'So, you'll risk me losing my job just to annoy me? How does that make any sense?'

Her mother growled and lunged at Ruby again, but this time she was ready. She grabbed her mother's arm and pushed it high behind her back, before clamping her free hand firmly around her mother's other arm and frogmarching her from the kitchen.

'Get your hands off me! I'll bloody kill you.'

As her mother screamed and turned the air blue with her curses, Ruby shoved her along the hallway, hitching up her mother's arm until she yelled with pain. Ruby fumbled with the latch on the front door, finally managing to swing it open.

With an almighty push, she put her mother out onto the street, slammed the door and collapsed back against it. Stars floated in front of Ruby's eyes and her heart raced as her mother's kicks rattled the door.

Taking a strengthening breath, Ruby pushed away from the door and rushed upstairs into her mother's room. Grabbing whatever clothes lay about the bedroom, she shoved them into an empty bag, walked to the window and threw the lot out onto the street.

'Just go, Ma. You can come back tomorrow. Tonight, you're out.'

Pulling the sash window firmly closed, Ruby started

to laugh, adrenalin seeping from her body, leaving her head pounding. What in God's name had just happened? She had no idea, but her victory felt good.

She rushed across the landing to Tommy's room. 'Are you all right, sweetheart? It's safe now. You can open the door.'

Scraping and shuffling sounded behind the door and then Tommy pulled it open, his face pale and streaked with tears. 'Where's Ma?'

'Gone.' She pulled him into an embrace and kissed his hair. 'For tonight, anyway.'

'You threw her out?'

'She'll find somewhere to sleep, don't worry about that.' She held him at arm's length and forced a wide smile. 'Come on. Let's get you washed and in your pyjamas.'

Tommy headed for the bathroom as Ruby took some clean pyjamas from his drawer and laid them on the bed. Tears pricked her eyes and her hands shook as her earlier euphoria faded. How could it be that a mother and daughter came to blows? Her and Tommy's lives were passing by in a home that was unsafe. A house that held no love except for what lay between her and her brother. She had to find a way out.

She entered her bedroom, listening as water splashed behind the closed bathroom door. Walking to her wardrobe, she retrieved a locked box and pulled the key, hanging on a string, from around her neck.

Opening the box, Ruby lifted out the trinkets she'd collected as a child. A shiny pebble, half a silver locket, a twisted satin sash that had once seemed so grand before she'd started working at Pennington's. Now she knew there were riches enough for anyone prepared to work and dream.

Pulling out an envelope from the bottom of the box, Ruby emptied her savings onto the bed and counted her hoarded booty.

It still wasn't enough, but it grew with every pay packet.

It was possible she had enough for two, maybe three months' rent if someone would be willing to give her and Tommy lodgings. The small amount of cash wouldn't get them more than a single room, but at least they'd be away from Ma.

'I'm in my pyjamas, Ruby!'

Tommy's shout came from across the landing and Ruby quickly gathered the money, put it beneath the trinkets and locked the box. Returning her stash to the wardrobe, she breathed deep, her gaze wandering to her washbag on the windowsill.

Inside was a razor blade she'd glided across her wrists time and time again whenever desperation sent her spiralling into a dark abyss. Sometimes she felt she had no way of protecting Tommy. No handle on her feelings for Victoria. No decent clothes. No decent food.

Her life was a mess, but . . .

'Ruby? Are you going to say good night?'

She did have Tommy.

She would always have Tommy.

She dragged her gaze from the washbag. And he would always have her.

17

Amelia walked from the second-class dining room, her head held high as she tried her best to embody the posture and confidence of a high-born lady. After three nights aboard the *Titanic*, she'd finally managed to convince Mr Weir she could be trusted to walk alone for an hour or so. It was becoming torturous not being able to venture into first-class and see the wonders she'd undoubtedly discover.

She touched the beading along the low neckline of her navy and silver evening dress, revelling in the sensation of the long hem trailing behind her. The feeling of being a princess in a fairy tale had remained ever since she had dressed three hours before. Its beautiful lace sleeves brushed over her shoulders and an intricately woven belt cinched her waist, a beaded pattern of intertwined ivy winding over and around the long skirt. With her smart navy shoes, beaded purse and feathers in her hair, Amelia embraced her renewed confidence.

Heading for the grand staircase, she surveyed the people around her, hoping no one stopped or challenged her. Nerves tumbled in her stomach, but she kept her head high. She had to see her mission through. Had to prove to Elizabeth — to herself — that she deserved the assignment given to her.

She was about to ascend the stairs when her heart sank.

Officer Murphy gave a semi-bow. 'Miss Wakefield. Good evening.'

Damnation. How was she supposed to sneak into the first-class lounge now? She forced a smile. 'Officer Murphy.'

His brilliant blue gaze lingered a brief moment on her lips. 'Walking alone on such a beautiful night?'

Her cheeks warming from his appraisal, she looked around them. Couldn't the man lower his voice? She faced him. 'Is that forbidden?'

'Of course not.' His smile faltered. 'You know, I'm not your enemy. It wouldn't do you any harm to be a little civil to me . . . on occasion.'

Amelia stilled. She hated being rude to anyone, but instinct told her to be wary of Officer Murphy. To keep her distance. He was a man who clearly enjoyed the pursuit of women. She neither wanted nor needed his attention.

'You are no more an enemy to me than I am to you,' she said, glancing towards the staircase. 'If you must know, I was curious to see the first-class deck. I assume you won't stop me from doing so?'

He raised his eyebrows, his gaze amused. 'Can I ask why I should allow that to happen considering you hold a second-class ticket?'

She lifted her chin. Officer Murphy was no more in charge of her than any other man aboard this ship. Mr Weir included. 'The less you know, the better.'

His attention, once again, dropped to her mouth and Amelia held herself still, determined not to fidget under his scrutiny. 'Well, then, maybe I could escort you?' He offered her his arm. 'It would be my pleasure.'

Indecision warred inside of her. He certainly knew the ship better than her. It would also cause less curiosity from other passengers if she had a chaperone.

Especially one who was so tall, so imposing, so annoyingly handsome in his splendid uniform.

She slowly slid her arm into his. 'Well, if you insist, it would be appreciated. Thank you.'

They stepped onto the stairs and a perplexing tension simmered between them that Amelia had no idea how to dispel. Why did she have to run into him of all people? It was as though he'd made it his personal mission to seek her out at every turn. Any other officer would have more than likely continued on their way, not caring what she was up to.

But it seemed for Officer Murphy, paying no attention to a woman alone was an impossible ask. He obviously suspected she was up to something, yet he had chosen to accompany her anyway.

Which gave her no idea of his intentions.

Swallowing her nerves, she glanced at his firm jaw and sweep of jet-black hair and had the sudden, unsettling urge to push the fallen strands from his brow. She quickly turned away, ignoring the increased thump of her heart.

'Here we are. The first-class deck. What do you want to see?'

His voice was lower now, more conspiratorial and she couldn't stem her smile. Maybe he could be an ally rather than an enemy. She only sensed warm amusement from him and was grateful for it. He didn't seem in any way lecherous, more intrigued.

Deciding the man deserved the benefit of the doubt, she exhaled. 'I want to see people. As many as possible.'

'People? What sort of people?'

'All sorts.'

'Toffs? Grand ladies? Professional gamblers? You'll

find them all aboard.'

'Then we'll seek them all out.'

'We?' He raised his eyebrows a second time. 'Am I now part of this espionage?'

Amelia frowned. 'I am hardly spying — '

'I'm teasing, Miss Wakefield.' He smiled as he led her into the lounge. 'Why don't I follow your lead?'

The lounge was a sight to behold and Amelia's reservations burst like popped bubbles as she was frozen by wonder. Four enormous windows surrounded the room providing panoramic views of the ocean; oak panelling with delicate carvings in warm wood tones covered the walls. At the far end, a huge marble fireplace dominated the space, surrounded by a wooden and mirrored mantel. Clothed tables bearing glinting crockery and flickering candles, their accompanying chairs upholstered in the most luxuriant material and style Amelia had ever seen.

'It's fit for a palace,' she breathed. 'I would be too afraid to even sit in here.'

'There are plenty of people around, we won't be noticed. Let's take a walk.'

She looked at him and he stared back at her, nothing but kindness in his ridiculously blue eyes. Accepting his company would allow her to achieve her goals and Amelia nodded, certain in the knowledge she'd be able to speak to people more easily with Officer Murphy beside her than she could if she had been alone.

He led her past a table where five gentlemen played cards, crystal tumblers filled with amber liquid beside them, cigars smouldering in an ashtray. On they walked until they reached an area dominated by women gossiping or exchanging praise for one another's appearances.

Amelia drank in every sight, sound and smell, inhaling the atmosphere deep into her lungs so that she might detail everything in her notebook in the morning.

'So . . .' Officer Murphy cleared his throat. 'Can I assume it is not just natural curiosity that compelled you to visit this part of the ship?'

She glanced at his handsome profile. What harm could it do to share some of her intentions with him? 'I'm aboard for business rather than pleasure, and my business is to see what people are wearing, carrying and using through every class on the ship.'

'Can I ask who you work for?'

'I'm a window dresser at Pennington's department store in Bath. Perhaps you know of it?'

'Bath?' He stopped, his eyes widening. 'You live and work in Bath?'

She frowned, disconcerted by his shocked reaction. 'Is that a problem?'

'More of a wondrous coincidence. I'm from Bath. I live near the river.'

'You do?' Amelia didn't know whether to believe him, despite the pleasure and sincerity in his eyes. Well, even if he spoke the truth, she would not be divulging her address to him so easily. 'Well, then, you must surely know Pennington's.'

'I do, but as for shopping?' He grinned. 'Hardly my area of expertise, I'm afraid, Miss Wakefield. However, if you wish to study the passengers while aboard, I will make it my business to help you. I assume you've given Mr Weir the slip?'

'The slip?'

'The old heave-ho. Made your escape. Running amok without his permission.'

The teasing in his voice wasn't mocking or spiteful. Instead, it spoke of his admiration.

She smiled. 'You assume right.'

They continued to walk slowly around the room until she was satisfied she had seen all she wanted to see. Officer Murphy led her from the lounge onto a sweeping promenade and they were surrounded by even more upper-class and aristocratic passengers. Dresses, hairpieces and adornments, glittering purses and fans sparkled and shone in every direction, jewels the size of Christmas baubles dangling from every female ear.

Glances were directed her way until nerves turned Amelia's hand clammy on Office Murphy's arm. Mentally admonishing herself, she squared her shoulders and continued to walk, avidly scouring the men and women.

'Good God,' Officer Murphy whispered. 'The value of the jewellery alone must be staggering.'

Pleased that he was no less overawed than her, she boldly pulled him forward, not entirely sure where her audacity had suddenly come from, but grateful for it all the same. 'Come, let's see if we can listen to a little conversation.'

'You want to eavesdrop?' His gaze lingered on hers. 'Well, clearly my first impressions of you were entirely wrong.'

Amelia's defences rose and she slipped her hand from his arm. 'Excuse me?'

'I apologise.' He looked along the promenade. 'I just thought you a little nervous when we last spoke.'

The reminder of how she had felt with the men appraising her before Officer Murphy approached on the deck the day before threatened to diminish her courage and Amelia pulled back her shoulders. 'Well, that was yesterday. Tonight, I am buoyant and eager to absorb absolutely everything.'

She stepped forward and nonchalantly lifted a glass of champagne from a passing waiter's tray before sidling closer to a small group of women conversing near a doorway.

'Say something,' she whispered as Officer Murphy came to stand beside her. 'Make conversation.'

He glanced at the women and started to speak, but Amelia wasn't really listening to his words. Instead, she focused on the women's dialogue.

'Oh, yes, I know Bath extremely well. In fact, my brother, Lawrence Culford, his wife and children live there. He owns the Phoenix hotel. Perhaps you've stayed there on your travels.'

Amelia almost choked on her champagne.

'Miss Wakefield? Are you all right?'

She took Officer Murphy's arm to steady herself and peered around him to look more closely at the women. Yes, she could see the resemblance. Not only had she met Lawrence Culford on account of him being married to Esther, her friend and mentor at Pennington's, but Cornelia, Lawrence and Harriet's sister, worked on the jewellery counter at the store. So, the woman regaling her audience must be Harriet, the sister she'd heard of, but never met. Why on earth would Cornelia be working at Pennington's if she came from such a wealthy family?

'Miss Wakefield?'

Officer Murphy gently squeezed her hand and she quickly withdrew it, the contact feeling oddly intimate. 'I . . . I'm quite all right.' She tried and failed to drag her gaze from Harriet Culford. She really was extraordinarily beautiful. 'I wonder if I could find a way to speak with her.'

'With who?'

Not realising she had spoken aloud, Amelia quickly faced Officer Murphy. 'The woman in the red dress is the sister-in-law of one of my closest friends at Pennington's.'

'Really?' He looked at Harriet Culford. 'Well, they do say it's a small world.'

'I need to find a way to introduce myself so that I might speak with her. There's every possibility she will enable me to spend a little more time in first class without people beginning to wonder who I am. After all, I can't stay with you all night.'

He looked into her eyes and Amelia could have sworn she witnessed a flash of disappointment before he smiled. 'Leave it to me.'

He moved her towards the group of women and Amelia's heart raced. What was he doing? They hadn't even discussed a strategy.

'Good evening, ladies. I'm Officer Murphy. How are you enjoying your voyage so far?'

Amelia stood frozen as their gazes none too subtly roamed over Officer Murphy's face and person. Amelia continued to smile but found their stares openly judgemental and condescending.

'Oh, I apologise, might I introduce Miss Amelia Wakefield. She is travelling to New York for business.'

'Business?' Harriet Culford's eyes widened. 'Well, aren't you a modern woman, Miss Wakefield. Can I ask the nature of your business?'

Amelia took a long breath, knowing her response could equally provoke a good or bad reaction. She had no idea how Harriet Culford's relationship fared with her siblings and Esther. 'I work for Pennington's in Bath.'

'Oh, my goodness. Well, that's wonderful.' Harriet laughed. 'My sister, Cornelia, works there. As did my sister-in-law, Esther, until she left to have her baby. Perhaps you know of them?'

'I do. In fact, Esther mentors me. Everything I have learned about window dressing, fashion and accessories came from Esther. I adore her.'

'Oh, then you must join our party this evening.' Harriet slid her arm into Amelia's, pulling her away from Officer Murphy. 'We'll have the most wonderful time. If you'll excuse us, Officer Murphy, we ladies have much to discuss. Good evening.'

He nodded and stepped back. 'Of course.'

Amelia held his gaze, mouthing a 'thank you' before she was pulled away. He smiled and she could have sworn his gaze remained on her back until she was out of sight. Yet, instead of shame and unease, rare attraction sped her heart — and that surprised her more than anything Harriet Culford might have to tell her.

18

By the time Samuel reached the second-class card lounge, there were only a few gentlemen remaining, cognac and cigars in hand, conversation pleasantly low. Luxuriant in its wood-panelled décor, the lounge was lit by glass domed wall sconces, music from the string quartet in the next room drifting through the gilded-double doors.

No matter how hard he tried to stop thinking about Amelia Wakefield, she continued to linger in his mind. He liked her spunk. Her independence. Her beauty. In fact, the depth of his interest in her had made him decidedly uncomfortable. His life had always been filled with too much worry, responsibility and work to consider romance. Now he was aboard a ship that could offer a life-changing opportunity — should he choose to take it — yet, instead of concentrating on whether or not to stay in America, his attention had been captured by a beautiful and mysterious woman.

Ladies had come and gone in Samuel's life. He was no saint, but honourable, he hoped. Mutual assignations followed by mutual separation. No heartbreak. No broken promises. That was all he had been capable of . . . all he *was* capable of.

So, why was it bothering him that he'd left Miss Wakefield in the clutches of strangers?

Because now her wellbeing felt like his responsibility, that's why.

She had an unusual and intriguing aura of vulnerability and strength, wisdom and uncertainty, that struck at something deep inside of him. Whatever it was, it made Samuel want to spend more time with her, to talk to her and get to know her.

He strolled through the lounge, glancing with disinterest at the games being played and the money changing hands. He could never afford to gamble the money he earned and considered the men who did complete fools.

Every penny he earned would always be accounted for, needed. Or else, spent wisely.

His shift had finished ten minutes ago and as he made his way back to the cabin he shared with Archie, Samuel tried to banish thoughts of Miss Wakefield and, instead, pondered New York.

Since his discussion with Archie and Harold, Samuel had tried to bury any possibility of staying in New York, citing the notion as ridiculous and impractical. Yet, wasn't Archie right in that Samuel had no set-in-stone obligation to return home? Morally, his selfishness, should he stay in America, could be assuaged by regularly sending money home, but that wouldn't lessen his mother's emotional need of him. Maybe without him there, Katherine and Fiona would think about finding their own employment and showing their mother some kindness and consideration.

Just as Samuel was leaving the card lounge, Mr Weir strode past him, his face etched with concern, his gaze manically flitting from side to side as though searching for someone.

Samuel immediately tensed. Hadn't Miss Wakefield returned to her cabin? He glanced at the wall clock. He'd left her over an hour ago.

Worry clenched like a fist in Samuel's gut and he hurried after Weir. 'Excuse me, sir. Mr Weir?'

The other man halted. 'Yes?'

'Is anything the matter? Only you seem — '

'Yes. As a matter of fact, I am looking for my ward. Miss Wakefield. I'm sure you wouldn't remember her, but — '

'I remember her quite clearly. Slim, dark, brown hair. Pretty.'

Mr Weir arched an eyebrow. 'Quite. However, when I knocked on her cabin door to check her safely abed for the night, the young woman sharing with Miss Wakefield confirmed she had not returned since before dinner. I agreed that she might take a walk about the ship but have not seen her since.'

Samuel glanced towards the doors. 'I see. Would you like me to look — '

'How am I to sleep tonight without knowing she is all right? My employers expect me to ensure she comes to no harm — '

'Allow me to help you locate her, sir.' Samuel smiled, trying to hide his anxiety. The last thing Amelia would want was Weir venturing into first class and embarrassing her. 'Maybe she has become lost. It is easily done, considering the maze of corridors, cabins and suites. What is your cabin number, sir? If I find her, I will ensure she lets you know she is safe and well.'

Weir continued to look about the decking, his brown eyes shadowed with worry, which, rightly or wrongly, reassured Samuel that the man wasn't quite the arse he'd thought him when they'd met previously.

'I'm in cabin E-78 and Miss Wakefield's cabin is directly opposite.'

'Good. Then I will go in the opposite direction from you and between us, rest assured, we will find her.'

Samuel headed along the deck and straight for the

grand staircase. It was already common knowledge among the staff that the first-class passengers were prone to going to bed much later than most of the other passengers. Their demands were higher, their capacity for alcohol consumption somewhat astounding, and their need for gossip and eavesdropping even more so.

He marched along, his boots stomping on the promenade planks, his eyes peeled for Miss Wakefield's distinctive hair. Sometimes brown, sometimes bronze, sometimes caramel, it was her hair that had initially attracted him. Since he'd seen her smile, her eyes lighting with mischief and possibility, he was more attracted to her than ever.

And now his heart was thundering that she could be missing, hurt or lost.

He sucked in a breath against the dropping temperatures and rubbed his hands together. At least there was little chance of her being outside. Her evening gown was low-cut and of a light gauzy material. She would be frozen to the bone should she be out here for any amount of time.

Yet, there were more couples and groups of gentlemen walking back and forth than he expected, their chatter subdued as the hour neared midnight. Samuel's concern deepened. There were no groups of women huddled together as there had been earlier in the evening. Understandably, most would have been in bed at such a late hour. So where was Miss Wakefield?

He headed back to the grand staircase and descended quickly, scanning the area around him. Finally, he emerged onto E-deck and headed for her cabin in the hope she had returned.

Finding Mr Weir's cabin, he put his ear to the cabin door opposite and heard quiet weeping.

Was it Amelia? Her roommate? Now what? Did he knock?

He gently tapped on the door. 'Miss Wakefield. It's Officer Murphy. Are you all right?'

The weeping immediately stopped.

Samuel strained his hearing and tapped on the door again. 'There's no need for alarm. Only, Mr Weir is looking for you and I wanted to make sure you are all right.'

'I'm fine, thank you, Officer.' Amelia's voice urgently whispered from close behind the door. 'If you could tell Mr Weir I am in my cabin, I would very much appreciate it. Good night.'

'Are you quite sure? Only — '

'Quite sure.' Her voice cracked. 'Good night.'

Samuel stared at the door. He couldn't leave her without at least seeing her face. If someone had upset her . . .

He stood back from the door and paced a few steps, his hand in his hair. He'd already witnessed a nervousness in her eyes and the last thing he wanted was to sabotage the improvement in their association.

The sound of the lock being turned halted his pacing.

Slowly, her door opened just a crack, then a little further until she peered out.

Her gaze met his and widened. 'Oh. I was just — '

'Making sure I had gone?' He smiled, hoping to reassure her that he meant no harm. 'I'm glad to see you are all right.'

'Officer Murphy, you must go,' she hissed. 'I am quite all right, and my companion is sleeping.'

She moved to shut the door. Samuel reached out, placing his hand firmly on the door. 'I heard you crying.'

Her cheeks turned pink and her throat moved as she swallowed. What in God's name had happened since he'd left her?

Why the hell *had* he left her?

She tightened her hand at the collar of her nightgown. 'I had some unwanted attention from a gentleman as I was walking back to my cabin. I dealt with the situation, but it has left me somewhat shaken. There is nothing to concern yourself about.'

Fury bubbled in Samuel's chest as he studied her, looking for any signs the bastard had touched her. 'Did he — '

'He grabbed me a little too tightly, but I managed to free myself and he walked away once I threatened to scream.' Her eyes hardened as she stood a little straighter. 'He's gone and I'm ready for bed. So, good night — '

'My name's Samuel, Miss Wakefield.'

'Sorry?'

He took a single step closer, wanting to delay their parting, wanting her to know she could trust him. 'My name's Samuel. If there is anything I can do, anything at all during the remainder of this voyage, I want you to seek me out. I need for you to promise me you'll do that.'

Slowly, she nodded. 'I will. Thank you . . . Samuel.'

He smiled to hide his rage at the faceless bastard who'd frightened her. 'You're welcome. Good night, Miss Wakefield.'

'Good night.'

Samuel backed away along the corridor, his head

reeling and his heart just a little too affected by Amelia Wakefield's distress. Just the thought of her being afraid or even merely shaken irritated him enough that he couldn't seem to unclench his fists as they swung at his sides. This was a ship of superior class, yet it seemed the same macho presumptions existed here as they did on the Southampton docks.

Well, as long as Miss Wakefield was aboard, she would now be under his careful watch.

19

Ruby descended Pennington's grand staircase, her steps unsteady under the weight of the dresses draped over her arm and the hats she carried in each hand. She nodded genially to customers as they swarmed past her in an endless stream. The store's *Titanic* window had caused quite the furore, and there had been a marked increase in the store's footfall over the last couple of days.

Pride filled her for the small part she'd played in the window's success.

As she headed for the stairs leading to the basement level design department, she looked around her and her smile vanished when she spotted Victoria speaking with an elderly lady and gentleman close by.

She had been purposely avoiding her for days and quickly dipped her head.

The cut and bruise on her cheek had blossomed into a rather fetching grey-yellow colour, accented by an ugly red scab. Her mother's mistreatment was more noticeable than ever and, where her design colleagues had been polite enough to withhold comment, if Victoria managed to corner Ruby she would undoubtedly insist on an explanation.

She quickly ducked deeper into the crowds, the myriad of bodies her cover. Having evaded Victoria, she breathed a little easier until Miss Pennington stepped into her path.

'Miss Taylor, could I possibly delay you for a moment?'

Inwardly cursing, Ruby halted and forced a smile. 'Miss Pennington, of course. Can I help you with something?'

Her employer's smile faltered as her gaze lingered on Ruby's cheek before she met her eyes, her smile widening too much to be sincere. 'Yes, I would like to speak with you and Mrs Lark once she's finished speaking to those customers.'

'Mrs Lark?' Ruby swallowed against the immediate dryness in her throat. 'Are you unhappy with how I've represented Accessories in the latest window?'

'Oh, no. Not at all. I'm very happy.' Miss Pennington raised her hand. 'Mrs Lark? Could I speak with you for a moment?'

Victoria turned from the elderly couple and said something before heading towards Ruby. Ruby's heart picked up speed. With her hands full, she had no way of hiding her face. Sweat broke out along her spine as she prayed Victoria stemmed her inevitable concern in front of Miss Pennington.

'Yes, Miss Pennington? Good afternoon, Miss Taylor.' Victoria's smile diminished as her gaze landed on Ruby's bruise.

Ruby quickly shook her head and widened her eyes, warning Victoria to keep her counsel. Victoria stared at Ruby a moment longer before facing Miss Pennington. 'How can I help, Miss Pennington?'

'I'm so glad I caught you both. I'd very much like you to work together on a new project. As Esther and Amelia will be away from the store for a while, I thought this the perfect time to give you a chance of creating a design of your own, Miss Taylor. Would you be open to the challenge?'

'Of course.' Ruby relaxed her shoulders, her concerns about her injury momentarily vanishing. 'I'd be delighted.'

'Wonderful. Then I'd like you to combine your design skills with Mrs Lark's expertise in accessories and devise a central atrium display.' Elizabeth looked across the crowded space. 'It's been too long since we have had something to stop customers in their tracks when they come through the door. To my mind, nothing catches a woman's attention more than accessories. I am thinking fans, parasols, sashes, belts, purses, gloves . . . and anything else you might think appropriate.'

Despite the heat of Victoria's stare burning into Ruby's temple, a rush of excitement stirred in her abdomen. This was the first time Miss Pennington had approached her for a design task of her own and it meant the world. To be valued and noticed at work mattered so much, and went a long way in eliminating her mother's criticism.

'Well, Miss Taylor?' Miss Pennington raised her eyebrows. 'Do you think you could come up with a design that Mrs Lark could bring to life? I want as much merchandise on display as possible. A big glass counter will be installed in the very centre, circular in design and directly in line with the front doors. That way, customers will have to walk around it in order to reach the stairs. It will be impossible to miss.'

'It sounds wonderful.' Ruby's imagination filled with possibilities at this chance to shine. She might one day be considered for a pay increase if she impressed Miss Pennington. 'When would you like my ideas to be presented to you?'

'As soon as possible.' Miss Pennington addressed

Victoria. 'Would you be free to discuss some preliminary ideas with Miss Taylor now? I know it's short notice, but it would be good if we can set to work today. I'll swap around some girls so that Accessories is sufficiently staffed.'

'Of course.' Victoria stared at Ruby, her green eyes filled with a persistent concern. 'I can come along with you to the design department now, if you like?'

Ruby swallowed, her smile strained. 'Wonderful.'

'Perfect, then I'll leave you to it,' Miss Pennington said, before she hurried away in the direction of Accessories.

Victoria immediately gripped Ruby's elbow. 'What on earth happened to your face? Did a man do that to you? Did someone strike you?'

'No. Yes, but — '

'What happened?'

Ruby nervously glanced over Victoria's shoulder, her arms aching under the weight of the clothes she was carrying. 'Not here. Let's go to the design department.'

Leaving Victoria to follow, Ruby walked towards the staff stairs as shame burned hot inside her. Dislike towards her mother rose on a tangible wave that Ruby must now bear the humiliation of confessing to Victoria just how bad things were becoming at home.

Tears pricked her eyes, but Ruby defiantly blinked them back.

She was not to blame for her mother's outbursts, her drinking or her sleeping with whichever Tom, Dick or Harry she invited back to the house. Every ounce of neglect, abuse and insult towards her children was her mother's fault alone.

To hell with her.

Ruby pushed open the design department's swing door and marched towards her station at the back of the room, carefully placing the hats on two stands before hanging the dresses on a mobile rack.

Drawing on every ounce of her minimal pride, she crossed her arms and faced Victoria. 'Before I explain anything, I do not want your sympathy. Is that clear?'

Victoria raised her eyebrows, irritation clear in her eyes. 'If I choose sympathy or anger, that is entirely up to me. What I won't abide is not hearing the truth. Who hurt you?'

Ruby stared into Victoria's eyes, her heart beating with the deep-seated desire she felt for her and had kept so carefully buried for months, but suspected others had guessed. It could only be Ruby's lack of discretion if her suspicions were proven true. There could be no doubt she behaved differently when she was around Victoria compared with anyone else. Slowly, patiently, Ruby had waited for Victoria to notice her and now, she could safely consider them friends. Good friends.

But, by God, she wanted so much more.

'Ruby?'

'My mother.'

Victoria's gaze turned incredulous. 'Your mother did that to you? Well, I hope you gave as good back. You are a grown woman, Ruby. No one, including your mother, has a right to put their hands on you.'

'I dealt with it.'

'Which means what exactly?'

'It will be awhile before she hits me again.' She looked past Victoria to the two colleagues working at sewing machines on the other side of the room. She lowered her voice. 'My mother is a drunk, Victoria.

A vicious, bitter woman who prefers the company of strange men to the company of her children.'

Victoria's jaw tightened. 'Then you must move out.'

Ruby laughed and uncrossed her arms, turning to the dresses on the rack behind her. 'Of course I should. I have no idea why I hadn't thought of that.'

'Ruby . . . ' Victoria's hand curled around Ruby's arm, forcing her to turn. 'I'm serious.'

Tears burned behind Ruby's eyes, her skin sensitive under Victoria's fingers. 'So am I. I can't leave. At least not yet. How can I keep Tommy safe without sufficient money? For the time being, I'm stuck. Stuck under Ma's roof for God's knows how long, but it won't be forever. I can promise you that.'

'No, Ruby, it won't be long and I'll tell you why.' Determination shone in Victoria's gaze. 'Because you and your brother are coming to live with me.'

20

Amelia closed her notebook and sat back in the desk chair inside her cabin.

It was her fifth day at sea and ideas for potential new merchandise and window displays for Pennington's were beginning to stack up. She couldn't wait to get to New York and discover more. Bumping into Harriet Culford had been a godsend, giving Amelia the opportunity to learn more about the upper-class way of life.

Speaking with moneyed people, spending social time with them, had provided a deeper insight into their wants and wishes. It had also helped that Miss Culford was incredibly fond of talking about herself and her possessions.

Amelia smiled as she walked to her bed and picked up her purse. Now, she and Mr Weir would be joining Harriet and some friends for lunch.

There was a rap on her door, and she hurried to answer it. 'Good afternoon, Mr Weir.'

'Good afternoon. Are you ready for our lunch date?' He inspected her dress. 'You look most presentable.'

Hardly an overwhelming compliment, but after the unwanted attention she'd received thus far, Mr Weir's words were sufficient. 'Thank you. Shall we go?'

He stepped back and Amelia pulled her cabin door closed.

Mr Weir cleared his throat as they walked. 'I still don't quite understand how you came to be speaking to Miss Culford when she is in first class and we are in second, but she must have enjoyed your company the other evening to invite us to lunch.'

'We got on very well,' Amelia said, scrambling to avoid an explanation of how she came to meet Harriet. 'Although, she couldn't be more different than Cornelia. In fact, it's barely comprehensible they are sisters when Cornelia is so humble and keen to help others. I'm not sure I can say the same of Harriet. At least, not yet.'

'Did she mention her sister's upcoming wedding during your conversations? I believe Cornelia and Mr Gower are to be married in the summer.'

Amelia frowned. 'No, she didn't mention it at all. Which seems strange now I think of it. No matter. I'm thrilled that Cornelia and Stephen have fallen so deeply in love. I'm sure their wedding will be beautiful.'

'Hmm.'

Amelia smiled at Mr Weir's clear dismissal of further wedding conversation. Stephen Gower had come to work at Pennington's the previous Christmas and it soon became public knowledge that he had once worked for Scotland Yard. Together with Cornelia Culford, Stephen had managed to track the killer of Mr Carter's first wife. A haunting event that had tormented him for years.

Even though such heinous events had initially prevented Cornelia and Stephen from a path of easy romance, they had prevailed. It gave Amelia hope that maybe all was not lost for her to one day find love, too.

They ascended onto D-deck and into the enormous first-class dining saloon.

Intimidation threatened as Amelia stared about

the space, fighting to calm her instinct to stare at everything and everyone.

The white-painted walls and leaded glass windows gave the feeling that they were not at sea at all but in a fancy restaurant in the middle of Bath. Decorative pilasters interspersed the windows and fluted urns stood in spaces throughout the room adding a regal atmosphere, perfect against the myriad of expensive clothes, hats, feathers and pearls. Expensive perfume and hair cream scented the air as Amelia passed the tables, smells of richly flavoured foods merging to tease her nostrils.

'Do you see Miss Culford?' Mr Weir peered left and right over the diners. 'I'm not sure I'd recognise her.'

Amelia surveyed the room and spotted Harriet seated around a table with four other people. Three additional chairs stood empty. Nerves clenched her stomach. She had not expected to dine with anyone else other than Harriet and her travelling companion, Susannah Varson. What if she couldn't keep up with the group conversation? Or someone asked her questions she wouldn't welcome being put to her in front of Mr Weir?

Harriet was beautifully dressed in a pale pink tea dress, her dark brown hair curled and pinned so that soft tendrils fell at her temples. Although a little on the slender side, she was no less beautiful than Cornelia.

Amelia smoothed her hand over the side of her dress, grateful once again for Elizabeth's generosity.

Whatever happened during luncheon, she was convinced Harriet would do her utmost to maintain a purposeful distance between them that would never occur to Cornelia to enforce. Well, that was fine. She was here to work, not make friends. Fingers crossed, that distance would also steer conversation clear of anything personal.

She straightened her shoulders. 'There she is. Just over there near the window.'

Mr Weir followed her gaze. 'Ah, yes. I assumed it would just be Miss Culford and her friend joining us, but I see our company has multiplied.' He glanced at Amelia, interest and more than a little pleasure lighting his brown eyes. 'This luncheon will undoubtedly expand on all you learned during your previous time in Miss Culford's company. Let us use this opportunity to our advantage, Miss Wakefield.'

Until now, Mr Weir had shown little enthusiasm for their information-gathering, behaving as though being aboard the grandest ship in the world was of little consequence. However, his eagerness for this lunch was palpable and Amelia had no doubt rubbing shoulders with the elite had altered his mindset. She bit back her smile. The more time she spent with Mr Weir, the more she liked him.

They reached Harriet's table and Amelia smiled. 'Good afternoon, Miss Culford. Miss Varson.'

'Oh, Amelia.' Harriet immediately stood and extended her hand. 'Everyone, this is Miss Amelia Wakefield and Mr Weir, isn't it?'

Mr Weir dipped his head. 'It is.'

'Please join us.' She looked around the table, her pretty blue eyes bright with happiness. 'Miss Wakefield and Mr Weir work alongside my sister and sister-in-law at Pennington's department store in Bath. It is such a coincidence to have them aboard. Miss Wakefield found herself in first class quite by accident when we met. Did you not, Miss Wakefield?'

Amelia opened her mouth to respond with an excuse, but Harriet had resumed her chatter.

'Take a seat, Miss Wakefield, Mr Weir, and I'll introduce everyone.'

Amelia sat and smiled at their dinner companions.

'You've met Miss Varson and this is Mr Benjamin Edwards. A profoundly astute and successful New York banker of the almost unforgivably modest character.' Harriet giggled, her eyes alight with blatant flirtation. 'And lastly, might I introduce the newly married David and Sophie Parker who are on their honeymoon?' Harriet's eyes visibly dimmed at she stared at the pair. 'It may come as a bit of shock for you both to meet Mr Parker under such romantic circumstances . . . considering he was previously married to my sister.'

The atmosphere turned icy and Amelia's cheeks heated even as she tried her best to offer Mr and Mrs Parker a smile. She had recognised David Parker the moment she'd been seated, having seen the man enraged and behaving in an unnervingly threatening manner towards Cornelia on the courthouse steps after their divorce hearing.

He was certainly a man to be wary of.

She quickly looked to Harriet before the part of her that no longer wanted to be seated at the table outweighed her determination to glean some New York shopping insight. It was highly probable most people present had visited America before this voyage. 'It was very kind of you to invite myself and Mr Weir to lunch, Miss Culford.'

'Not at all, and Harriet, please. We are all friends here. Whether first class or second.'

Amelia stared at Harriet's turned cheek. If the

woman had spoken sincerely, then Amelia was a millionaire. She could only surmise that Harriet's act of extending her hand across the class divide was a device to make herself appear tolerant and more forward-thinking in Mr Edward's eyes. It was obvious she had set her sights on the wealthy American banker.

Waiters approached the table carrying the first courses as others came forward to fill their water glasses.

Amelia glanced at Mr Weir and he raised his eyebrows, his eyes kind.

She smiled and relaxed her shoulders. If Mr Weir was happy to play a part in this undeniable charade, so was she. What did it matter if she failed to impress or inspire these people? They would be of use to *her*, not the other way around.

She turned to Susannah Varson. 'So, tell me, Miss Varson, where did you purchase your wonderful hat? Do you hope to find something new and exciting to take home from America?'

'I do. I bought this hat at Selfridges in London. Have you been?' The young woman beamed, pride showing in her pink cheeks. 'Papa is so generous with my allowance whenever I take a trip to the capital.'

And so the conversation began, and Amelia avidly listened, ears pricked for any and all information. Throughout the meal, she asked questions of Mr Edwards, his descriptions and knowledge of New York further fuelling her impatience to arrive. America seemed such an exciting place where societal and political changes took place at a much more rapid pace than they did in England.

Anticipation and expectation rose inside her.

Just a few more days and they would sail into New York harbour and then her adventure would truly begin.

21

As dessert was being finished in the second-class dining room, Samuel made a sharp exit, his cheeks aching from his continual and enforced smiling. The brief, duty-bound conversations he'd shared with twenty or thirty passengers throughout lunch had been nice enough, but claustrophobia throughout his 'entertainment' shifts was beginning to grow.

He entered the corridor, intent on taking some air.

The guests' chatter had often turned to the weather and how the temperatures were dropping at an unexpected rate. This evening, people proclaimed to smell ice or snow in the air. Coincidentally, the captain had voiced the possibility of icebergs, or even the emergence of an ice-field, as they sailed farther across the great ocean. Yet, no undue alarm had been raised and Samuel had reassured a few overly cautious passengers as best he could.

Whether freezing cold or not, he welcomed the chill if it meant ridding himself of the stuffiness in the dining room. For all the guests' amiable conversation, their haughty gazes and upturned chins were indication enough of their assumed superiority over him and the other staff.

He strolled along C-deck to the promenade and spotted Amelia Wakefield talking with Mr Weir as they walked in Samuel's direction. He hadn't seen her since he'd knocked on her cabin door, the night before.

She looked animated as she spoke with Weir, his

mouth curved into a smile that took Samuel by surprise. Maybe the man wasn't quite as grave as he'd first appeared.

Instead of addressing them, Samuel feigned interest in the view through one of the promenade's large glass windows. Did he speak with Amelia as he wanted? Or leave her alone to talk with Weir? Clearly, she was enjoying their conversation.

He regretfully chose the latter, albeit entirely convinced by forgoing the chance to speak to her, he was doing the decent thing for both of them. He liked her more than he should, but the apprehension in her eyes after her threatening encounter last night made it clear she was understandably averse to male attention.

And he would respect her wishes completely.

Whenever he thought of her being molested, his blood boiled. The last thing he wanted was to give Amelia further reason to distance herself from him.

'Officer Murphy? How are you?'

Her sweet voice carried across the promenade and straight into Samuel's chest. God damn it, he was caught like a fish on a hook. Plastering on a smile, he faced her and Weir, a pang of jealousy assaulting him to see Amelia's hand curved so easily around the older man's arm.

Samuel dipped his head. 'Good afternoon, Miss Wakefield. Mr Weir.'

Her dark eyes grazed over his face, a teasing smile playing at her lips. She looked exceedingly happy and a yearning to know why wound tight in his gut.

'I didn't see you at lunch,' Samuel said, as he shook hands with Mr Weir. 'Did you enjoy your meal?'

'That's because we didn't eat in the second-class

dining room.' Amelia smiled sheepishly. 'I managed to get an invitation to take lunch in first class.'

Samuel grinned, taking an infinite amount of pleasure in her satisfaction. 'I see.'

'Didn't I tell you I wanted to see how everyone on the ship behaves?' Her brown eyes shone with happiness. 'Learn of their dreams and wishes once they reach America?'

'You did.' He winked at her and two spots of colour leapt into her cheeks before she glanced down at her feet.

Weir's smile vanished as he assessed Samuel through narrowed eyes.

Samuel held his gaze, heedless of the disgruntled way Weir now studied him. Why shouldn't he engage in conversation — a little flirtation — with a beautiful woman? This was an adventure, a surreal moment in time. Not just for him, but for so many on this ship. He guessed the same could be said for the two people standing in front of him . . . despite Weir's loftiness.

Samuel raised his eyebrows. 'And you, sir. Did you enjoy your lunch?'

'I did, Officer Murphy. The first-class food is excellent, of course, but I have to admit no more impressive than what we've been served in second class. White Star has most certainly assured a luxurious journey for all.'

Was the man serious? Did he think only the comfortably or exceedingly well off were on this ship?

'Well, for some passengers, anyway.' Samuel glanced away, irked that Weir wouldn't consider the journey of third-class passengers, or worse, the poor sods packed into steerage. 'I wouldn't say everyone aboard is having the grandest of times.'

'You mean the third-class passengers?' Amelia studied him, her gaze sombre with interest. 'Are the conditions really that much worse?'

'It's hard to say if they are better or worse than the people travelling down there are used to, but the cabins and facilities are definitely more crowded and confined than second and third class.'

She frowned and faced Weir. 'Maybe I should venture to the lower decks, too.'

'I hardly think the lower decks are a suitable place for you to be venturing, Miss Wakefield.'

'But didn't I say I want to see everything? Miss Pennington did not send us on this trip to only view the wealthy. Pennington's welcomes everyone. She will expect me to know as much about the dreams of those passengers who couldn't afford the higher-class tickets as she will of the wealthy. If you have no wish to accompany me, then maybe . . . ' She looked to Samuel, her dark eyes pleading with him. 'Officer Murphy wouldn't mind?'

Weir flinched. 'Miss Wakefield, Miss Pennington asked that I ensure your safety. You have wandered off before for such a time that I had to enlist Officer Murphy's help in finding you. No, I think it best we keep to the second- and first-class areas.'

Amelia's gaze turned steely as she glared at Weir's turned cheek and Samuel looked away, his admiration for her mounting. She really was quite a woman, and his wish to know her, spend time with her, deepened.

'Mr Weir, I am determined to see the whole of this ship, with or without you,' she said firmly. 'Now, you either grant me consent to do just that, or I will have no choice but to ask Officer Murphy for his help in sending a wire to Miss Pennington asking for her permission to carry out my investigations in any way I see fit.'

'Miss Wakefield, I will not stand here and allow you to speak to me — '

'The only other alternative is that you trust Officer Murphy to ensure I come to no undue harm.'

A vein rose in Weir's temple as he looked at them both, before facing Amelia. 'Miss Wakefield — '

'Do we bother Miss Pennington with this or not? That is the only thing up for dispute.' She snapped her gaze to Samuel. 'Will you ensure my safety this afternoon, Officer Murphy? Be so kind as to escort me back to my cabin once I have seen everything I wish to see?'

Samuel fought to contain a sombre expression. 'Of course.'

She turned to Weir, one eyebrow raised.

Weir looked as though he might burst a blood vessel but, slowly, he stepped back. 'As you wish. Officer Murphy, I expect you to knock on my cabin and let me know when Miss Wakefield is safely returned. Do you understand?'

'Yes, sir.'

'Good.' Weir turned to Amelia. 'On your head be it if your quest to see everything gives you sleepless nights. I will bid you good afternoon.'

'So, my afternoon is yours, Officer Murphy.' She grinned, her brown eyes glinting with mischief. 'What delights will you show me first?'

22

Ruby bent her head to the sewing machine in Pennington's basement. All afternoon her fingers had worked the complicated row of stitches, but her thoughts remained jumbled and unsure.

Because you and your brother are coming to live with me . . .

Victoria's words ran on a continual stream through Ruby's mind. It didn't matter that she'd protested against Victoria's offer. It didn't matter that she'd told her she couldn't afford to pay her a decent amount of regular rent.

Victoria had been adamant, and now Ruby was torn between accepting her offer, which would undoubtedly give her and Tommy a chance to escape their mother . . . or to steadfastly refuse. The sensible first option would mean enduring the torture of not just seeing Victoria at work and occasional social outings, but living side by side, night after night, with a woman she desired heart, body and soul.

How was she to hide her feelings in such intimate circumstances? Would she see Victoria in her nightclothes? Walking from the bathroom with only a towel covering a body Ruby longed to touch and kiss? Yearning tingled through her and Ruby pressed her fingers tighter to the material she worked on. Such wanton lust in a woman towards a man was shameful enough, but to want Victoria as Ruby did was mortifying . . . and futile.

Across the room, her colleagues worked diligently

at their machines, but Ruby's cheeks burned that they might have sensed her incongruous thoughts.

Footsteps at the doorway turned her head and Ruby inwardly groaned as Hazel Price sauntered into the room, her weasel-like face further accentuated by her pinched smile and small, beady eyes flitting left and right as she sought her unfortunate prey.

Her gaze landed on Ruby and satisfaction immediately lit Hazel's eyes.

What in God's name did the woman want now?

Day after day, Hazel Price haunted Ruby on the floors and departments of Pennington's like an annoying beetle, scurrying and skitting about, spreading her spite and negativity. There could be no doubt she knew of Ruby's secret love of Victoria, that her desire for her went beyond the platonic. The question was, what did Hazel intend to do about it?

'Miss Taylor, just the person I was looking for.' Hazel walked closer, her expression predatory. 'I've been sent up with some material for you from the workroom. Mr Carter said you will know what it's for.'

Ruby stood, her spine ramrod straight, braced for whatever Hazel was ready to launch at her. She took the bolt of ivory satin. 'Thank you. Can you tell Mr Carter I will be in a position to start working on a wedding display in the next week or so?'

'Weddings. Funny things, aren't they?' Hazel strolled around Ruby's workspace, her long fingers sweeping over the material swatches and lengths of ribbon. 'They're so banal, don't you think?'

'If you say so.' Ruby laid the material on a chest of drawers and crossed her arms. 'Is there anything else you wanted?'

'Hmm?'

'You've delivered the material. If there's no other reason for you to stay, I'd like to get back to my work.'

'Oh, your work . . . is that all you have occupying your mind today, Miss Taylor? Only . . . '

Ruby curled her hands into fists, her nails pinching into her palms. 'Only what?'

Hazel stopped and held Ruby's gaze, her eyes burning with familiar malice. 'Only, I understand from Mrs Lark that you will soon have matters far more pressing than anything Mr Carter or Miss Pennington might demand of you.'

Ruby felt the colour drain from her face as her mouth dried. 'What are you talking about?'

'You don't know?'

'Why would I ask if I did?'

'Well, let's just say I'm all for the modern woman. Modern situations. But really, Miss Taylor, you and Mrs Lark living together when it's clear the relationship is so much more than *friendly*. Everyone has seen the desirous way you look at her. Your feelings are clearly written in your eyes. In fact, your interest in Mrs Lark is quite the topic of interest in the workroom. I daresay the same will be true throughout the entire store by the end of the week.'

'I have no idea what you're talking about.' Ruby turned away, her fingers trembling as she rearranged some needles on her table, her heart racing. 'Mrs Lark and I are friends. Nothing more, nothing less. I'd thank you not to spread your malicious, unsubstantiated gossip around the workroom or anywhere else, for that matter.'

'Gossip? About your inappropriate interest or you moving into Mrs Lark's house? Oh, well, I know for certain the moving in is not gossip, at least. I heard it straight from the horse's, or should I say, Mrs Lark's mouth.'

Ruby slowly turned, sickness rolling through her. Surely, Victoria would not have made her offer of a room to Ruby public knowledge? And to Hazel of all people?

Hazel grinned spitefully. 'So, it *is* true. Look at the colour of your face. Well, such open flaunting of such a repulsive relationship is quite unorthodox, I must say.'

Anger swept through Ruby on an undulating wave. How dare she? She trembled as she fought to stem the urge to slap the woman. Ruby squared her shoulders. She would not waver in front of Hazel. Or anyone else. She and Victoria, if she chose to live with her, would be doing nothing wrong.

She crossed her arms. 'Mrs Lark is a widow. Living with her maid in a house she owns. She has offered for my brother and me to stay with her while I'm going through a few difficulties. I have neither accepted nor refused. So, why don't you reel in that nasty tongue of yours, swallow whatever ridiculous conclusions you've jumped to and leave this department? Right now.'

Hazel's smile widened, her eyes alight with glee. 'Or what?'

'Or . . .' Ruby stepped closer, her hand hovering over the pair of scissors next to her. 'I might not be able to contain my patience as I am now. That's what.'

Hazel's gaze shifted to the scissors and her smile wavered for a brief second, before she lifted her chin. 'I'll be on my way then. I look forward to seeing how this little story plays out. Good day, Miss Taylor.'

Ruby held herself rigid, the stares of her colleagues burning into her from every direction. She kept her focus on Hazel, met her glare when the witch threw a parting glance over her shoulder.

Swallowing hard, Ruby returned to her sewing machine and sat, the fraught silence of the room pressing down on her. She had to say something. Do something. She was more or less in charge of the department while Amelia was away, and Miss Pennington was coming to trust her. Rely on her. She could not let her down and wane in the authority she'd been granted.

She purposefully met the open stares of her colleagues. 'Do you need more work, ladies? Or should I tell Mr Carter this week's display will not be ready in time, and we'll not be able to start on the wedding display next week as planned?'

All three women mumbled a 'no' and turned back to their work.

But not fast enough for Ruby to not notice their smirks, their undisguised delight, in all that Hazel had just purposely played out in front of them.

No doubt her and Tommy living with Victoria would soon be the subject of word by word scrutiny.

Ruby faced her machine, hating that her vision blurred behind her tears.

She had to make a choice.

To stand up and accept Victoria's offer with proud finality or bury her shame and vow never to speak or bother Victoria again, in the hope she escaped the store's speculation.

23

Amelia walked beside Samuel, trying her hardest not to think about his handsome face, broad shoulders and dangerously disarming smile. The strangest, unexpected sensation had skittered over the surface of her skin when he'd winked at her in front of Mr Weir. A sensation that felt far too much like attraction . . . something she had begun to think herself incapable of feeling after the rape.

Yet, she *was* attracted to Samuel. Exceedingly so.

He touched a secret part of her soul, of her heart. Never before had a man given her such undivided, unconditional attention. He listened when she spoke about her work and seemed to understand her passion for it, taking an interest in her cause to explore every part of the *Titanic*. What she was beginning to feel for Samuel went beyond his extraordinary looks.

Time and again, she searched for any indication his interest in her might be grounded in an ulterior motive or come with a clause that he would reveal in time. Yet, she saw nothing but kindness in him. A gentle attentiveness that she enjoyed, rather than turned away from.

Regardless, she had to remain mindful that she had been caught in a similar situation before. Softened by the helping hand of a man she'd thought considerate and, instead, had been a monster.

'So, what would you like to see first, Miss Wakefield?' Samuel glanced at her, his brilliant blue eyes happy. 'I don't have access to the cabins, I'm afraid, but I can show you the dining room and common areas?'

Amelia stopped, her confused intuition about him overtaking her politeness. 'Why are you so determined to help me, Officer Murphy? Not that I don't appreciate it.'

'It's Samuel, remember? Especially when we're alone.' He smiled, his eyes gentle on hers. 'I want to help you because I like you.'

Heat crept into her cheeks, pleasure warming her heart. 'But you barely know me.'

'True, but I like what I know so far. Is that so bad?'

'No, I don't suppose it is . . . Samuel.' She carefully studied him as a delicious happiness rippled through her. 'And I'd very much like you to call me Amelia. Especially when we're alone.'

His grin lit his entire face. 'Come on. Let's start with the dining room.'

He offered her his arm and, once again, instinctive self-preservation rose. Amelia hesitated and tried her hardest to fight her demons. *Samuel is not a monster. He won't hurt me like the master did.*

She slipped her hand onto Samuel's arm and exhaled shakily. 'We should tell each other a little more about ourselves. You already know I work for Pennington's and have for about two years. I started in the workroom, stitching and sewing buttons and gradually worked my way into the design department. I love my job. Do you enjoy being a seaman? Is sailing on the *Titanic* a dream come true?'

'Not a dream come true, no.'

The rare disquiet in his voice surprised her. 'Oh?'

He stared ahead, his jaw a hard line. 'The *Titanic* is my temporary, maybe even permanent, escape from responsibility.'

'Surely there can be no responsibility more arduous than being a crew member of such a phenomenal vessel? People all over the world are mesmerised by this ship. That must put an enormous amount of pressure on everyone involved.'

'Maybe, but the job isn't the responsibility I'm referring to. I love sailing. Love being on the water. I'm referring to the obligations I have at home. Financial and emotional.' He hesitated as though trying to decide whether or not to elaborate, before he abruptly stared ahead. 'My father was a seaman, too. He died suddenly from an accident on the Southampton docks. So, with his death, I became solely responsible, at the grand old age of nineteen, for my ma and sisters.'

'They don't work?'

'No, I wouldn't necessarily want Ma to. In fact, I'm no longer sure she could. She's been . . . fragile since my father's passing. He looked after her from the day they married. As for my sisters . . . ' He shook his head. 'I'm beginning to think they're a lost cause. I swear, Ma considers them ladies of high breeding rather than daughters of a sailing man.'

'I see.'

But she didn't see at all. How could his sisters, who were clearly capable of working, leave their brother solely accountable for their prosperity? She had worked in some form or another her entire life. Dark, hard memories pressed down on her and Amelia glanced at Samuel, afraid he might see the self-pity in her eyes. He continued to stare ahead, seemingly lost in thought.

She cleared her throat. 'I can't imagine what it's like being part of a family. I'm sorry so much has fallen to you.'

'You're an only child?'

'Yes.'

'And your parents live in Bath?'

Amelia swallowed, afraid to talk about her private life, but wanting to just a little with Samuel. Would it really hurt to tell him something of her childhood? 'My mother died birthing me.'

His soft gaze searched hers. 'I'm sorry.'

She quickly looked away lest she fell into the ocean-blue kindness in his eyes. 'There's no need for your sympathy. I've managed well enough.'

'And your father?'

'Was forced to give me up to an orphanage. Having been born out of wedlock, neither his family nor my mother's wanted anything to do with me. I stayed at the orphanage, learned to sew and knit and when I turned fifteen . . . '

Further words caught in her throat. She could not tell him about her time in service. Samuel had a way of looking at her that made her want to share too much with him. To unburden herself for the first time in her life. She had no idea why. The connection she felt with him made no sense.

Yet, she instinctively sensed she could trust this man — this relative stranger.

Absolute, unsubstantiated foolishness that she needed to stem.

'I worked as a maid in a grand house until I got a position at Pennington's.' She forced a smile. 'And I haven't looked back since.'

He studied her before he winked in that toe-curling way of his. 'A strong woman then. Just as I thought.'

Despite the words of warning to herself, an undeniable pride burned inside of her as they walked on. No one had ever called her strong before. Talented, yes. Hardworking, most certainly. But strong? Never. She stood a little taller, risked another glance at Samuel's profile and a warmth stirred deep in her chest that was as delightful as it was terrifying.

He led her down a set of steps to the lower deck and she gently pulled him to a stop at the bottom of the stairs as realisation dawned. 'Do you mean you won't be returning from America? Is that what you meant by a permanent escape?'

He eased her hand from his arm and swiped his hand over his face, a sudden tiredness clouding his eyes. 'I shouldn't dwell on what ifs and maybes. They'll most likely come to nothing.'

'But that's what you meant? You could possibly stay in New York?'

'My friend thinks I should stay in America, but Archie's a dreamer. Thinks anything in this world is entirely possible.'

Didn't she believe the very same thing? 'And you don't?'

He glanced along the corridor. 'I've had dreams in the past, but quickly learned such thinking is futile.'

His frustration was palpable, and Amelia had the sudden urge to comfort him. 'Even now, when you are aboard a ship bound for America? Surely, a year, two years ago, you could not have envisioned yourself here as you are now? Isn't that proof enough that we have to think bigger than ourselves? That we have the right to imagine the unimaginable and revel in our dreams when they come true?'

His gaze wandered slowly over her face. 'You're a breath of fresh air, do you know that? You have such . . .'

Her heart beat a little faster. 'What?'

'Such wilfulness.'

She laughed. 'Wilfulness?'

'Yes.' He grinned. 'Like you believe life is exciting, bountiful and true.'

Amelia's smile dissolved, and she turned away from his admiring gaze as a fire lit by disappointment, hurt and rape twisted inside of her. 'Life is full of challenges and ways of making us turn away from the light. From opportunity.' She faced him, lifted her chin. 'But I have vowed to never allow anything, or anyone, make me waver in my wish to have a good life and inspire the same in others ever again.'

A deep line appeared between his brows as he studied her. 'Did something happen to you, Amelia?' he asked softly.

Amelia purposefully held his gaze, her heart racing. 'That is neither here nor there.'

Several seconds passed before he gave a firm nod, understanding seeping into his gaze. 'You're right, it isn't. Archie thinks there is nothing to stop me from sending money home, finding my own life. Maybe he's right, but dreaming about escape is one thing, actually doing it is another.'

Amelia touched his arm, willing her passion to ease as she softened her voice, lest he think her ever so slightly mad. 'But wouldn't it be an unbelievable adventure if you were to stay?'

'Yes. Yes, it would.'

She stared at him as her imagination ran wild with ponderings of what it would be like to start a new life across the Atlantic. Her stomach knotted just imagining what excitements would lie ahead for Samuel if he took that leap. Of what awaited *her* on this trip to a new land.

'You're beautiful, do you know that?'

She blinked, words catching in her throat.

'Really, really beautiful.' He smiled. 'Shall we go?'

Her steps lighter, they ventured deeper into third class towards the dining room. He had called her beautiful and said so many other wonderful things to her . . . about her.

Amelia briefly closed her eyes and forced her focus to her work, the increased noise of the engines providing the perfect excuse to not indulge in further conversation.

As they neared a set of double doors, a uniformed steward straightened his shoulders, eyeing them with clear suspicion.

'Leave this to me.' Samuel strode forward and touched his hat in greeting. 'Good afternoon, is it possible we can access the dining room? Only, Miss Wakefield has possibly left her gloves at one of the tables.'

The steward merely smirked and assessed Amelia from head to toe before raising his eyebrows. 'Am I to believe you to be a third-class passenger, Miss? Only, it seems a number of first- and second-class passengers find it an amusement, a distraction, if you will, to venture to the lower decks to view the furnishings and clientele as objects of fascination. We are under strict orders that no one other than third-class are allowed in these rooms. These passengers deserve the same amount of respect as anyone else.'

Shame washed over Amelia that she might be considered a voyeur of other people's unfortune or daily struggle. Why had she not thought of how condescending it might seem to third-class passengers to have someone from second-class come down on what could be deemed as a slumming expedition?

Samuel cleared his throat. 'Miss Wakefield merely wishes — '

'It's quite all right, Officer.' She touched Samuel's arm and faced the steward. 'I apologise. I am a second-class passenger and you're right, I shouldn't be here. I merely wanted to see the dining room and hopefully speak to some passengers for my work.'

'Your work?'

'Yes, I'm a window designer for a prestigious department store. It's Pennington's mission to ensure our clothes, accessories and all other areas of merchandise are available to everyone. Whatever their walk in life. Believe me, sir, if my employers were not funding this trip, I would most certainly be travelling third-class. I meant no offence. I'll go.'

'What is it you'd like to see exactly?'

'Just the dining room. Maybe the lounge?'

He looked from Amelia to Samuel, who shrugged, and then back to Amelia. 'All right. As lunch is finished, you may see the dining room, but that's it. Most of the passengers have left anyway. There will be a few staff you might want to speak with.'

'Thank you.' Amelia smiled. 'That's very kind of you.'

He nodded and stepped back, opening the doors.

The third-class dining room was, indeed, emptying of its remaining diners but the differences between the class areas were immediately plain. The third-class dining saloon didn't have the fancy wood panelling of second class, or the columns and pilasters of first, yet it was pleasingly decorated in whitewashed panelling and teak furniture, giving an airy feel, with comfortable-looking chairs and decently clothed tables.

Amelia walked slowly, casting furtive looks at the remaining diners as they strolled towards the exit. Everyone seemed happy enough, their eyes and body language not as downtrodden and morose as Samuel's response to Mr Weir's comments earlier had led her to believe.

All were decently dressed, even if flat caps and lace or ribbon hair adornments donned their heads, rather than the flamboyant women's hats and gentlemen's top hats of the upper classes. The colours of their clothes were a little more subdued but were as close to the current fashions as possible on a lower income.

Pleasure swept through Amelia as she walked, Samuel's quiet footsteps behind her.

The ambience of the dining room was inspiring. As though the design and décor had been purposely considered as a way of giving third-class passengers a sense of luxury, of importance, no matter their work or reasons for travelling.

Could not Pennington's inspire the same in their merchandise? Surely, whatever ideas Amelia returned to Bath with for the upper classes, each could be made in cheaper, more affordable materials for the lower classes. Thus, giving everyone the chance to feel proud, fashionable and important.

She faced Samuel. 'I've seen enough. Let's go.'

'Are you sure? I can persuade the steward to let us see the general room. I'm pretty sure there's a smoking room and bar, too.'

'No, I already have ideas of what needs to be done at Pennington's. My ideas around manufacturing and window designs are beginning to form splendidly.' She grinned. 'I'm sure Miss Pennington will agree with what I envision. Let's leave the staff to their work.'

He stepped back, gesturing with a sweep of his arm for her to lead the way. As she brushed past him, the escalation of her confidence and ambition urged her to encourage Samuel in his. The need to talk to him alone took over her common sense.

'Samuel?'

'Yes?'

'Might we meet later?'

His gaze was intense on hers. 'For?'

'I'd like to talk to you alone. This evening.'

His eyes flashed with surprise before he looked past her. 'My shift in the control room doesn't finish until eleven. How will you possibly — '

'Leave my excuses to me. I will meet you on the promenade then.'

Before he could respond — or she lost her nerve — Amelia headed for the dining room doors.

24

Samuel stared through the control room window at an endless sheet of shining black ocean, his thoughts swimming with possible explanations of why Amelia had asked him to meet her. What did her request mean? Did it mean anything at all? Did he even want it to mean anything when a ship-bound romance would undoubtedly bring more problems than satisfaction?

Amelia might be a working woman, but she was also a woman of class and strength. Yet, her quiet sophistication, soft voice and beautiful smile contradicted the pain he'd seen in her eyes when she had spoken with such fervour about nothing standing in her way of building a good life for herself.

How in God's name did someone who had been orphaned retain the spirit and heart to rise? Not just rise, but forge a successful occupation at one of the country's most illustrious department stores. He was by no means a shopper, but even Samuel had heard Pennington's mentioned in the same sentence as Harrods and Selfridge & Co while aboard the *Titanic*.

The woman should be dressed to the nines and sipping a cocktail in first class under the admiring glances of a millionaire or two, not wandering around with a seaman in tow.

'Penny for them, Sam?'

He started. 'Archie. How are you?'

'Good. All the better for seeing you. I looked for you after lunch but couldn't find you anywhere.' He wiggled his eyebrows, his brown eyes teasing. 'Didn't duck out of your entertaining shift, did you?'

'I was around.' Samuel turned his attention back to the ocean. 'Not that I find everything about those shifts entertaining.'

'No?'

The teasing in Archie's voice caused Samuel to face him. 'What?'

'I heard you went walkabout with a certain lady.' He nudged Samuel's shoulder. 'I hope you weren't up to no good.'

Samuel made a show of checking some switches. 'I was escorting Amelia around the deck, if you must know.'

'Amelia, eh?' Archie grinned. 'Wasn't that the name of the lady you couldn't take your eyes from when she boarded? Hair the colour of melted chocolate and a face that would give an actress a run for her money?'

For the first time ever, Samuel didn't find Archie's jesting about a woman Samuel might be taken with remotely amusing. Amelia was different. Intelligent. Kind. Caring. She deserved the utmost regard . . . from everyone.

'As a matter of fact, it was her. Her name is Amelia Wakefield and I'd thank you not to speak about her in any way other than respectful.'

Archie's eyebrows shot to his hairline as he let out a low whistle. 'Whoa, someone is a little smitten, I'd say.'

Samuel glared, protectiveness for Amelia *and* himself unfurling inside him. 'So what if I am? She's a nice girl. A great girl, in fact.'

'Well, you won't get any interference from me, my friend.' Archie slapped Samuel's shoulder. 'We're aboard this ship for three more nights, why not enjoy some female company if you can? Could be two nights, considering the way the captain keeps pumping up the speed. You should tell her about your plans to stay in America, she might join you.'

'Don't start with that again.' Samuel turned to check some papers beside him. 'I'll be back on the return ship, same as you.'

'For the love of God, man.' Archie's smile vanished. 'Why don't you stay? Jobs are going begging, people making money hand over fist in America. I know you think it's none of my business what you do with your life, but I've got a strong feeling America will be the making of you. You could create a life of dreams there, Sam. Why waste this opportunity? When I get back, I'll visit your family and tell them you've decided to stay. You can wire some money as soon as we come into dock. Keep them sweet for a while until you find work. Nothing could be simpler.'

'Nothing could be simpler . . . ' Samuel murmured, frustration simmering as he gripped the papers harder. 'There is nothing simple about my family. You know that. They need me, Archie. Ma, especially. I'm the only one bringing money into the house. I can't just up and leave her without warning.'

'Why not? When does she ever wish you luck, Sam? Ask when you're going to settle down and marry? Never, because she's scared when you do, you'll be lost to her. She's never going to give you a choice to leave so you have to damn well make it yourself. Stay in America. I mean it.'

Archie stormed away and Samuel closed his eyes.

He hated the rare arguments he had with his friend. Archie was his constant. A friend and ally in Samuel's work and personal life.

If it really mattered that much to Archie that Samuel stayed in America, could his friend be right? If he didn't take this opportunity, would his entire life begin and end in Bath or Southampton? Alone and unhappy, potentially working year after year on the docks and aboard ships without building any sort of personal happiness?

The next shift crew slowly filed in and Samuel gave a final check over the statuses in front of him, noting them down for the officer who came to stand beside him. 'All yours. I'll see you in the morning.'

Samuel walked from the control room, taking the stairs two at a time, and entered the maze of corridors and stairs that eventually brought him to the Boat Deck. He and Amelia had agreed to meet on the promenade, close to the second funnel.

As he stepped through the door, apprehension stole through him and he sucked in a breath from the drop in temperature. He looked to the sky. It was a sheet of black, a million and one stars sparkling like diamonds, no clouds marring their beauty, the ocean a dark, motionless sheet. Still and unmoving, not a single wave breaking its crest.

Samuel shivered and rubbed his hands together, hoping Amelia wasn't outside waiting for him in these near-freezing temperatures.

But she was.

Although the deck was practically deserted, she sat on one of the benches, a stole tightly drawn around her shoulders and one of the ship's complimentary lap blankets tucked around her legs. She stared across the sea, her brow furrowed and expression grave. Samuel had no doubt she was working, her mind whirling with plans and ideas.

He had never met anyone so industrious, so passionate about their work and it made him want to find his vocation. A job that might light him up from the inside, too.

Samuel smiled as he approached her, touched that she would keep to their plans regardless of the cold.

'Amelia, what are you doing?' Fondness for her swelled behind his chest. 'You should have waited for me inside. I would have found you.'

She smiled sheepishly. 'There's every possibility I could be hiding from Mr Weir more than waiting for you. All the second-class public areas are closed and most of the lights extinguished but, thankfully, he met with Mr Parker who invited him to first class for a drink. He wasn't happy when I declined to join Mrs Parker in the first-class lounge, but I insisted he stay. I am almost certain we have at least an hour before he comes to my cabin to check I'm readying for bed.'

'Seems I'm going to have to be mindful of your tactics.'

'There's not much people can make me do against my wishes anymore.' A flash of determination burned in her eyes before it dissolved, and she tossed the blanket from her knees to stand. 'Have you ever seen the water so still? It's like a sheet of ebony.'

He followed her gaze across the ocean. Nothing stirred. Not a wave. No ice. Nothing.

'It's kind of eerie,' he said, quietly. 'In all my years at sea, I don't think I've ever seen water so completely calm.'

'It's beautiful.' She sighed and faced him. 'Let's go inside. We'll find a quiet spot somewhere.'

'A quiet spot? Do you think that's such a good idea?'

She briefly dipped her gaze. 'I want us to be alone somewhere so we can talk and not have Mr Weir descend on us the moment we're not looking.'

Before he could protest or give her a hundred reasons why them being alone was a bad idea, Amelia stepped towards the door beside them. Samuel stared after her, his feet welded to the deck and his mind reeling. If a senior officer caught him alone with a passenger without a feasible reason, he would be reprimanded. Possibly given a much lowlier role than he had now.

Cursing, he followed her. What other choice did he have when he already cared so much for her and desperately wanted to hear what she had to say?

She led him through the empty lounge and along a corridor where she stopped.

When she lifted her eyes to his, they were filled with worry. 'I don't want you to think me presumptuous or improper asking to be alone with you like this, it's just . . . '

Her uncertainty was palpable, but Samuel didn't think her presumptuous or improper. He took her confidence to be alone with him as a sign she trusted him and that pleased him more than she could ever know.

'It's fine.' He smiled, hoping she saw the sincerity in his eyes. 'You can trust me, Amelia. I'd never do anything to upset you.'

A strange look passed through her gaze that he couldn't decipher.

The skin at her neck shifted as she swallowed, indicating her heightened nerves, but Samuel also recognised her familiar determination as she stared resolutely ahead, her jaw tight.

Then she smiled back at him and his heart stuttered.

Christ. Despite trying to be a gentleman at all times, imagining how it would feel to make love to Amelia rushed into his mind. Worse, so did the horrible notion of how it would feel when they had to go their separate ways when they reached America. She mattered. He had no idea why she should so quickly or so deeply, but who was he to dictate his heart?

A young couple arm-in-arm passed by, giggling and whispering, their intentions absurdly plain. He glanced at Amelia and she held his gaze.

Rare heat travelled over his neck. 'What?'

'You're blushing.'

'So are you.'

She quickly looked to the floor. 'I didn't ask to see you alone to . . . '

He looked into her eyes. 'I know.'

'I just . . . enjoy talking to you. Want you to be happy.'

'And I am. Especially now, like this. With you.'

25

Ruby's need to slide her fingers across the accessories glass countertop and touch Victoria's hand taunted her, longing painfully twisting her heart.

Hating her shameful desire, Ruby quickly looked from Victoria's beautiful green eyes to the stands of necklaces behind her. 'If Hazel Price is so gleeful in talking about the possibility of me and Tommy coming to live with you, I can only imagine what other staff are thinking, too.'

Victoria raised her eyebrows, her gaze irritated. 'And that worries you?'

'Of course. For you, not me.' Ruby's deeply embedded protectiveness for those she loved rose. 'I don't want people talking about you. Undermining you and insinuating things that just aren't true.'

'Such as? What did Hazel say exactly? You do know what a spiteful madam she is, don't you?'

'Oh, I know only too well, but that doesn't make it any easier to accept your offer and have the whole store talking about us.'

'But we aren't doing anything wrong, Ruby.'

Victoria gently touched Ruby's hand and she flinched, snatching her hand from the countertop.

'Don't,' she snapped. Hurt flashed in Victoria's eyes rending a painful slash across Ruby's heart. 'I mean, it's just what they want to see.'

'What who wants to see?' Victoria's eyes darkened, her colour high as she moved away to rearrange some scarves. 'This is silly. If you don't want to move in with me, then don't. I was merely trying to help you and Tommy remove yourselves from a home which is clearly dangerous. If you'd prefer to keep things the way they are, that's your choice.'

'But I don't want that.' The need to touch Victoria, to reassure her, rushed through Ruby as she quickly moved along the counter and gripped the edge, her heart aching that Victoria might, for a single moment, think she would reject her in any way. 'I just don't want to bring trouble to your door, that's all.'

'If you think I'm the type of person to listen to gossip, be affected or upset by it, you don't know me at all. As for you? I think you need to consider what you are forcing Tommy to continue to endure should you remain living with your mother.'

Ruby stepped back. Never before had she seen such fury in Victoria's eyes, such quiet venom in her voice. 'Victoria — '

'No.' Victoria glanced at the other staff staying late for Pennington's monthly stock take and lowered her voice. 'This is your choice, no one else's. I spent most of my married life with a man who worshipped me. A man who saved me from a father who thought no less about striking his daughter as he did his sons. You have a chance, Ruby, an opportunity to leave. If you stay, then there is nothing more I can do to help you.'

'Excuse me, Mrs Lark. Could you help me?'

'Of course, Milly.'

Victoria moved away to help a colleague, leaving Ruby standing alone and feeling like a castaway on a deserted island. She had no idea that Victoria had lived with violence. No idea the same scars must be as deep in her heart as they were in Ruby's. The knowledge only served to deepen her love, her connection, to a woman who would never return her affection in the same way.

Ruby slowly walked away, her mind reeling with Victoria's words and heated conviction. She was absolutely right. The decision to leave her mother had no bearing on her feelings for Victoria, or the speculation and opinions of others. It had to be grounded in saving Tommy, saving what positive hope he and Ruby had left, before all was destroyed completely.

They had to leave. There was no other choice.

'Ruby?'

She squeezed her stinging eyes closed as customers hurried around her, the noise suddenly unbearable. Taking a strengthening breath, Ruby turned and forced a smile. 'Miss Pennington. How can I help you?'

'I've just been struck with a fabulous idea for the wedding window.' Excitement gleamed in Elizabeth Pennington's dark green eyes. 'Esther thinks that we could . . . Ruby? What is it?'

Ruby's cheeks warmed as a lone tear slipped over her cheek. *Why did I have to cry now? Right here. Right in front of Elizabeth.* An employer who had the keenest eye and the most attuned intuition of any woman Ruby had ever met.

'I . . . ' She swiped at the tear. 'It's nothing. We'll go to the department now, shall we?' Ruby asked, grateful that Tommy was staying at a friend's house tonight, or else nothing would have delayed her in getting home to him.

'No, I think my ideas can wait.' Elizabeth's intense gaze settled on Ruby as she took her elbow and steered her towards a quieter spot by the jewellery counter. 'Please, Ruby. You must tell me what it is bothering you. I don't like to see you this way. I don't like to see any of my staff this way.'

'I'd really rather not speak about it.' Ruby glanced around her, inwardly cursing as she caught Hazel's eye. The vile woman sauntered past and wiggled her fingers in a semblance of a wave. Ruby shot her a glare before facing Elizabeth. 'I am quite all right.'

'Are you sure? We could go to my office to talk, if you'd like.'

'I'm quite sure. Thank you.'

An uneasy atmosphere descended as Ruby fought to not fidget under Elizabeth's scrutiny. At last, Elizabeth raised her hand in surrender. 'All right, if that's what you want. Let's walk together and I'll just give you a brief overview of what I have in mind. We can talk more tomorrow.'

They walked through the atrium and as she passed Accessories, Ruby looked at Victoria who was busy pouring over a ledger, her shoulders high and her brow furrowed. Fear clenched Ruby's stomach. Had she lost their cherished friendship as well as an opportunity for escape?

I am such a fool.

'If another member of staff is upsetting you, Ruby, you must tell me.'

Ruby turned. Elizabeth watched Victoria through narrowed eyes, her back rigid.

'I will not stand for tension between my staff. Pennington's prides itself on care for its customers *and* its workers. If you're unhappy, I want to know. You are becoming a valuable part of the design team. I wouldn't want to lose you.'

'Oh, you won't lose me, Miss Pennington. You can be assured of that.'

They walked on and Ruby straightened her spine.

And neither would she lose Victoria.

To hell with Hazel or anyone else who wanted to talk about them. Tomorrow she would tell Victoria that she and Tommy would like to gratefully accept her offer for them to move in with her.

26

Amelia inhaled a strengthening breath, but it did nothing to soothe her nerves. She stared into Samuel's brilliant blue eyes, so bright in the semi-darkness, with no idea what she was doing, or thinking, by inviting him to talk with her this way. She could have spoken to him in a more public space, yet she sensed his reluctance to veer from the professional whenever there were other passengers present.

Yet, she had an explicable and urgent desire to know him better; to learn of the dreams that lay in his heart.

His gaze grew intense on hers and her heart beat a little faster as something pulled low in her abdomen, shocking and arousing. A mysterious sensation she had heard much talk of, but never experienced. Was this intoxicating connection between a man and a woman a phenomenon? Or a normality? She had no idea.

'Why am I here, Amelia?' He didn't move, just continued to look at her, his gaze soft as it travelled over her face. 'What do you want me to do?'

She stilled. 'To do?'

'There's usually always something passengers need me to do. This . . . my being here like this . . . what do you need?'

She swallowed. What did she need? She had no idea. All she knew was she had to do all she could to persuade him that he must seize the chance of a new life in America. To reach for success, liberty . . . love. How could she explain to him that knowing he was in a position of imminent freedom, her own ambitions would be bolstered? If Samuel was to make a life far, far away, grabbing his future with both hands, who was to say the same wouldn't be true for her one day?

That she might one day have the blessed promise of forgetting what had happened to her and start again.

A man's loud laughter boomed from further along the corridor and Amelia jumped, her eyes wide as she spotted Mr Carlton and Mr Weir.

She snapped her gaze to Samuel's and gripped his arm. 'Quickly.'

He glanced over his shoulder and spotted Weir. 'Damnation.'

Amelia pulled him along the corridor until they came to a deserted staircase. She hesitated, her nerves jumping as she fought back her demons with everything she had. How was she to move forward, to bolster Samuel's courage, when she showed none of her own?

'In here,' she whispered, pulling him gently beneath the staircase until their backs were against the wall, their presence concealed in the shadows. 'No one will see us here.'

She stepped closer to him until only the smallest space separated them, praying her nervousness didn't show through her enforced bravado. Purposefully, she met his impenetrable gaze. 'I want you to stay in America. Stay there and make a life for yourself. Let me live vicariously through you. Let me know what it is to not have to worry about your reputation, your past, convention and propriety. America is a new world. A place anyone can make their fortune. You must go. For me. Please.'

Confusion shadowed his eyes. 'What are you

talking about?'

She sought the right words, the right conviction to make him understand how he had ignited a wish in her for more, just by speaking about his possible escape. 'Don't you see?' She shook her head. 'Opportunities like this don't happen for people like us.'

'Like us? What do you mean *us*?'

Heat warmed her cheeks that he might think she in any way meant to insult him. She clutched his hand. 'People who work hard every day, Samuel. People who are the backbone of England. This is your chance to be more than that. To be a risk-taker, a pioneer, a person in charge of his own destiny.'

He slowly pulled his hand from hers and stepped back, pushing the fallen hair from his brow, his eyes boring into hers. 'And if all that is possible for me, why is it not for you, too? What is there to keep you in Bath? Are your commitments holding you captive any more than mine?'

Words battled on her tongue. Didn't he realise how free he could be? How the responsibilities holding him back could be assuaged with regular money wired home, telegrams and letters. For her, everything was different. Everything was tainted in violence. Rape. Reputation. She had to stay on a regulated path. Keep her head down, work hard, pay her rent and hopefully retain some friends along the way.

This entire world was a man's, and Samuel was entirely male without need for proof or struggle. He was rapidly becoming the most different of men as any she had ever met. Kind, thoughtful, pensive and passionate. A man who articulated his feelings, found amusement amid responsibility. A man who made her smile, stand taller and made her dare to dream that anything was possible.

If that wasn't the measure of a true man, she might as well give up hope of ever finding one. Finding a man with whom to share her life had not occurred to her since the attack. Now Samuel had evoked all sorts of emotions in her. Emotions that were terrifying. Yet, still, she wanted so much for him.

She closed her eyes. 'It's not the same for me.'

A heavy, ensuing silence lingered, the pressure of sharing more with him growing with each passing second. But she wouldn't. Couldn't. How could she bear to see the disgust in his eyes if he should learn of her being so soiled, so violated?

He gently touched his finger to her chin, and her eyes popped open.

Yet, he didn't step back or recoil as though he'd overstepped an invisible mark. Instead, he placed his thumb beneath her chin, holding her softly, yet firmly, so that he might look deep into her eyes.

Did he see her pain? Her shame?

'Samuel . . .' Heat infused her body from head to toe. She could not think. She could not breathe. 'You must understand.'

'What must I understand?'

Tears pricked her eyes and she blinked, sending a single tear slipping over her cheek. 'I am not free like you. I'm a woman. We don't have the same liberties as men.'

'Why don't you? Am I really to believe you care what others might think?' His thumb traced the tear as it travelled to her jaw. 'I know you don't have a family as I do, but you love your occupation. Still, I know there is more to you than Pennington's. Don't you, too, want to discover what else is possible?'

Hope sparked inside her and a little of the tension left her shoulders. 'So, you do want all the things I spoke of? Liberty? Success?'

'Of course, but it doesn't mean I can act on my wishes. I've already explained what awaits me back home. I'm not the sort of man who turns his back on his family or his friends.'

He had no need to tell her such a thing, she instinctively knew how reliable he was, how steadfast. 'I see.'

'Do you? Because . . . I have no idea why, but it's important to me that you understand the sort of man I am, Amelia. That you know you can trust me, that I like you.'

She couldn't stem her smile. 'I like you, too.'

Their eyes locked, his filled with relief and then something else. Longing.

'Might I . . . kiss you?'

Fear started a steady thrum deep in her chest and her mouth drained dry. 'What?'

He smiled softly, his eyes gentle. 'Can I kiss you?'

Her heart picked up speed even as she nodded, even as she slowly licked her lips. An overwhelming, uplifting anticipation passed through every nerve in her body. How was he to know she had never willingly let anyone kiss her before? That nobody had ever asked her permission before taking from her what he wanted?

'Yes.' She nodded. 'You can.'

Desire mixed with admiration in his eyes, darkening them to a midnight blue that was completely and utterly mesmerising. Slowly, he inched forwards and Amelia's eyelids drifted closed, his breath a soft whisper against her mouth.

His lips were gentle at first, his hand moving from

her face to lay softly on her cheek. An alien stirring twisted deliciously low in her stomach and she inched closer, pressing her mouth just a little more firmly to his. She wanted him to know, to feel, that she wanted this. Wanted to be in his arms, in his protection.

He eased back and whispered, 'Amelia.'

Indescribable power rippled through her body making her reach for him. She gripped his waist and pulled him back to her. This time, it was her leading the connection, the intimacy.

She pressed her mouth to his, a soft whimper escaping her as she kissed him, relishing in the new, unexpected sensations that overtook her every emotion.

Then the moment was cruelly sliced by a sudden shuddering vibrating through Amelia's body and she pulled back, her gaze moving past the staircase. 'What was that?'

27

At first, Samuel had thought he was trembling rather than the momentary and irregular movement of the ship, but Amelia had clearly felt something, too.

His trained ear picked up an interference in the usual pattern of the engines. 'Maybe it was — '

The vibrations escalated, followed by urgent chatter farther along the corridor.

'Something's happening.' He reluctantly released Amelia and stepped out from beneath the staircase. When they had sought privacy, only two or three couples had been in the area, but now a number of people milled about, confusion etched on their faces as they garbled questions to whomever was closest.

Amelia came up behind him. 'What is it?'

An older gentleman turned, appraised Samuel's uniform and came forward. 'You there. What's happening? I heard a strange noise.'

The engines stopped.

What in God's name was happening for them to halt? Dread knotted Samuel's stomach. Something must be seriously wrong for the Captain to shut down the engines. Tension stiffened his shoulders as several stewards hurried along the corridor carrying life-jackets and shoving them, one by one, to the nearest person, their strides long and their expression serious. 'Put these on, please and make your way to the Boat Deck. Quick as you can, please.'

Samuel faced the gentleman. 'Can I suggest you return to your room, sir? I will speak to the stewards and find out what's going on.'

'I will do no such thing. I felt something hit the ship, I'm sure.'

'Samuel?' Amelia gripped his forearm. 'Is it bad?'

Whatever its foundation, every instinct in his body told him that whatever had caused the ship to list was serious. The last thing he wanted was to trigger unnecessary alarm. He fought to keep the concern from his face. 'I'm sure everything is fine.'

'Ladies and gentlemen.' A steward stopped in front of the group. 'Please immediately return to your rooms and dress warmly before donning your life-jackets. This is just a precaution. The ship has hit an iceberg, but it's nothing to worry about. The Captain has insisted passenger safety is a priority. Please make your way calmly to your rooms.'

He hurried away along the corridor, towards the second-class cabins. 'Make haste to the Boat Deck. Dress warmly. Lifejackets to be worn.'

The others scattered, making for their cabins and Samuel turned to Amelia. 'Do as he says. I have to get to the control room and do what I can to help.'

'But — '

'Please. Do as I ask. Find Weir. Everything will be all right. I'll come and find you as soon as I can.' Without thinking, or concern for who might see them, Samuel pressed a kiss to her lips. 'Promise me you'll do as I say.'

'I will, but what about you?'

'I'll be fine. See you soon.'

Samuel strode away from her, his heart beating fast. Why in God's name had stewards been sent armed with lifejackets moments after the collision if it wasn't immediately considered serious? Why the urgency and why the grave expressions of every member of staff he passed?

'Sam! Sam!' Archie grabbed hold of Samuel's arm. 'Where the hell have you been? I went to your cabin. We've been hit bad.' He lowered his voice. 'We'll have to do what we can, but I swear to you, she's going down.'

'What the hell are you talking about? This ship is the most advanced the world has ever seen. It would take more than a brush with an iceberg to send her down.'

'It wasn't a brush.'

'What?'

'She hit and scraped along the side. Water is pouring into six of the forward watertight compartments. Andrews told the Captain we have less than two hours before she sinks. Just hurry, for God's sake. Get your lifejacket on and meet me on the Boat Deck, we've been ordered to get as many women and children as we can into the lifeboats.'

Without bothering to get his lifejacket, Samuel bounded after Archie as they reassured and directed the deluge of passengers who had been roused from their beds. The noise was deafening as they climbed towards the Boat Deck.

When Samuel and Archie finally emerged onto the deck, the sights and cacophony of the passengers' chatter and shouting, steam and creaking metal, drew them into a moment of paralysed shock. Side by side, he and Archie stared around them, the freezing air cutting through Samuel's uniform and stinging his cheeks. A few women milled around, their arms tightly folded over their thin evening gowns, their gentlemen companions, arms slung around their wives' shoulders, dressed in black suits and crisp white shirts.

There seemed to be more first-class passengers already on deck than any other. Had they been warned first? Or had the iceberg hit that area of the ship more directly? He and Amelia had only felt a tremor beneath the staircase.

The ship sat tilted in the water, one of its violated funnels releasing steam on a constant, ear-splitting scream. Passengers moved back and forth along the deck, men holding children, women cradling babies, the elderly clinging to one another.

Some faces showed confusion and panic. Whereas others seemed utterly convinced there wasn't anything to worry about. Samuel had no doubt that nonchalance would soon change.

Briefly closing his eyes, he tried to get a hold on the rapid beat of his heart. The terrifying knowledge that whatever was happening would not be brought under control any time soon pulsed like a drumbeat in his head. Full out panic would begin soon enough. The shudder had been felt less than fifteen minutes ago and already the irregular angling of the ship was heart-stoppingly obvious.

They were going down.

'Holy Christ.' The blasphemy whispered from between Samuel's lips. 'What the hell do we do for these people, Archie?'

Now that the engines had stopped, the steam coming from all eight exhausts made it damn near impossible to think straight, let alone be heard.

His friend pulled him into a tight embrace and yelled gruffly into Samuel's ear. 'We do what we can. Take care, Sam.'

Their eyes locked and Samuel tried to stem the

gnawing dread that unfurled inside him. 'I'll see you soon.'

Archie nodded and took off.

Sam watched him until he was swallowed up by the crowds and then raced towards the lifeboats on the port side. There were fewer people this side and things appeared calmer. Samuel looked around, assessing where he could be of the most assistance, his mind constantly filled with Amelia and how she fared. He prayed she'd appear on the port side soon. He would make damn sure he handed her into one of the lifeboats himself.

The First Officer stood farther along the deck, waving the sign for all hands on deck as lifeboats began to be lowered. Samuel sprinted to the closest lifeboat and set about hauling and coiling the ropes, ready for lowering. Every minute of their limited training aboard this ship and the years he possessed as a seaman came to the fore as his mind focused.

The clamour of shouting and the screeching of metal and steam made it impossible to speak with his fellow crewmen, but each worked methodically and confidently. It was only the lack of eye contact that gave any indication that his shipmates' fears mirrored his own.

A bellowed message was yelled along the port deck.

'Women and children only. Women and children only.'

Samuel glanced at the men around him. Each of them was likely to perish out here in the darkness, in the icy-cold ocean right alongside him. Sickness coated his throat as his Ma's and sisters' faces rose in his mind's eye, regret for all he had planned to do for them no longer relevant. If to die on this ship was his fate, then he'd damn well do all he could to save as many lives as possible before his time came.

He clenched his jaw and stepped towards the closest people to him. A mother and father in their twenties and two young children. He clasped the father's arm. 'Sir, we need to get your family aboard a lifeboat. There is no time to waste. Please, this way.'

Thankful the man broached no argument, Samuel led the way to the lifeboats.

'You there.'

Samuel turned to face a senior officer. 'Yes, sir.'

'I'm putting you in charge of getting passengers aboard this lifeboat. For God's sake, man, put this on.' He grabbed a lifejacket from a passing steward and pushed it into Samuel's hands. 'Not everyone will be able to get on the lifeboats. Keep calm at all times. Show nothing on your face. Do you understand?'

Samuel nodded as he donned the jacket. 'Yes, sir.'

With a final lingering assessment of the growing crowds, the officer left, leaving Samuel in charge. He inhaled a long breath and then yelled orders as he and other crew helped women and children aboard the lifeboats. The weeping goodbyes and promises of reunion gripped Samuel's heart and conscience, but he remained tight-lipped even as guilt pressed like a lead weight on his chest. Most people remained entirely unaware of the imminent fate of almost everyone onboard.

Anger and frustration, fear and loss swelled inside him. Who in God's name was responsible for this? How had a ship so magnificent, so enormous, been reduced to a vessel that would sink, taking thousands of lives with her? And what of the damn lifeboats? Why had his senior officer been so certain that so many would not be saved?

A hard slap landed on his shoulder.

'What's your name, son?'

Samuel saluted the senior officer. 'Murphy, sir.'

'I've just learned you have experience of sailing vessels as well as steam ships. Correct?'

'Yes, sir.'

'Good. You are one of two seamen charged with rowing a lifeboat to the rescue ship. I will send your second along once I've ascertained the next best person and which boat you are to command. In the meantime, supervise the lowering of as many as possible. You are doing a fine job and I want you in charge until the last moment. You are not to climb aboard a boat until I give the order.'

'I would prefer to stay aboard, sir.' There was no way in hell he was abandoning ship when so many others would surely perish. 'I can be of help to the end.'

The officer's fairly amiable expression immediately darkened, his eyes aflame with urgency and anger. 'This is not the time to play the goddamn hero, Murphy. You are in service. You are abandoning nothing. You are assigned to get women and children to safety.' He glanced left and right. 'You are saving their damn lives. Now get to it.'

The officer shoved his way through the mass around them, leaving Samuel standing rigid with indecision. What the hell was he supposed to do? He couldn't get in a lifeboat knowing hundreds of civilians would die. If he survived and others didn't, how was he supposed to live with that?

'Samuel! Samuel!'

He sharply turned.

Amelia pushed her way to the front, her hand at Mr Weir's wrist. 'Thank God, I found you,' she yelled. 'I was so worried.'

He stared at her beautiful face, willing his racing heart to calm. 'You need to do get in this lifeboat, Amelia. Right now.'

'But — '

'Now.' He clenched his jaw, his eyes never leaving hers. 'I mean it.'

The momentary relief he'd seen in her eyes when she'd found him slowly evolved into confusion and then comprehension. A tiny flicker of fear passed through her gaze before she pulled back her shoulders. 'No, I will help as many others as I can. I know more than most how it feels to be left for dead. For knowing life can change in an instant through no fault of your own. I am not leaving. Not yet.'

'Amelia — '

'I said, I'm not leaving.' Her glare locked with his. 'I told you before, no one will make me do something I don't want to do ever again. Including you.'

28

Amelia dragged her gaze from Samuel's, hating that she had to defy him, but how could she save her own skin rather than do all she could to help the terrified families around her? She was alone. Without loved ones. These people had so much to live for.

This entire situation made her deeply regret that she had been reduced to such a state of sadness to contemplate taking her own life. Yet, a second chance had seemed impossible after her attack. Being here, like this, when so many people's lives would be taken, when they so much wished to live, made Amelia vow eternal gratitude for the gift of life.

Determination swelled inside of her.

She would do everything she could to ensure at least some of these people had a chance of survival, bury her own terror and fear and stand strong when so many innocent people were at risk . . . innocent people with innocent children.

She faced Mr Weir. 'We must do all we can to help. Go farther along the deck and point people towards the boats. I'll do what I can here.'

'Miss Wakefield . . . ' He looked at Samuel and then the lifeboat, his eyes reflecting his concern, but his calmness palpable. 'I really think you should climb aboard. Mr Carter will never forgive me if he learns I failed to convince you — '

'I will get in a boat once I've done all I can for these poor families. I promise. Please, Mr Weir, I can't stand by and do nothing.'

He stared at her before giving a curt nod, his eyes filled with a strange sadness. 'We should exchange something.'

Amelia frowned, glanced at Samuel who now had his back turned to her, helping a young woman and her child aboard. 'Exchange something?'

'Yes, in case we . . . just in case.'

'But I don't understand. Just in case of what?'

He drew his pocket watch from his waistcoat and placed it in her hand, closing it into a fist and holding tight. 'Here. Now, let me have that comb in your hair.'

Her concern deepened, her eyes still locked with Mr Weir's as she reached up and drew the ivory comb from her hair, placing it gently into his outstretched hand.

He softly smiled. 'Thank you.'

'But — '

'Good luck, Miss Wakefield.'

His gaze lingered on hers before he turned and walked away.

Amelia stared after him until he disappeared, a horrible foreboding knotting her stomach. What just happened? Why would Mr Weir insist they exchanged a possession with one another?

Swallowing hard, she inhaled a deep breath and strode to Samuel's side. 'Who's next?'

He turned and looked over her shoulder. 'Where's Weir?'

'Gone to help. What can I do?'

'You can get on this lifeboat.'

'No.'

Her heart beat hard in her chest, but she did not look away or falter.

His jaw clenched before he gave a firm nod. 'Fine.

Go back and try to encourage as many women and children forward as you can. Their reluctance is foolhardy, but understandable. We have to be firm. These people will soon realise their fate.'

The night was bitterly cold, but it wasn't the temperature that touched icy-cold to Amelia's bones. Samuel was a seaman. A sailor with experience and expertise. He would understand what was unfolding more than many of the thousands aboard. And, in that moment, Amelia entirely understood, too.

People would die. Drown. Perish.

Fighting the tears that burned the back of her eyes, she drew her gaze over Samuel's face once more before turning away.

Shouting came from along the deck.

'First-class passengers to the front, please. First-class women and children, this way.'

Amelia's anger ignited as officers reached into the crowds and blatantly picked out the wealthier dressed families, urging them forward and physically holding back others. Narrowing her eyes, she strode towards the uniformed imbecile who clearly thought himself God to pick and choose who would be given a chance to live.

'Everyone is equal, are they not?' she yelled, pulling at his sleeve. 'Whoever is here first should be put into a boat. Class is of no distinction. Especially now.'

'Either get in a boat or get out of my way.' The officer yanked his arm from Amelia's grasp. 'This is not the time for female hysterics.'

Amelia glared at his turned back before elbowing her way through a row of richly dressed passengers to some people dressed less grandly standing anxiously behind. She stormed towards a family who stood huddled together, the children's eyes wide with fright and their parents looking confused and afraid. In their arms, they seemed to carry the entirety of their meagre possessions. Small wooden boxes and belongings wrapped in material lay in their arms as though they'd grabbed all that they could physically carry, worn clothes and knitted scarves wrapped around their thin bodies. She had heard some women yelling at their maids to return to their cabins in order to retrieve jewels, furs and money.

The comparison in need and importance to these people was sickening. Sickening and wrong.

'Quickly, come this way.' She smiled at the family. 'I'll find you a boat. Everything will be all right.'

For every mother and child she helped into a boat, Amelia breathed a little easier, her heart a little calmer. Her arms ached and her legs were tired, but brute determination rose up inside her time and again, filling her with strength and purpose. The sky was filled with a million stars, the sea as calm and still as a millpond. Yet, inside, a turbulent mix of fear and apprehension ebbed and flowed through her. Every now and then, she would look across at Samuel, his face etched with determination and care. His strong arms lifting children to safety, his smile flashing and his eye winking as he offered all the possible comfort and reassurance he could.

Admiration swept through her and a sudden nonsensical thought of what could've been between them rose in her mind but, in reality, she had no relationship with Samuel. They'd known each other a matter of days. It could only be fear making her consider him with such longing.

The screams of women and the cries of children

increased as families were wrenched apart, having little choice of whether or not to leave their husbands and fathers behind. The fear and grief in some of the mothers' eyes made Amelia want to turn away, her heart breaking, but she held fast.

'Come, you must think of your child,' she said, urging a young woman and the babe she held into one of the boats. 'The men will be put on boats as soon as the women and children are away.'

The woman searched Amelia's face, her face shining white in the moonlight. 'Do you promise?'

Amelia's heart and conscience ached with guilt. What did she really know? She had not even spoken to Samuel who would undoubtedly know more than her. She forced a smile, guilt clawing at her. 'I promise.'

The woman glanced at her husband before climbing into the boat and it was immediately ordered to be lowered. Amelia crossed her arms tightly across her body as the boat listed and jerked towards the inky-black water. Surely, more people could fit into these boats? There certainly seemed to be room for twenty or more people in the one she watched descend.

She glanced towards Samuel and stilled, tension inching through her shoulders. He spoke with another officer who gestured frantically towards the lifeboat next to Samuel. They appeared to be in some sort of altercation. Amelia kept her gaze firmly on Samuel as she shouldered her way through the crowds towards them. Something was causing Samuel to fling his arm towards the boat, his face dark with anger. When she was close enough to hear their shouts above the thunderous belching of the tunnels, the steam hot and persistent, she stopped.

'This is it, Murphy,' the officer yelled. 'It's your turn. Get in the boat and row these people to safety. That's an order.'

Amelia's breath caught like broken glass in her throat. Samuel was leaving.

Time stood still, her pulse a steady thrum in her ears . . . and then Samuel raised his hand in a firm salute.

The officer nodded and strode away.

Hundreds of people now stood or ran around the Boat Deck, cold and frightened with no idea of whether they would live or die. Death seemed to hover over the ship, its corpselike state a dark and dismal blanket shrouding them all, pulling them towards what would assuredly be a bleak and slow ending.

Elizabeth and Esther's faces filled Amelia's mind. The store. The park. Every place where she had managed to find peace and escape in the beautiful city of Bath . . .

'Amelia!'

She started and faced Samuel, the soles of her feet stuck to the deck.

'Quickly!' He waved her forward, his gaze intense. 'You're coming with me. Right now.'

29

Samuel kept his hand outstretched towards Amelia, his heart thundering.

How was he to reach her — keep her safe — when so many people separated them? He couldn't leave the lifeboat and, if Amelia bolted, he would have no possible way of catching her . . . of having the chance to maybe love her.

Chaos was breaking out around them, the smell of oil and grease, fear and desperation merging and spreading like the water that grew ever higher. Samuel dragged his gaze from Amelia, indecision and terror tormenting his heart and mind. He was under orders to stay in the lifeboat, but how in God's name could he leave without Amelia? God damn it, he shouldn't be leaving at all. Not when so many people were destined to die. Yet, if he could save just a few . . .

At last, Amelia moved towards him, her steps steady and sure, her chin raised as though the screaming and shouting wasn't all around her, pressing into their space and stealing their courage.

The moment she slipped her hand into his, relief and strength flooded through him. They would do what they could for these people together. Side by side. She carefully lifted her foot into the boat.

'Wait. Please, wait.'

A young mother lunged forward and pushed her baby into Amelia's arms.

'Please,' the woman cried. 'Take her with you. I can't leave my husband. Take her. Give her a chance to live. Please.'

The woman turned and ran as though unable to bear the force of her heartbreaking decision. Amelia's eyes were wide on Samuel's as she clutched the crying babe to her chest. 'Samuel . . . '

'Everything will be all right. I'll make sure you and the baby are safe.' He squeezed her arm and prayed she understood his promise. Come what may, he would ensure she *and* the baby survived.

Amelia climbed into the lifeboat and sat on the wooden bench beside two women wrapped in furs. The jewels around their necks and in their ears glinted beneath the flickering lights as they clung to one another, tears flowing in silver tracks down their cheeks. Amelia sat upright, her spine rigid as she stared resolutely ahead, her jaw tight. If memory served him right, she'd met these women during her investigative trips to first-class. He thought their names to be something like Parker and Culford.

A senior officer came forward. 'Officer Murphy. Lower the boat.'

'But I can take more, sir. There's room for at least —'

'Now, officer.' The man's face was a mask of detachment, except for his eyes which blazed with underlying panic. 'We have no time to lose. Lower or face the barrel of my gun.'

Samuel clenched his jaw, his heart pumping before he nodded and forced his gaze to the passengers standing above them, lest he ever forget the distress and terror in their eyes. This was why he was on this boat. To give something to these poor men who could do nothing to help their loved ones. He would stand where they had not been given the chance.

Tears glistened in the eyes of these husbands, sons and brothers as they stared at the females they knew or loved. Samuel's heart filled with their pain and he caught the eyes of a few before doubt in his capabilities rose and he quickly looked away, the threat of losing hold of his sanity edging in.

'Lower the boat,' he yelled. 'All aboard.'

A bitter nausea coated his throat under the knowledge more passengers could have boarded their vessel. It was clear how hysterical things would soon become once the *Titanic* started its inevitable descent into the ocean. He forced himself to concentrate on the job in hand.

A flare whistled into the black night sky and exploded like a pink-red rocket. The collective gasps of the passengers cut through the roar and screech of the ship.

Now people would know the *unsinkable ship* was in dire distress. The atmosphere aboard would veer from a place of reasonable control, to out and out chaos. Drawing in a shaky breath, Samuel worked the ropes as they approached the sea's surface, burying the conflicting emotions ricocheting through him and making him want to shout aloud at the injustice of what was unfolding.

Did the designers of the ship — the Captain — really think these lifeboats offered anyone guaranteed survival? He'd heard officers saying there weren't enough boats for all aboard and if Samuel's wasn't completely filled and had been ordered to sea, then most certainly other seamen were receiving the same instructions. There was a chance every passenger, every member of crew would perish. His thoughts turned again to his family. His mother and sisters. How would they manage without him? Without his money? His words of encouragement and optimism? They had already lost their husband and father, now they would most likely lose Samuel, too.

He inwardly cursed his arbitrary thoughts. Why was he worrying about his kin when they were safely in Bath? Right now, he had other people's relatives under his care. He had Amelia under his care.

Samuel looked at his fellow rower and Archie's face came into his mind's eye. He hoped to God his best friend managed all right. Hoped to God he, and thousands of others, survived.

Taking a deep breath, Samuel shouted, 'I ask that you all remain as calm as possible so myself and Officer Lansman can row you to safety.' Another flare lit the night sky, showering white sparks like falling diamonds before they disappeared on snaking wisps of smoke. 'It's imperative you let us concentrate. We must get away from the ship as quickly as possible.'

The *Titanic* had grown eerily still on the water even as her tilting grew ever more pronounced. The ship was sinking and if he and his colleague didn't get the lifeboat far away, as quickly as possible, there was every chance their small vessel would be drawn into the deep, dark depths of the ocean by the sheer force of the ship's enormous suction.

Gripping the oars so tightly his knuckles ached, Samuel met Amelia's steady gaze. 'Pull!'

His arms soon burned from exertion, his fingers welded to the oars by the freezing, early morning temperatures. Onward Samuel rowed, gritting his teeth and focusing on moving them away from the *Titanic*, away from the screams and terror echoing across the ocean from the passengers still trapped aboard.

Every face was focused on the ship behind him. Amelia's hand was at her throat, her face so still it could have been carved from marble.

Samuel's mouth burned with bile as he forced himself to turn.

The ship was slowly descending from the head. There could be absolutely no hope of delaying her sinking.

He estimated that the *Titanic* would be beneath water within an hour.

Swallowing hard, Samuel faced his charges, keeping his gaze on Amelia's and ignoring the terror in his heart. 'We will survive. We have to survive for everyone left behind. Do you hear me?' He gripped the oars, braced and pulled. 'We will survive!'

On and on they rowed, the weeping of some of the women contradicting with the absolute silence of others. The baby in Amelia's arms was quiet and he prayed her sleeping. Something in the distance caught his eye and his heart jolted. It couldn't be . . . could it?

'A light,' he whispered. 'A light,' he said a little louder. He smiled. 'A light!'

They all looked across the ocean to the flickering in the distance.

'We will all be saved.' Samuel pulled on the oars, his exhaustion and terror miraculously lifting with his hope and prayers. Strength and fortitude powered through his body, pushing him on. He heaved on the oars. 'Fear not, we will all be saved.'

With an almighty roar, he pushed on, not really knowing if the light was real or imagined but determined to reach it. As much as he hated being given the chance to survive when so many could die, if or when they reached America, he would stop at nothing to build the life he and every other person aboard the *Titanic* had dreamed of.

His family would receive his money, but Samuel would never again return to England.

30

The decision had been made and Ruby felt liberated. She and Tommy would move in with Victoria as soon as she could accommodate them.

Filled with optimism, she entered Pennington's through the staff entrance.

Another vile row with her mother last night had been the deciding factor that had pushed Ruby over the edge. Tommy had stood in their living room, his spine pressed hard against the faded wallpaper, his face etched with fear, his eyes watering as his sister and mother became enveloped, once again, in a physical confrontation.

Ruby had yelled at him to go upstairs, but Tommy had remained frozen to the floor by fear. The sight of him quivering had been too much and Ruby had immediately surrendered, allowing her mother to push her to the floor, thus finishing the fight. Her mother had then stalked from the house, foolishly triumphant.

Thankfully, leaving Ruby and Tommy to a night alone.

Residual anger simmered inside of her as Ruby marched through Pennington's brightly lit atrium, nodding hello to the passing customers. It was barely past nine, but already the aisles and central areas buzzed with activity. No matter the month of the year, Pennington's hummed with an invisible pulse, a beating heart that fuelled its staff and the public alike.

With its innumerable sparkling chandeliers,

polished mahogany staircase, endless arrays of rainbow-coloured merchandise and smartly uniformed staff, Pennington's presented a magical shopping experience. Somewhere people swarmed to see and be seen. A place of opportunity for women like Ruby who longed to make something of themselves. A place for men, women and children to see, touch and taste things they might not anywhere else.

It was a prime example of what anyone could manifest in their lives. What she wanted to manifest in *her* life.

Miss Pennington and Mr Carter were the walking embodiment of financial and romantic success who inspired Ruby to reach for more every day. She was under no illusion of the magnitude of work that must go on in the executive offices to ensure the continued, ground-breaking success of such a store, but her employers' love and respect for one another outshone even their work.

Ruby smiled as she walked. The glances and touches between Miss Pennington and Mr Carter were subtle on the shop floor, but their shared energy was tangible to all who witnessed it. Maybe one day she would go somewhere where abiding to the rules of propriety and convention wasn't the only way. Where principles were a little less strict than they were in England. Where she could be with a lover — a woman — and not live under a constant shroud of fear, revulsion and the threat of violent opposition.

In the staff quarters, she quickly locked away her coat and hat before heading to the stairwell that led to the design department.

'Good morning.'

Ruby started, her heart jolting to see Victoria

standing outside the design room.

'Good morning.' Ruby offered a tentative smile, unsure of Victoria's mood. Her green eyes were unreadable, her arms crossed, yet her shoulders relaxed. They had barely spoken a word in days. 'Is everything all right?'

'Everything is fine.' Victoria dropped her arms and came forwards, taking Ruby's elbow and leading her away from the department door. 'I need to know if you've made your decision about coming to live with me.' Her eyes softened. 'I shouldn't have spoken to you the way I did. I'm sorry. It's just . . .'

Ruby drew her gaze over Victoria's face, her wonderful hair. 'It's just what?'

'It's just . . .' Victoria's eyes filled with sadness as though she held back tears. 'I couldn't bear it if one day something happened to you or Tommy at home, Ruby. Please, come and stay with me.' She smiled. 'I've spent the last two nights clearing out my spare room. There's plenty of space, if you and Tommy don't mind sharing. I have two beds, a wardrobe, a chest of drawers. I've laid a lovely rug on the floor. There's — '

'It sounds wonderful.' Ruby touched Victoria's face, a dangerous, yet necessary gesture that sped Ruby's heart. 'We'd love to.'

'You let me babble on like that when you have already decided?' She laughed, her cheeks reddening. 'I feel like a foolish, eager youth now.'

Ruby smiled, her heart near bursting with love for this wonderful woman. 'Let me know when we can move in and we will be there.'

Concern shadowed Victoria's eyes. 'And your mother? What will she do? How will you tell her?'

'You leave my mother to me.' Ruby lifted her chin

against the treacherous nerves that took flight in her stomach. 'I will tell her bluntly and with finality. You are not to worry.'

'But if she protests? Or tries to stop you?'

'Unfortunately, I've been pushed countless times to prove my superior strength, both physically and mentally, over my mother. Tommy and I will be leaving. Have no fear.'

'Oh, Ruby. I'm so pleased.' Victoria pulled Ruby into her arms and squeezed her tightly. 'We are going to get along so wonderfully.'

Ruby closed her eyes and inhaled Victoria's soft, floral perfume. She took this blessed moment to revel in the closeness, the soft roundness of Victoria's breasts against her own. The sound of her satisfied sigh in Ruby's ear . . .

31

Sounds and smells that had enveloped Amelia during their horrifying escape and eventual rescue from the *Titanic* filled her senses, images floating behind her closed eyelids as she sat huddled beneath a blanket in the *Carpathian*'s saloon. Climbing aboard the ship under the brute strength of the crew, ropes and pulleys should have been a terrifying experience but gratitude she was alive, when so many were dead, had not left Amelia's heart or consciousness for a moment.

She squeezed her eyes more tightly closed, battling to keep her tears at bay. She hadn't cried once from the time she'd been in Samuel's arms when the iceberg struck to now, almost ten hours later.

Convinced her grief had been paralysed by shock, cold or pure adrenaline, her tears had not fallen. But now, as they sailed towards New York, fear, confusion and desperation clawed at Amelia's psyche. What on earth would she do now? There had been no sign of Mr Weir and she would soon be forced to presume him dead. Sickness unfurled inside her as Amelia opened her eyes and surveyed the desolation and grief surrounding her, men and women sitting and standing in dazed disbelief.

Since they'd been brought aboard, the *Carpathian*'s care of the *Titanic* survivors had been incomparable. They were immediately given blankets and brandy in an attempt to warm them, each suffering from varying degrees of hypothermia and hysteria. Her lips had been so frozen from cold and fear, Amelia had barely been able to drink from the rim of the offered glass but, with Samuel's gentle persuasion, she had swallowed the burning liquid and taken comfort in watching him to do the same afterwards.

He stood across the room in deep conversation with a member of the *Carpathian*'s crew and she wondered what they were discussing. She and Samuel had briefly spoken about what they'd been through, what they'd seen, thought and felt, but now she was warmed with hot coffee, sandwiches and cake, her thoughts dwelt on the present and the future.

She had no doubt Samuel's mind was filled with the same.

How would they ever enjoy anything of their futures when so many of their fellow *Titanic* passengers had succumbed to the icy waters of the North Atlantic ocean? She had overheard whispers among the *Carpathian* crew that barely a third of the passengers had survived. That meant the death toll could well be over one thousand souls.

She could only imagine the pain and heartbreak the families of those poor, lost souls would suffer once news of the tragedy filtered to Britain and the States. Amelia closed her eyes. She had no doubt the press would treat this disaster as sensational and squeeze every last drop of blood out of the tragedy.

Grief and resentment wound tight in her throat as Amelia clenched her hands together, vowing that whether she had days, months or years to live, she would not waste a single moment. Fury and a thirst for survival burned deep in her chest just as it had when she'd managed to rise from her master's bedroom carpet after he'd raped her. Just as it had when her landlady had saved Amelia from leaping to her death . . .

She'd fought her way out of a deep dark abyss before and she would again.

Samuel came towards her, his gaze soft on hers as he sat beside her.

Taking her hand, he raised it to his lips, pressing a kiss to her knuckles. 'They think we'll be in New York in two, possibly three days.'

Sadness for those who would never see the Statue of Liberty appearing on the horizon squeezed her heart. 'And the number of survivors hasn't changed?'

'No, and for that I am sorrier than I can say. We must make their deaths mean something.' He shook his head. 'I won't be coming back to England, Amelia. I can't. Not now.' His gaze drifted over her face, lingered at her lips. 'We've been given a second chance that we must act upon. We owe it to all of those who died to live our lives in the fullest way possible.'

'I agree. I thought your friend was right before all this, but even more so now.' She exhaled a shaky breath and gently pulled her hand from his, lest she never let go. 'As for me, I have to go back to Bath. Elizabeth was good enough to give me this opportunity and I must deliver what I promised.'

His eyes filled with what looked to be disbelief. 'You still call this trip an opportunity? After everything we and thousands of others have been through? You really are the kindest, most generous woman I've ever met. Do you know that?'

'Kindness and generosity describe Elizabeth, not me. When she asked me to go to New York, she had faith in me to do a good job. To see, listen, taste and touch everything New York has to offer and how America is advancing in retail. Whereas I saw the chance to elevate myself, to travel and discover new things. The sinking and my survival only shows my selfishness.'

'You were spared for a reason.' His jaw tightened. 'You have to believe that and push on. The sinking means you were chosen. To *be* more. To *do* more.'

'Oh, believe me. I will never take my life for granted ever again.' She stared at the weeping women around them. 'And never again will I just think about myself. I want to help the families of those who died, but have absolutely no idea what can be done.'

He brushed some fallen hair from her face. 'I wish to do the same and we will. Somehow.'

She stared into his beautiful blue eyes. 'Are you scared?'

'Now?' He frowned. 'No. I'm not sure I'll ever be scared again after surviving this.'

'I am.' She inhaled a long breath. 'I'm scared I'll never be able to set foot on a boat again. I'm scared I'll never be enough for all those who lost their lives and they'll look down from heaven and think I've wasted every moment of what they've lost. I'm scared . . . ' She looked at him. 'That I'll never be truly happy.'

Part of her longed to have Samuel take her in his arms and kiss her as he had before. The other part feared receiving comfort from him. Feared how it would provoke her to lean on him when she'd not leaned on anyone her entire life.

Yet, she sensed that Samuel would never bend nor forsake her.

'You *will* be happy, Amelia.' His gaze burned with confidence. 'You will succeed at anything you put your mind to, and you will live a wonderful life.'

Hope painfully twisted her heart and she looked at their joined hands. 'I assume there is no news of your friend? I had hoped he might have been assigned to row one of the other lifeboats.'

'No. No news.'

She looked up and, to her dismay, tears filled his eyes before he blinked and quickly stared across the room.

'Samuel . . . I'm so sor —'

'Don't go back, Amelia.' He sharply turned, his gaze intense on hers. 'Stay in New York. Stay with me.'

'What?'

'I met you on a ship destined to sink to the bottom of the ocean. We spent time together as crew and passenger. Time that wasn't strictly allowed. Yet, somehow, we managed to be together again and again. I kissed you. I held you. Stay with me. Let's see what America has to offer together. Let's take this opportunity to become the people we are meant to be.'

The insanity of his suggestion echoed in her mind, but it was superseded by the excited thump of her heart, the wrenching pull in her stomach urging her to accept his proposal. To take his hand and leap into the unknown with a man she instinctually trusted.

'We could find work,' Samuel continued, the eagerness in his voice gathering strength, the light in his eyes brightening. 'We could see the Statue of Liberty and Times Square. We could see it all. Together.' He lowered his voice and looked deep into her eyes. 'I promise I'll look after you. Always.'

32

Samuel tightened his hold on Amelia's hand, ignoring the voice screaming in his head, asking him what in God's name he was doing. 'This is a chance like neither of us has had before. I'm not suggesting such a leap lightly. I just . . .' He shook his head. 'We've been given a second chance. How can we not act on that? How can we not stay in America and seek our fortunes the way so many people on the ship intended? Don't we owe it to them to do that much, at least?'

Her cheeks had paled, and she studied him with a look in her eyes he couldn't decipher.

'Amelia — '

'I understand what you're saying, but I'm not you, Samuel. I don't take risks. I don't sail around the world.' She slipped her hand from his. 'I have no skills, except for what I've been taught at Pennington's. Of what I learned in service. Scrubbing grates, changing beds. Good stitching and sketching will hardly ensure me a fortune. Whereas you have charisma, charm and confidence. I have none of those things.'

His gut clenched with annoyance that she would even think she lacked any of the things she claimed he had, much less say it. 'Do you not see what you are? *Who* you are? You are kind, brave, determined and beautiful. What else do you need to start a new life somewhere else?'

She shook her head, her gaze hardening. 'You need more than those things. You need tenacity and strength, a will that refuses to bend. Unfortunately, I have a tendency to please people, to immerse myself in other people's wishes and a will that . . . most certainly bends.'

'I have seen nothing other than steel in you. The way you were determined to visit every area of the ship in your mission to serve Pennington's. The way you stood up to Weir and those snotty women in the lifeboat. God, Amelia, the way you held that baby so close to you until she was safe. The way you are here now and looking me straight in the eye means you are strong. Strong and unbreakable.'

She stared at him, her gaze unblinking. 'You're wrong.'

He frowned, concerned by the tremor in her voice. 'Why am I?'

'You just are. I don't want to talk about this anymore.' She looked away. 'Your life is your own and I'm happy you are staying in America. I think it's absolutely the right thing for you.' She faced him, her gaze determined. 'But it's not for me.'

Frustrated, he reached for her, but she leaned away and hurt slashed his chest as he swallowed hard. 'Why is wanting to carve out a life of your own selfish? Does a person not have the right to make themselves happy? To do what they love and earn money from it?'

'I thought so, once upon a time.' She glared at him. 'But that sort of dreaming was stolen from me . . . by a man. And now here you are, asking me to trust you. To leave everything I have in England, take your hand and walk into the sunset. No, Samuel, I won't do it.' She abruptly stood, her shoulders trembling and her gaze angry. 'I am not worthy of anything more than what I have right now. I have a good position at Pennington's, I have housemates I adore and, for the first time in my life, money of my own. I don't need to dream, and I don't need to run away. Not anymore.'

She moved to walk away and he quickly stood, grasping her elbow. He wanted to take her in his arms, to hold her until she stopped shaking. 'Amelia, there is more for me than providing for my family. All I've ever really wanted was a good job, a wife and family. To be settled and happy. I don't think that's too much to ask, but if I return home, the passion that's been stirred awake now that we've escaped death will be extinguished. Will be sucked out of me the moment I walk through my door and back into the role that was determined for me by my father's passing. I can't do it. I can't go back.'

Her beautiful, dark brown eyes glinted with tears and when she spoke, her voice was softer. 'And I wouldn't want you to. Look at these people's faces.' She looked around. 'Nothing will ever be the same for them or us, ever again.'

He followed her gaze around the darkened saloon. People sat in chairs and on the floor, cradling glasses of brandy or steaming cups of tea. Their listless eyes stared at the walls, their hands or the floor. Numbed with shock and loss, no one had any idea of what would happen next, of how they would get home or even if they could, or should, continue with the plans they'd had when they had boarded the *Titanic* just a few short days ago.

Most had lost the entirety of their money and belongings, possibly had nowhere to go until they received funds sent from home. It was true that more first-class passengers seemed present than second or third, but it did not mean they felt the loss of husbands, brothers or sons any less keenly.

A hollow sickness rolled through him and Samuel swiped his hand over his face. 'The desolation in this room is only the beginning. Once full realisation hits, God only knows how these people will fare.' He looked at her. 'We're not just lucky we survived, we're lucky the people closest to us weren't on that ship, too.'

Amelia nodded, tears glistening on her lashes. 'You're right,' she said softly. 'Do you know, I have no idea if Mr Weir has a family. I should send a wire to Elizabeth once the families have sent theirs. If Mr Weir had a wife and children, she will want to help.'

'She sounds like a wonderful employer.'

'She is, and a wonderful inspiration to so many of us at Pennington's. I owe her everything. I refuse to use the chance she's given me for my own gain. I can't stay in America. I have a job to do in New York and then I will return to Pennington's.' She hesitantly ran her gaze over his face as though unsure whether to say more, before she inhaled a deep breath. 'I have had nothing and won't risk being in that position ever again. I have to go back.'

'I understand, but can't you see what you've already achieved? How strong you are? Miss Pennington might have given you the position at Pennington's, but it was you that worked so well that you rose higher and higher until she felt confident enough to put you on a ship to another country. You can rise again in America, Amelia. I know you can.'

'I can't.' The skin at her throat moved as she swallowed, her gaze drifting from his to look defiantly across the room, her cheeks mottled. 'I won't be able to do it all over again. You don't know anything about me and, more than that, you are wrong.'

‘Why?’ His heart beat out the silent seconds, fuelling his frustration and admiration of this wonderful woman. ‘What happened to you to make you think yourself so unworthy?’

She snapped her eyes to his, her gaze blazing with fury. ‘Why should I explain such a thing to you? Do you think because you ensured me a space on the lifeboat, I owe you the rest of my life?’

‘Of course not. I care about you. Is that so bad?’

She glared at him, her cheeks reddening. ‘Yes. Yes, it is.’

‘But —’

She stormed away from him, the blanket around her shoulders slipping unheeded to the floor as she marched out of the saloon and, undoubtedly, out of his life.

Samuel closed his eyes. Instinct told him that he and Amelia were meant to meet on the *Titanic*, were meant to get to America and start again. Together.

But why did he believe such a thing so vehemently? How in the world could a meeting of two people hold such certainty? He was a fool. He clenched his jaw and stared towards the door that Amelia had disappeared through. Well, he’d had enough of being a fool. It was time he became the king of his own world.

With or without Amelia.

33

'Ruby! Come quick.' One of the store's lift attendants burst into the design department.

Ruby immediately leapt to her feet. 'Henry? Whatever is wrong?'

Young Henry stood in the doorway, his eyes glowing with excitement and his cheeks flushed. 'Mr Carter sent me to tell all the design staff to join him in the atrium. He's gathering everyone right now. Customers, too.'

Ruby put her hands on her hips. 'What on earth has happened — ?'

'It's the *Titanic*. She's sank!'

Ruby froze, unable to even react as chair legs scraped along the tiled floor, other design staff abruptly standing. 'That's impossible.'

'It's true. Hurry. Mr Carter and Miss Pennington are coming to the grand staircase. They're going to tell the whole store what is happening. Quickly!'

He ran off leaving a pregnant silence lingering in his wake.

Slowly, Ruby turned, her eyes catching those of one of the young women working with her. 'It can't be true. What if . . . what if people are dead?' She clamped her hand to her throat. 'Amelia was on that ship. Mr Weir, too.'

'Oh my God . . . '

'We should go.' Ruby made for the stairs, her heart pounding. Surely Amelia hadn't been killed? Dread pulled deep in her stomach even contemplating that one of the few people who had shown her such kindness should have perished. Sometimes Ruby suspected that Amelia had guessed of her shameful inclination and accepted her anyway. Maybe now she would never have the chance to tell Amelia how much her discretion meant to her.

She reached the atrium and joined the crowds of customers and staff gathered in front of Mr Carter where he stood on the steps on the grand staircase. 'Ladies and gentlemen, I can confirm the rumours and speculations of the press have been proven to be true. The *Titanic* has indeed sank . . .'

Ruby's intake of breath joined those around her as she struggled to hear Mr Carter over the thudding of her pulse. How was it possible for such a mammoth ship to sink?

Mr Carter continued to speak, his words faltering, gathering strength and then faltering again. Even when he'd finished Ruby couldn't quite believe what she'd heard.

Pennington's staff and customers dispersed as Mr Carter slowly walked down the last few steps of the grand staircase, his expression dazed and his gait unusually hesitant.

Shocked and afraid, Ruby crossed her arms to hide her trembling. People everywhere mingled, their hands reaching for each other as they offered shared condolence and support. Pennington's had never been so quiet, so static. Grief and sympathy for the many families who would be affected by the tragedy unfurled inside her as Ruby dropped her arms and turned to Victoria.

Tears shone in her eyes. 'What is to be done, Ruby? All those people . . .'

'I know.' Ruby shook her head, her gaze once more drawn to the stunned crowd as many moved towards the exit, shopping forgotten. 'But I'm sure Miss Pennington will gather us soon. There must be something we can do.'

Victoria nodded, her gaze burning into Ruby's as she squeezed her arm.

Mr Carter's speech once more resonated in Ruby's mind. He had been sensitive but firm as he'd tried his best to reassure the families and loved ones affected by the *Titanic*'s sinking that they would have the store's unwavering support. It just didn't seem real that such a thing could happen.

Ruby stared towards Pennington's main window. 'Something will have to be done immediately about the *Titanic* display.'

Before Victoria could respond, Elizabeth Pennington hurried towards them, her face ashen and her green eyes shadowed with disbelief. 'Ruby, we must dismantle the *Titanic* window as soon as possible. Come with me.' She looked to her left. 'Mrs Lark, would you please go to the ladies and men's departments, also Homewares, and ask that two members of staff are spared from each department? They are to bring with them all the boxes for the merchandise used in the *Titanic* display.'

'Of course, Miss Pennington.' Victoria's eyes were wide on Ruby's. 'I will speak to you later, Ruby.'

Elizabeth led the way to the main window and the small holding area behind it. Opening the concealed door, she entered the window and Ruby followed.

'Close the curtains, Ruby. News of the sinking is being handed out by every paperboy, on every corner of the city. The last thing we want is people to think us insensitive at such a dreadful time.' Elizabeth shook her head, her hand at her throat. 'I have no idea what to do. Amelia and Mr Weir . . . my God, Ruby, how could this have happened? Mr Carter is trying to get in touch with the authorities to see what procedures are in place to locate missing passengers, but I'm not Amelia's or Mr Weir's family. I have no idea how much the people in charge will tell me or how I will possibly find out more.'

Seeing Elizabeth's usually calm composure was cracking, Ruby moved to the curtain to give her employer a few moments to collect herself. Sympathy and understanding twisted inside her as she pulled on the curtain's rope with trembling hands, Amelia's face looming in her mind. Surely, such a shining light could not be extinguished when Amelia was barely twenty-three years old?

The curtain closed on the gawping passers-by outside and Ruby turned.

Elizabeth was busy gathering the nautical paraphernalia they had used to decorate the window and even though her face was etched with the staunch focus her staff expected of her, there was no hiding the stiffness in her shoulders and the pallor of her face. She was entirely shaken.

'Why don't you let me strip the window, Miss Pennington?' Ruby asked gently. 'I'm sure you have a hundred and one other things that need your attention. I will get everything taken down in no time.'

Elizabeth sat back on her haunches. 'I can't bear to think how many people who work here had family, friends or associates aboard that ship.' Her eyes glinted with tears. 'I must check on Mrs Culford.'

'Esther? But she is at home with her baby and Mr

Culford, isn't she?' Ruby felt sick. Surely Pennington's previous head window dresser hadn't been aboard the *Titanic* too? Was that why Amelia had been sent on the trip to America? On a special assignment with Esther? 'Oh, Miss Pennington, surely Esther wasn't — '

'No, she is safely at home, thank goodness.' Elizabeth shook her head, her gaze full of despair and sadness. 'But her sister-in-law travelled on the *Titanic* and also Cornelia's ex-husband and his new wife, too. I went to the jewellery department and informed Cornelia before I made the announcement and she has gone home. But how many more staff will be in shock and suffering such heartbreaking loss? How I am to help them, comfort them, when I don't know all my staff as well as I'd like?' She swiped at her cheek. 'I try so hard to ensure my staff are happy, but what can I do to bolster them now?'

The door to the window opened and Victoria entered, carrying several boxes with other members of staff following behind, also armed with packaging. Her eyes immediately met Ruby's and she raised her eyebrows, silently asking if she was all right.

Ruby nodded, her heart lifting just a little that Victoria's concern should be for her at such an awful, universal time.

Elizabeth rose from the floor and Ruby touched her arm. 'Go, Miss Pennington. I will oversee everything here. I won't leave until everything is removed from the window and returned to the various departments. I promise.'

After instructing the staff to pack up the merchandise from their relevant departments, Ruby embraced the unexpected anger and disbelief that so many lives had been taken on a trip that, for many, was most likely a once-in-a-lifetime opportunity for a better life.

This was the misfortune that rained down on people. They were given a chance, only to have it cruelly snatched away again. They were given freedom, only to be caged once more. All the loved ones left behind would not have the lives they had before; everything had changed. Fury burned inside her. Life was precious and she would not stand by one more day and let her mother destroy any more of the brief and happy moments her children might be blessed with.

Emboldened, she strode through the chaos towards Victoria only to be intercepted by Mr Evans who worked in the men's department.

'Ah, Miss Taylor. Might I ask how you came to be in charge of us? It seems to me you are taking this tragedy and turning it into an opportunity.' He sneered at her, his cold, beady eyes boring into hers. 'I wouldn't even begin to get above your station. There is more than enough talk surrounding you as it is.'

Ruby drew her hands into fists, her heart pulsing in her ears. 'Really?'

'Yes, really.' He sniffed and glanced towards the back door where she knew Victoria was working. 'It seems you have a much closer relationship with Mrs Lark than most. People are talking of you being in love with her. Nobody can fail to miss how you look at her and take every opportunity to touch her.'

Sickness coated Ruby's throat. 'Is that so, Mr Evans?'

'It is. Yes. Some might assume such abhorrent goings on are only among decidedly repulsive men, whereas I have it on good authority that there are just as many females guilty of the same behaviour.'

'Well . . .' Ruby's pulse thumped in her ears, self-preservation and protection for Victoria rising as she stepped closer to Mr Evans and lowered her voice. 'I would advise you to take your wisdom and stick it in your own thick ear before dishing it out to the rest of us. I've heard that you don't take kindly to female rejection. It really wouldn't do for Miss Pennington to hear of your over-interest in the shop girls, would it?'

His cheeks turned red and his eyes bulged. 'Why, you — '

Ruby spun away and marched towards Victoria, her determination well and truly at its height. She clasped Victoria's elbow and looked deep into her eyes. 'Is tomorrow too soon for Tommy and me to move in with you?' she whispered.

'Tomorrow?' Victoria glanced over Ruby's shoulder. 'Well, no, that's fine. If you're sure?'

Hating that Victoria felt the need to check for listening ears when all too soon Hazel Price would learn of their cohabiting and gossip and judgement would echo from every corner of the store. 'I'm sure, but are you?' Ruby's heart beat fast with her need to escape her mother's domination. 'Because if you've changed your mind, I understand. Either way, Tommy and I will be leaving. Tomorrow.'

Victoria's eyes flitted again from person to person before she looked at Ruby and lifted her chin. 'I'm sure. Entirely sure. Tell your mother this evening, and I will have everything ready for you anytime.' Her gaze grew intense on Ruby's. 'If things turn nasty when you go home, you grab whatever you can and come to me tonight. Anything else you need, we can collect another day.'

Ruby raised her eyebrows, inappropriate pride warming her. 'We? You would really face my mother?'

Victoria gave a curt nod. 'For you, yes. I'll see you later.'

She hurried through the window's back door and Ruby stared in stunned silence after her. *For me? What did she mean?* Could she dare to hope Victoria's feelings might be straying past platonic?

'Miss Taylor? We need your direction over here.'

Blinking from her stupor, Ruby strode towards the front of the window, her focus on work, even if Victoria's words, and their meaning, continued to circle her mind.

34

Amelia walked onto the Boat Deck of the *Carpathia,* her gaze steadfastly averted from the lifeboats lining the ship's edge. If she never saw another lifeboat — another ship — in her life, she would be grateful. Yet, it was a plain and simple fact that she would need to get back to England and the only plausible way was by boat.

She pressed her hand to her unsettled stomach and stared at the people wandering around the deck. The air held a chill, and most were in coats and hats, some with blankets over their shoulders, others dressed in suits, their arms tightly crossed in an effort to keep warm.

It wasn't long before they were due to sail into New York harbour, but still dismal blankness showed in every pair of the survivors' eyes; their slumped shoulders and bowed heads reflecting the heavy weight in their hearts. Her own heart twisted with profound sympathy for so many who had lost so very much. She was alone in this world, yet she'd survived. She doubted the guilt of her survival would ever leave her.

Amelia swallowed the lump lodged in her throat. She had never felt so very alone and her heated exchange with Samuel had only enhanced her solitude. Their argument had left her shaken and upset and they had steadfastly avoided each other for the last two days. Would today be a third day of them not speaking?

His distance pulled painfully at her heart.

Despite being brought up in an orphanage and

going straight into service, all Amelia ever sought and needed was the company of others.

And she'd found that at Pennington's and with the suffragist group in Bath.

She'd found it with Samuel.

Forcing her mind away from the man she was falling in love with, Amelia wondered how the staff and her associates fared. The suffragist society she belonged to provided a much-needed hand of friendship and when it had been extended by Esther Culford, Amelia had immediately clutched it. Would Esther and the others know of the sinking by now? Would Pennington's? Elizabeth and Joseph's faces swam in her blurred vision and she quickly blinked away the threat of tears.

She had to send word to Elizabeth that she was alive and well. As for Mr Weir . . . Amelia glanced around the small trios and groups of men and women, she could only assume him dead. They had been aboard for three nights. If Mr Weir was alive, he would have found her by now. After all her moaning and protestations about him before they'd set sail, she would have given anything to see his harassed face spot her in the distance and have him come barrelling towards her in reprimand.

She briefly closed her eyes before pulling back her shoulders and walking purposefully towards a group of crewmen.

As she neared, one of them saw her and broke away from the group. 'Might I help you, ma'am?' he asked, touching his hand to his hat. 'Is there anything you need?'

'I was wondering how I might go about sending a message? I believe someone is in charge of sending them home for the first-class survivors? Only, if the courtesy has been extended to second — '

'First-class, you say? Well, of course, ma'am. If you'd like to come with me, I'll take you to an operator and he'll arrange for a wire to be sent for you. Were you not in the saloon when the announcement was made that first-class passengers would send wires initially, before being quickly followed by second and third?'

'I wasn't, and I'm not actually first-class.'

'You're not?' The young officer appraised her from head to toe as though she was dressed finely rather than in clothes that had been sodden and dried, her hair bedraggled and stuffed beneath her hat and her shoes no longer really resembling shoes at all. More leather and rubber held together by God's generosity. 'Well, pardon me, ma'am, but you certainly have a look of class about you, if you don't mind me saying.'

Amelia's cheeks turned warm and she dipped her head. 'Thank you. That's very kind.'

'Nothing kind about it.' He winked. 'It's the truth.'

Her smile faltered as he strode ahead of her. For a fleeting moment, she'd been flattered that an officer had mistaken her for first-class, when maybe he thought her nothing more than pretty. A face. A woman to cajole and flirt with. A woman to charm and manipulate. She narrowed her eyes at the officer's back as she followed. Were there any different men in the world?

She silently admonished herself. Samuel was different.

Her anger lifted. Maybe if she could pass as a first-class passenger, it was a sign she was meant for bigger and better things. Samuel's fiery determination to forge a whole new life for himself in New York wouldn't leave her thoughts or conscience. Was he right? Shouldn't every survivor take the chance they had been given and do something extraordinary?

'Here you go, ma'am. I'll leave you with Officer Jordan.' The crewman touched his hat again. 'Nice to meet you. Be sure to be back out on deck soon. You don't want to miss your first glimpse of the Statue of Liberty.'

Amelia took a seat next to the operator and folded her hands in her lap, her back straight. 'I'd like to send a message to Elizabeth Pennington at Pennington's department store, Bath, England . . .'

Fifteen minutes later, Amelia emerged from the operating room and back out onto the Boat Deck. The first person she saw was Samuel.

He had his back to her talking to some officers. She smiled to see his overuse of hand gestures as he explained his conversation to the other men. The mannerism seemed so familiar to her already. The way he used his hands to aid his words amused and softened her. It was something she had not seen so exaggerated in a person before. Something that she knew she would always see as uniquely Samuel if she had to pick him out in a crowd.

He met her gaze.

The concentrated look immediately left his face and was replaced with a flash of pleasure and then, if she was right, uncertainty. Their parting had been unpleasant, to say the least, and now she was sorry. Neither of them had the right to waste time on trivial arguments. Not now. Not ever.

She slowly wandered towards him, her mind scrambling for the right thing to say. How to apologise, but not have him reassert his request that she remain in

New York. The notion was impossible and, anyway, she'd now written to Elizabeth confirming she would return in two weeks if she would be generous enough to send funds to enable Amelia to find room and board now that all of her possessions had been lost.

But every time she looked at Samuel, her stomach knotted and her heart hitched with love. His morality and ethics, his devotion to his family and friends, even his pursuit of her and his excitement for their futures attracted her. His dreams were vast, and she applauded him for that more than he could know, but how was she to trust him? To stay in a strange land with a strange man was madness, but part of her understood just how wonderful it would be to start life again where no one knew them.

'Hello.'

She looked into his eyes and her heart softened to see such affection in his. 'Hello.' She smiled. 'I've just sent a message to Elizabeth. If she didn't know before, she'll soon know of the sinking and that I am safe.' Her smile dissolved. 'I also told her there has been no sign of Mr Weir.'

Samuel's sad gaze slid gently over her face before he offered his arm. 'Walk with me?'

She hesitated and then slipped her hand into the crook of his elbow, unable to entirely ignore how natural it felt to walk with him this way.

Just the two of them.

35

Samuel led Amelia along the *Carpathia*'s deck, passing crew and survivors gathered to catch the first glimpse of the Statue of Liberty. His heart raced and his hands were clammy with anticipation — or maybe trepidation — of what awaited them once they docked. Maybe Amelia was right to be afraid to look too far into the future, to think that they might not have the right to make plans or pursue dreams.

Yet, he could not lessen the certainty that his destiny lay in the great lands of America.

Whether or not she felt the first stirrings of what Samuel believed to be something special between them, he wanted Amelia to understand just how amazing a person she was, how much potential she had to make a difference in this world. His decision to explore the opportunities New York had to offer didn't have to come with the proviso that she shared them with him; he wanted her to throw herself into the adventure by her own choosing.

A loud, collective gasp broke his thoughts, followed by a burst of cheering and clapping. The faces surrounding him that had been so nondescript, so paralysed with shock and grief, now grew euphoric with relief and joy.

'Quickly.' He grinned and tightened his hold on Amelia, as he pulled her to the railing. 'They must see the statue.'

They gripped the railing and, through the thin mist that hovered around her, the Statue of Liberty stood, her torch held high and the spikes of her golden head piece glinting in the hazy sunshine.

'My God, there she is.' He turned to Amelia. 'Can you see her?'

Amelia stared in the direction of the Statue, her face expressionless before she smiled, her mouth stretching wider and wider. She looked at him and the happiness in her eyes took his breath away. Words lodged in Samuel's throat as hope rose in his chest.

'She's beautiful, Samuel. Truly beautiful.'

So *are you*. 'Isn't she just?' He dragged his gaze away from her to stare across the water, his heart pounding. Did she feel it now? Feel the opportunity? The intensity of their God-given gift to live on? To do more? See more? Love more . . .

'What does she represent?' Amelia asked. 'I should probably know, but I don't.'

'Freedom.' He turned, pride swelling inside him. 'The abolition of slavery. Opportunity. New beginnings.' He hesitated and then leapt into the fire and touched her face. 'What is possible . . . for us.'

She looked deep into his eyes. 'Samuel . . .'

He slowly dipped his lips towards hers, giving her ample opportunity to lean back and reject his kiss. Instead, she came forward. Her mouth touched his, tentatively at first, and then she pressed her body closer and he moved his hand from her face to cradle the back of her head. He deepened their kiss and she responded, a soft murmur escaping from somewhere deep inside of her.

After all too brief a time, he reluctantly pulled back, not wanting to push his luck. Her eyes were glazed, but also filled with passion and fire. He slipped his hand into hers. 'So? What do you think?'

She smiled. 'About the kiss? Or the Statue of Liberty?'

'Either.' He laughed and brushed a fallen curl from her brow.

Her gaze lingered on his mouth before she stared towards the Statue. 'I think you're right. I was foolish to believe I could continue with my work in New York as I intended. Everything has changed. Possibly forever.' She faced him. 'We survived and, as you said, for some reason, God put our lives above others. We owe it to Him and them to do all we can to uncover the reasons why.'

Relief powered through him making it impossible to resist kissing her again. This time, she pulled *him* close, kissing him until he thought he might lose the ability to breathe.

When she stepped back, her eyes glittered with hope. 'I'm no longer saying no to you about staying in New York, but I'm not making any promises either. I have little money and means. Elizabeth will most likely be good enough to send me sufficient money for the two weeks I am supposed to be here, but after that — '

'I have money at home. We will find somewhere to stay and I'll ask my mother to send me some of the money I have put by. She might not like it, but she knows that money is my earnings, not hers. I will see you are all right, Amelia. I promise.'

Slowly her smile dissolved. 'It's that sentiment that worries me.'

Confused, he touched his finger to her chin, lifting her eyes to his. 'That I want to take care of you?'

'Yes.'

'But why? We are both stepping into the unknown.

If my caring for you bothers you, don't consider it as me looking after you, but sharing something with you.'

'But don't you see? If I let you look after me this way, you are pursuing the same life as you did in England. Nothing would have changed for you. Once more, you are financially responsible for someone else. I don't want that for you and I'm sure, once you're thinking clearly, you won't want it for yourself.'

'I have never thought more clearly in my life.' He took her hand and held it to his chest, praying that she heard him. 'My mother and sisters weren't my responsibility by choice, they became my responsibility when Dad passed. This, us, is entirely different. I *want* to look after you. I *want* to share in this adventure with you, however long it lasts. I'm not asking that you pledge your life to me. Just step into the arena with me. After that, destiny will take over, but I really believe we have to at least try for the lives we've always dreamed of.' Tears pricked his eyes. 'God knows I owe Archie that much, at least.'

She squeezed his hand. 'I know you do, and I'd never stand in your way, but . . . ' She studied him, uncertainty alight in her dark brown eyes. Then she curtly nodded, her gaze dark with determination. 'I will stay two weeks and think of adventure and opportunity but, after that time, if I want to return to Pennington's, that is what I will do.'

Disappointment threatened, but he wouldn't push her. Wouldn't risk her being beside him out of obligation rather than desire. 'Of course.'

'You promise me that when the end of the two weeks grows close, you'll respect my decision? Whether that be to stay or go?'

'Yes.' He swallowed, his heart a panicked beat that there was every chance in fourteen days, he'd never lay eyes on this woman again. 'I promise.'

36

Ruby stuffed the rest of her belongings into her carpet bag, before standing back from the bed. She crossed her arms. Now packed and ready, she just had to get Tommy sorted out before their mother returned from wherever she'd chosen to go that evening.

Dinner had been torturous. Somehow, she'd managed to finish her meal despite planning to leave the house within the next two hours. A maelstrom of guilt, fear and misplaced worry for what might befall her mother had unexpectedly swirled inside Ruby's heart and conscience. Somehow, she'd found the inner strength to tolerate her mother's jibes and criticisms from across the table, fully aware the hour that stretched like three might be the very last she'd ever have to spend in her mother's company.

As was usual once she'd eaten her fill, her mother had stood from the table, grabbed her cigarettes and purse with a shout over her shoulder for Ruby and Tommy to get into bed and not wait up.

Neither of them ever had, so her mother's words were wasted.

Leaving her bedroom, Ruby walked to Tommy's door and gently knocked before entering.

'How are you doing, Tommy? Are you packed?'

Her brother turned from where he sat on the floor, his eyes wide with fear. 'Won't she be extra mad when she finds us gone?'

'Mad?' Ruby raised her eyebrows and ruffled his hair. 'Why on earth are you worried about her being mad? Mad is Ma's natural state. I don't think I can ever remember her being anything but mad. Can you?'

But Tommy didn't smile. Instead, he turned back to his bag and put his bedtime teddy bear, worn and tattered through the upsets and tears the poor thing had soaked up countless times, on top of his clothes and few precious story books.

'Hey.' Ruby sat on the floor and pulled Tommy into her arms, pressing a kiss to his temple. 'You will really like Mrs Lark. She is kind, sweet and funny. I'll be able to cook us meals and tuck you in at night. You can come home from school and look at your books for as long as you want without anyone making fun or disturbing you. Won't you like that?'

His head bobbed beneath her chin.

Fighting the tears that pricked her eyes, Ruby squeezed him and then pulled back so she could look at his face. 'You have to trust me that leaving now is the right thing to do. Nothing is ever going to change if we stay here, Tommy. I want a good future for us both. Ma is getting worse and I can see no end to it.' She held his chin between her thumb and forefinger, willing him to believe her. 'Staying with Mrs Lark is just temporary until I can save enough money to get us a room all of our own. It won't be forever. I promise.'

His sad, pale blue eyes stared back at her and Ruby could've sworn she heard a splinter crack across her heart.

Slowly, he nodded. 'I love you, Ruby.'

'And I love you.' She pulled him close and a treacherous tear rolled over her cheek. Quickly swiping it away, she stood and pulled Tommy to his feet. 'Now, let's close your bag and get out of here, shall we? I bet you're looking forward to seeing where you'll be sleeping tonight.'

He tentatively smiled. 'Will we be sharing?'

'Yes.'

He grinned. 'Then I want to go now.'

Laughing, Ruby led him by the hand onto the landing, collected her bag and they walked downstairs. Once in the hallway, she buttoned Tommy into his coat and playfully plonked his cap on his head. She pushed her arms into her own coat and stared along the narrow hallway and staircase, glanced into the living room. She shivered as years of violent memories assaulted her, re-filling her heart with the ugly resentment that lingered there like a stubborn bruise.

Ruby liked to imagine that she loved Victoria, that she was capable of building a future with someone she could give herself entirely to. Yet, deep inside, she doubted who she was a hundred times a day. Was she really capable of feeling anything for anyone when her mother had taught her nothing but disparagement and degradation?

Opening the front door, she put her hand on Tommy's shoulder and walked him outside into the night. Closing the door, she dropped her key into her pocket, hating that something inside of her couldn't make her leave it behind. Despite all that her mother had done, Ruby wouldn't be able to live with herself if her mother needed her and she couldn't access the house.

If the call came for help, Ruby would be there.

'Not that you deserve it,' she mumbled as she exhaled a shaky breath and urged Tommy along the cobbled street.

They quickly walked towards Victoria's townhouse

on Laura Place, a pretty residential area where a beautiful, ornate fountain held centre-stage. As they passed the fountain, Ruby threw an imaginary penny into its waters and sent up a wish that this move was the right thing for Tommy. No matter what her mother's actions, he loved their mother and Ruby would do all she could not to further taint her in his eyes. As long as their mother remained a safe distance from him and let him grow, that was fine. If Tommy wanted to speak to her again sometime in the future, Ruby wouldn't do anything to prevent that from happening.

At least, she wouldn't when he'd grown six feet tall, broad-shouldered and man enough to defend himself.

They came to a stop outside Victoria's house and Ruby stared up at its façade. The sand-coloured stone glowed beneath the streetlamps, the dark blue door gleaming, and its brass knocker shining. The windows were so clean, she could make out the dark swirls on the drapes inside and see the porcelain trinkets lining the inside sill.

Part of her knew that living here might not be any less difficult to bear than living with her mother . . . albeit for entirely different reasons. She was infatuated with Victoria and she held Ruby's stupid heart in her hands and most likely had no idea of her inappropriate desires. To think that Ruby might see Victoria in her nightclothes, spend nights side by side with her in front of the fire, run her a bath or maybe help wash her hair would be torture beyond anything she had already endured.

So why was she here? Ruby swallowed against the dryness in her throat. *Because she offered me a way out. She looked into my eyes and said, 'For you.'*

She slid her arm around Tommy's shoulders. 'Everything will be all right.'

Lifting her chin, she walked to the door and firmly knocked.

'You're here!' Victoria's face was alight with pleasure as she stood back to let them in. 'I've been looking out of the window like a madwoman. Come in, come in. And you must be Tommy.'

Ruby's throat clogged as she looked down at her brother who solemnly took Victoria's hand. When she met Victoria's eyes, the immediate fondness she saw in their beautiful depths tipped Ruby a little deeper towards inevitable heartbreak.

'Let me take your coats.' Victoria practically shook Tommy out of his and hung it on the stand behind her before doing the same with Ruby's. 'Leave your bags there and come through to the parlour, my maid, Susie, will take them up to your room. I've made some sandwiches and a chocolate sponge. I hope you like chocolate, Tommy.'

He shyly smiled and nodded.

'Good, because — ' she whispered behind her hand ' — I know that sister of yours is like an animal when she sees chocolate, so we'll have to be super quick to get a slice first.'

She grabbed his hand and hurried into the parlour, leaving Ruby to follow.

Once she could move her feet.

Tommy's giggles drifted through the open door like music to Ruby's ears. Why, for the first time in forever, did she feel as though she'd come home?

37

His shoulders stiff with tension and unable to stop his foot tapping on the floor, Samuel sat on a wooden chair in the Grand Central Station offices and sent up a silent prayer that he would walk out of here in new employment. He needed this job for himself, for Amelia and for Archie.

He looked along the row of young men sitting alongside him. Most of them seemed to be around his age, expressions of nerves mixed with desperation etched on their faces which no doubt matched his own. Naively, he hadn't expected quite so many people to be here looking for employment when the building work had been going on for so long. He couldn't help wondering, as he was newly arrived from England, whether his chances of gaining work over these New York men would be considerably lower.

He had heard the stories of thousands of immigrants flocking to America looking for work and the possibility of a better life, but he'd also learned of the prejudices that had been dumped on them from every direction.

Rising at dawn, he'd taken his first awe-inspiring walk through Times Square, marvelling at the amount of motorcars and cabs on the roads and the number of people walking the streets at such an early hour. Southampton and Bath could hardly be considered ghost towns, but the small amount of New York he had seen so far had crept under his skin and lit his imagination with excitement and ambition.

And now he was at Grand Central Station with its foundations laid and gargantuan ironwork erected, following the dream Archie had wanted him to reach for. As God was his witness, Samuel vowed to do all he could to take the first step on this new journey as his best friend would have wanted. Tears burned behind his eyes. Archie had been lost among hundreds of others and, in truth, Samuel was unsure how he would fare for the rest of his life without Archie's constant, unshakeable optimism urging him on.

'Next!'

The shout came from a man in his mid-forties, his salt-and-pepper hair neatly trimmed and his navy-blue, pin-stripe suit of a quality that illustrated a successful man.

Taking a deep breath, Samuel stood and approached with his hand outstretched. 'Samuel Murphy, sir.'

'Mr Murphy. Good to meet you. Malcolm Denning. Come on through.'

Samuel followed Mr Denning into a small office, sparsely decorated with a metal shelfing unit against the far wall and a steel desk behind which another man sat reading some papers.

Mr Denning gestured towards a chair on the other side of the desk. 'Take a seat, Mr Murphy. This is James Winston, one of the overseers here at the Grand Central.'

Samuel nodded. 'Nice to meet you, Mr Winston.'

The man looked up from his papers, nodded and returned to his reading.

'So . . .' Denning settled into a chair beside Winston. 'You're British.'

'Indeed, sir. I previously worked in Southampton.'

'Southampton?'

Winston looked up and mirrored Denning's wide-eyed stare.

Samuel frowned, unsure why mentioning Southampton should cause such a shocked reaction.

'Are you a *Titanic* survivor?' Winston lowered the paper he'd been reading, pushing it away, his gaze firmly on Samuel's. 'You were on the fated ship?'

There was no indication in the men's expressions of whether admitting such a thing would be beneficial or detrimental, so Samuel inhaled a long breath and nodded. 'Yes.'

'Holy mother of God.'

'A real *Titanic* survivor right here in our offices.'

Denning and Winston spoke over one another, insensitive grins spreading across their faces, their eyes alight with awe. Samuel's gut knotted with revulsion as he held their gazes. For crying out loud, did these two imbeciles not realise how many people had died? The pure terror of what it was like in those final hours? The clawing guilt the survivors battled with every minute since; the mourning they suffered for those they'd lost?

Samuel clenched his jaw, anger simmering deep inside of him.

'Mr Murphy . . .' Winston stood and offered his hand across the desk. 'It is an honour to shake your hand. I cannot imagine the sights you've seen or the hell you've been through.'

Samuel slowly took his hand. 'I'd rather not revisit my memories right now, sir. If you don't mind.'

'Of course, of course.' Winston held up his hands, his smile dissolving as he glanced at Denning before facing Samuel again. 'The trauma will take a long time to heal, I'm sure.'

Samuel held his tongue.

'So, you're looking to stay in New York?' Denning asked. 'You'd like to play a part in building Grand Central?'

'Yes, sir.'

'You have experience on the railroads?'

Samuel sat a little straighter and looked Denning straight in the eye. 'No, sir, but I'm a quick learner and I work hard. I have experience with mechanical engineering and have a mind and inquisitiveness about the workings of all transport. I worked on Southampton's docks for years and learned about sailing from the bottom up. Promoted from sailing boats to steam, to liners, and eventually given a prominent role in *Titanic*'s control room. I like to think that given the chance to work on the railroad, I'd have the same success here as I did in England.'

Denning's brow furrowed, his gaze unconvinced. He turned to Winston.

Samuel held Winston's gaze.

The look in his eyes was a lot more encouraging than Denning's, giving Samuel hope. He recognised the look. He'd seen it half a dozen times before. A man who liked a challenge. A man who liked to take raw talent and mould it into a practised expertise. A man who liked to give others a chance.

Winston leaned forward and picked up a box of matches. 'How long do you intend staying in New York, Mr Murphy?'

'As long as I can. Perhaps forever.'

Winston lit his cigar and puffed, the end sparking red and then orange until smoke drifted making Samuel feel nauseous.

'Well, then, if you're willing to work from the

bottom up . . .'

'I am, sir. I'll prove to you what I'm capable of.'

Denning cleared his throat. 'The railroad isn't easy, Murphy. It's tough work. You'll need strength of character as much as muscle.'

'That was true of the sea, too, sir. I have strength. Challenge me in any way you see fit and I'll overcome. I guarantee you that.'

Denning studied Samuel through narrowed eyes before turning to Winston with a shrug.

Winston grinned and offered his hand to Samuel a second time. 'Welcome to Grand Central, Murphy. Leave your details with Denning and we'll see you first thing Monday morning.'

Fifteen minutes later, feeling as happy as he had when he'd stepped off the *Carpathia* and onto solid terra firma, Samuel hurried back to the hotel, desperate to tell Amelia of his success. Pride burned inside him, and tears pricked his eyes once again as Archie's face filled his mind. Despite Samuel's fears of what would happen in New York, how long he'd last here or if he'd stay forever, he'd done what his friend had asked of him.

He was staying in New York and he was going to work the Grand Central railroad.

Now he wanted to have Amelia share in his euphoria, have her see his face and want the same feeling of anything being possible. The two of them could make a life here, he was sure of it. Whether or not that would be together romantically was too early to hope for — to assume — but either way, why would Amelia want to go back to England?

He understood her passion for Pennington's, but she could work in one of the huge department stores he'd passed that morning. She could rise higher than she'd ever dreamed, or could, in a small city like Bath. He sensed her ambition. Loved her determination and innovation. She was perfect in every way. He just had to try to find a way for her to see it, too.

Up ahead, Samuel spotted a post office and reached into his pocket. He should have just enough change to send home a wire. The White Star Line had given each surviving passenger a small amount of money to start them on their way until they could arrange for funds to be sent from home. He needed to be frugal but updating his mother was paramount. With a job secured and the promise of him sending money her way as soon as possible, she shouldn't resist too much about sending some cash to him urgently.

Well, he bloody hoped not. Surely, she'd be pleased to hear from him, that he was alive, rather than upset about the idea of his not returning home for a while?

38

Ruby sat in Elizabeth Pennington's office, her notebook tightly clutched in her lap. She surreptitiously watched Elizabeth finish her conversation with her husband, Joseph Carter, whom she had asked to join their meeting.

'So, Ruby . . . ' Elizabeth smiled as she and Joseph joined Ruby in the comfortable seating area by the window. 'I hope you've had a little time to think about what we can do next with the main window. It's been three days since we cleared the *Titanic* display and I'm keen to start work on something to cheer and inspire the public. We all need a burst of something beautiful to get us through what will be a most horrible time for so many.'

Joseph sat down beside his wife on the settee. 'I have put several workroom staff on standby if you need some extra stitching and altering done, Miss Taylor. The new window must be a priority. A large part of Pennington's reputation and attraction are our windows. With the curtains closed, it only reminds people of the *Titanic* tragedy, rather than giving them hope for the future.'

The importance and expectation of Ruby's ideas was obvious, and she sat a little straighter in her chair, battling the tumble of nerves in her stomach. 'It's very generous of you to allow me use of your staff, Mr Carter. Their help will be most welcome. I've written up notes for two ideas, but I am leaning towards one more than the other. I'm quietly confident it shouldn't take too long to design and erect the display if we get to work as soon as possible.'

'I'm glad to hear it.' He smiled and glanced at his wife. 'Have you shown Miss Pennington?'

'No, not yet. I — '

There was a knock on the office door before Mrs Chadwick, Elizabeth's secretary, walked briskly into the room, her glasses perched on the end of her nose. 'Miss Pennington, I have Esther Culford here. She wondered if she might impose on your time for a few moments?'

'Of course.' Elizabeth immediately leapt to her feet, pleasure brightening her green eyes. 'Show her in, please.'

Ruby swallowed, her nerves escalating. As Pennington's previous head window dresser, Esther Culford's reputation preceded her. Arguably, she'd had as much of a hand in Pennington's new, equal opportunity philosophy as Elizabeth and Joseph before Esther had left the store to birth her baby. Her eye for detail, innovation and excitement for change, had played an integral part in bringing Pennington's into the twentieth century.

Ruby's mouth dried. How would she ever measure up to Esther? Would Elizabeth ask Ruby to share her ideas in front of Esther? The notion was terrifying.

'Esther! Oh, my love, it is so wonderful to see you.' Elizabeth embraced her friend. 'Haven't you brought darling Beth with you?'

Esther laughed. 'No, your namesake is happily playing with her brother and sister at home. I made my escape and left them with Helen. Our nanny is a godsend, you know that.' She turned and nodded at Ruby. 'Hello, Ruby.'

'Hello. It's nice to see you, Esther.'

'You, too.' She opened her arms to accept Joseph's embrace. 'Joseph.'

'Come and join us,' he said, waving towards an empty armchair. 'You might have some helpful input into Ruby's plans for the main window.'

Ruby's heart sank and her hands ever so slightly trembled. Any hope of Esther not being involved had been futile. Well, she was here now so there was no other option than to dig deep and find the confidence to get through this meeting with passion and verve. Prove herself capable of executing a good job.

'I'd love to,' Esther said, as she sat down. 'My mind has been filled with worry and grief ever since the sinking. Lawrence is beside himself trying to get Harriet home. We think she will be on the first ship to leave America for England. At least, we hope she is.' Her eyes filled with concern as she looked around the group. 'The sombre tone of her telegrams indicated she is much changed. Not herself at all. I cannot imagine what she's been through.'

Elizabeth took Esther's hand. 'I have the same concerns about Amelia. Her telegrams have convinced me she was trying to be happy when she really isn't at all. She wants to stay in New York and continue with the scouting assignment, but I worry she wants that for fear of disappointing me should she abandon everything we had planned.'

Esther set her bag on the floor and sighed, tiredness shadowing her gaze. She pushed a blonde curl behind her ear. 'Well, there is little any of us can do when the survivors are thousands of miles away. Harriet wants to get back to Culford Manor as soon as possible and . . .' She looked at Elizabeth and then

Joseph, a silent something passing between the friends that Ruby couldn't decipher. 'She wants Lawrence, me and the children to come and live with her there. Permanently. I really think we have no choice but to agree, considering all Harriet has been through.'

'Surely you won't go?' Two spots of colour leapt into Elizabeth's cheeks. 'After everything that happened in that house, how Harriet was so awful to you when . . .' She blinked and looked at Ruby as though suddenly remembering she was there.

Ruby immediately stood, her cheeks burning that she had been party to a conversation that clearly concerned personal and private matters. 'I should go. It was lovely to see you again, Esther.'

'Oh, no, Ruby stay.' Esther's hazel eyes softened, her smile kind. 'I'd love to hear your plans. It will be a welcome distraction, I promise.' She looked at Elizabeth and Joseph. 'Why don't you both join Lawrence and me for dinner tonight at the house? We can talk more then.'

Joseph nodded. 'We'd love to.'

'Absolutely.' Elizabeth squeezed Esther's hand before turning to Ruby. 'I'm so sorry, Miss Taylor. I fear I am no more myself than anyone else these past few days. Why don't you share your ideas with us and Mrs Culford?'

'Of course.' Ruby sat down and pushed her fears away. This was yet another chance that Miss Pennington was giving her. An opportunity for Ruby to show what she could do and hopefully gain the added benefit of Mr Carter's and Esther's approval too. 'I would appreciate everyone's opinion.'

Inhaling a strengthening breath, Ruby opened her notebook and scanned her notes before studying each of the three faces in front of her. All their eyes were upon her, alert and interested.

'Considering the pain and suffering happening across Great Britain and America at the moment, I think it would be good for the public to see a display at Pennington's that can only provoke feelings of hope, optimism and happiness.'

'Hear, hear.' Joseph Carter leaned forward on the settee, his blue eyes gently encouraging. 'What do you have in mind?'

Ruby pulled back her shoulders. 'Weddings.'

'Weddings?' Elizabeth frowned. 'Surely weddings are the last thing anyone will want to think of when so many have lost husbands, wives, sons and lovers? Wouldn't a wedding theme risk being insensitive?'

Ruby's throat dried. For two days she'd agonised over a premise to bring smiles to people's faces, to lift their hearts and look to brighter horizons. Had her overwhelming instinct that weddings were the ultimate symbol of hope been wrong?

'I disagree.' Esther stood and walked behind the settee, her gaze firmly on Ruby's. 'Tell us more. What can you see in the window?'

Ruby cleared her throat and mustered every ounce of her floundering confidence. 'Well, I was thinking a country chapel background with an entire family wedding party present, along with a few farm animals, flowers, blue skies and sunshine. A June bride. Puppies and kittens . . . ' Her heart picked up speed as her vision filled her mind's eye. 'A pretty sister holding an infant and her husband proudly standing beside his new family. Rebirth, hope, starting again . . . a family dream for the future, love and care. A much-needed dose of buoyancy showing our customers that as much as we have been struck down by pain, loss and grief, we will rise again to a better future.'

The only sounds in the room was the swish of tyres through the rain-sodden street outside the open window, interspersed with the odd snatch of raised voices and a crying child. Heat slowly inched up Ruby's neck to burn in her cheeks as Miss Pennington, Mr Carter and Esther stared at her, their expressions still and considering.

'Of course, if this idea is not to your liking . . . ' she babbled, 'then I can show you the ideas I have for maybe a baby theme or just family as a whole or — '

'Weddings . . . ' Joseph Carter murmured, his gaze on Ruby as he slowly nodded. 'What do you think, Elizabeth?'

Miss Pennington turned to her husband and then Esther. Esther's staid expression slowly softened as her smile grew wider.

Elizabeth grinned and faced Ruby. 'Superb idea, Miss Taylor. Truly inspired. I cannot think of anything more fitting to rouse people's spirits and look to happier times. Weddings mean family and friends united and hopeful for a young couple who have their whole lives ahead of them. Your idea will remind people of what matters. Love, trust and care. Family, children and loved ones.' She looked at her husband and Esther a second time. 'Are we all in agreement?'

'Absolutely.'

'Without a doubt.'

Ruby exhaled as her relief rushed out a whoosh of air. 'Oh, I'm so pleased. I was so worried that you — '

'No need to worry anymore,' Miss Pennington laughed. 'Go back to the design department and further your ideas. As soon as you know what you need to get started, let me know and you will have mine and Mr Carter's full support. We have just over a month to bring your idea to fruition. As of the 1st of June, Pennington's will unveil its new, hopeful main window. Congratulations.'

'Thank you so much.' Ruby clutched her notebook to her chest, desperate to escape the office so she might hurry to the shop floor and tell Victoria her news. 'Shall I get started straight away?'

'Absolutely.'

Ruby left the office and walked as fast as her legs could carry her along the wood-panelled executive corridor. Once inside the lift, she leaned against the wall and grinned, ignoring the attendant's curious glances.

At last, everything in her life seemed to be taking a turn for the better. First, escape from her mother and now a Pennington's window all of her own. She had never felt so blessed.

39

Amelia stood in the atrium of RH Macy & Co in utter stupor.

She tried to take a forceful step forward in her mission to see how American department stores differed from Pennington's, but her feet remained stuck to the floor. Her initial observation of her very first New York store, was that *everything* was different.

The store was at least five or six times bigger than Pennington's, its entrance twice as grand. But it wasn't just its size that had frozen Amelia's boots to the floor, rather the mania surrounding her — no, that infused her. Crowds of people walked around, their faces eager and seemingly hypnotised by an overwhelming need to spend, spend, spend.

Lights shone, music played, chatter exploded, and laughter rang unrestrained. Where Pennington's held a mysterious and exciting aura, RH Macy's held an abundance of enjoyment and frivolous frivolity. People tipped their heads back and laughed aloud, women strode at lightning speed, their arms intertwined and pulling each other along to see the next counter and the next.

Someone bumped hard into her shoulder and Amelia stumbled forward.

The man gripped her elbow, grinned and doffed his hat. 'Sorry, miss.'

'Not at all,' Amelia managed, trying not to laugh. The man didn't look in the least bit sorry, but his delightful gaze and wide smile wiped away any annoyance she might have felt. 'Good afternoon to you.'

He winked and sped off into the crowds, entirely out of sight before she drew a second breath. Amelia moved into the throng, her purse tightly clasped under her arm as she stared at everything and everyone. The merchandise barely differed from the wonders that could be found at Pennington's, the clothes on offer as diverse and affordable, the jewellery shining just as brightly. The biggest difference was most definitely the atmosphere and Amelia grew profoundly heady.

Excitement and power swept through her as she pulled back her shoulders and headed for a side staircase leading to the next floor. People shouted and called to one another with abandon, their beaming faces looking into their children's as they were carried in their parents' arms or on their shoulders.

There was little decorum and even less politeness among the customers, but it didn't matter or affect what they were here to do.

Shop.

She entered the toy department and once again her steps faltered. Light, laughter and love seemed to seep from every doll, train set and teddy bear. Children ran amok, their parents and guardians chasing after them, each looking as youthful as their charges. A tangible excitement bounced from the walls making adults and children hurry to the cash desks with the toys they just had to have.

All the neglect and emptiness of Amelia's childhood fell away as she looked into the faces of these delightful children, her heart swelling with a certainty she had never known. Her mind had been filled with fashion and accessories while at Pennington's, influenced and mentored by Elizabeth and Esther, she never once considered toys her passion.

Yet, suddenly, she had a deep yearning to be a part of this mad euphoria, to acquire new toys and games and watch these children relish in the discovery and buying of them. Why she felt this way she had no idea, but it was as though she was shedding an old skin and being enveloped by a new one . . . one that would make her stand taller, prouder and happier than she'd ever thought possible before now.

The blinkers fell from her eyes.

If she were to remain in New York, she could be whomever she wanted to be. No more hiding her past, hiding her assault and the shame that marked her a used woman. Here, she could become someone brand new. A woman who worked in retail and did everything in her power to bring children joy. Nothing had ever felt so completely right.

She whipped her notebook and pen from her purse and set to work.

Dusk had begun to fall by the time Amelia emerged from RH Macy's and the moment she stepped out into the softly falling drizzle, she wanted to turn around and go back inside. Maybe even hide until the store's lights were extinguished and she could walk around inside, unnoticed in the darkness.

She was giddy with excitement and, as she strode along the street towards her hotel, all she wanted to do was seek out Samuel and tell him all she had seen, heard and talked about with the customers and shop girls at the phenomenon that was RH Macy's.

Would Samuel listen to her about such things? Was he a man with any interest in shopping? Maybe not. Amelia smiled. But he did care about her. Memories of his kisses tingled on her lips and her body heated.

He was such a good man. A strong man. A caring man. So very different, in fact, from any man she'd ever met.

He had a rawness to him that was unique. An almost dangerous intensity that should have set her running in the opposite direction yet held her in its thrall whenever he looked at her a certain way, with a certain desire.

She walked into the hotel lobby and looked around at the people cradling early evening drinks as they relaxed with family and friends or business associates. Not seeing Samuel among them, she slowly walked towards the bar area, a little apprehensive about entering alone.

Then she spotted him.

Taking a moment to study him unnoticed, Amelia breathed deep and tried to work out these new feelings Samuel Murphy had provoked in her. It was an impossible task when she had no idea what her attraction and interest in him meant or what she was to do about it. For all the possibilities her visit to the department store has aroused in her, her life was in Bath . . . at Pennington's. The thought of turning her back on her security was terrifying, but the *Titanic* sinking had irrevocably changed her — would possibly change the whole world, once more and more people learned of the tragedy.

Life changed all the time. Maybe it was time hers did, too.

She approached Samuel where he sat alone on a high stool at the bar. Feeling brave, she gently placed her hand on his shoulder. 'Good evening.'

He slowly turned, and Amelia immediately pulled her hand away, her stomach knotting with apprehension. His gaze was angry and glazed, his mouth drawn into such a tight line, his lips showed white.

Fear whispered through her and she stepped back, feeling foolish. 'Are you drunk?'

'Yes. And so what if I am?' He turned back to his glass and drained it. He lifted it to the barman. 'Another.'

Alarm wound around her heart and squeezed until she worried how she would take her next breath. Memories rushed her mind as the brandy-filled smell of the master's breath on her cheek and neck rose in her nostrils, his heavy body pressing against hers as he clawed and pulled at her blouse, the buttons ripping and her cries going unheeded in such a huge and empty house . . .

'I . . . I'll go.' She moved to walk away when Samuel reached out and grabbed her wrist, his gaze burning into hers. She lifted her chin and hissed, 'Let go of me, Samuel. Right now.'

He held a second longer before releasing her, raising his hand in the air. 'Sorry.' He closed his eyes and turned away from her. 'God, I'm sorry. For everything.'

Amelia stared at his turned cheek, uncertain even as her fear began to dissolve. Why was he in such a state? Had the sinking suddenly paralysed him? Sent him into a swirl of disbelief and confusion?

'What has happened?' she asked, softly. 'Why are you being like this?'

'Just go, Amelia. I was wrong about everything. I'm trapped. The life Archie wanted for me was a pipe dream.' He picked up the filled glass the barman had put on the bar and drank. 'I shouldn't have painted you a picture of what is surely impossible. I shouldn't have even tried to make you see the world differently. This is it. What we have now is what we'll always have.'

She slowly slid onto the stool next to him and curled her hand around his where it lay limply on the bar. 'Who have you been speaking to?'

He turned and her heart jolted to see tears in his eyes, his gaze glazed in distress. 'I've had a telegram from my mother.'

40

Samuel stared into the amber depths of his glass, unable to bear the weight of the disappointment in Amelia's dark brown eyes. He mentally willed her to leave him to wallow in his self-serving pity. To keep his neck tight in the noose that his mother's neediness had pulled taut enough to choke his dreams. Just as it always had and, no doubt, always would.

But Amelia didn't leave. Instead, she raised her hand to the barman. 'A lime cordial, please.'

Samuel closed his eyes, his hand gripping his glass. 'Can't you join me?'

'I'm here, aren't I?'

'In a proper drink, I mean.'

She raised her eyebrows, her gaze challenging. 'Why? Will it make you feel better?'

He swallowed as shame threatened before he lifted his chin, feigning arrogance. 'As a matter of fact, it will, yes.'

Her gaze wandered over his face to linger a moment at his lips before she faced the bartender. 'Excuse me? Sorry, could I change my order to a glass of white wine?'

'Of course, miss.'

Samuel bounced his foot against the footrest on his stool, his moroseness giving way to embarrassment. 'I didn't mean to talk to you like that. When you came into the bar, I mean.'

'I know you didn't. Thank you.' She accepted her glass of wine from the barman and sipped. 'Why don't you tell me what your mother said?'

'She's begging me to return home. My sister is pregnant, and I can only assume the father is nowhere to be seen.' He pushed his hand into his hair. 'How in God's name can I abandon them now?'

Concern shadowed her gaze. 'I see.'

'On top of that, how can I realistically go on here when I have no idea what I'll do until I get paid. I can probably afford another three nights at this hotel, at a push, or else six days somewhere cheaper.' He stared at her, his fingers itching to touch hers. 'I don't want to leave, Amelia, but I don't think I have a choice. I thought we'd have at least two weeks together before you decide whether or not you want to stay. Now it seems I could be leaving before you.'

Her eyes never left his as Samuel's heart beat out the seconds, willing her to say something . . . say she'd come back to England with him if that's what it would take for them to be together.

She exhaled a shaky breath and lifted her drink. 'Tell me how you got on at the station. Did you get a job?'

Confused by her change in subject and how Grand Central even mattered anymore, Samuel frowned. 'I did, but I don't see —'

'Then you shouldn't be so hasty in your urgency to abide by your mother's bidding.' She took a long sip of her drink as though fortifying herself. 'I spent a couple of hours walking around RH Macy's department store today. It was mesmerising.' Her eyes immediately glittered with excitement as her mouth curved into a wide smile. 'Like nothing I've ever seen before.' She gripped his forearm where it lay on the bar. 'You have to see it, Samuel. I thought Pennington's was the most glamorous place on earth and it probably is, but RH Macy's has an . . . energy, a pulse. People were just running around as though afraid they might miss something. Children laughed and played. Friends joked and nudged one another. Even the elderly seemed perfectly content to be jostled amid the madness. It was intoxicating.'

Samuel's gut clenched with trepidation. Had she even heard that he was leaving? Or had her trip today turned her mind to staying in New York regardless of anything or anyone? He sipped his drink, sickness rolling through him. For all his persuading, had he unwittingly lost her? This wasn't the serious woman he'd met on the *Titanic.* A woman intent on doing the job she was sent to America to do. To impress her employers and rush back to report her new ideas for Pennington's future. Now, Amelia wore the look of fascination that surpassed the intention of leaving everything she knew behind. Was everything he'd wanted, everything he'd been determined he and Amelia do together when they reached New York now lost to him because he had little choice but to return home?

Selfishness and frustration simmered inside of him and Samuel drained his glass, hating the way he was feeling. 'Which means what exactly?'

'It means you were right. New York is a place where anyone can start again. Where anyone can be whoever they want to be.' She sipped her drink. 'It's a land of freedom, just like the Statue of Liberty represents. If any of the other stores here have half the excitement of RH Macy's, I cannot see myself returning home.' She laughed a little hysterically. 'Although how I'll ever tell Elizabeth that I'm not sure. And which department captured my fascination most firmly? Go on, guess. You'll never believe it.'

Darkness shrouded him and Samuel looked away from her bewitching gaze, ignoring her question. 'If you stay, you'll be staying alone. Clearly, you haven't listened to what I told you about my mother and sister. *I* have to go home.'

The ensuing silence pressed down on him, and with each passing moment he sensed the joy slipping out of her. His tone and words had slashed at her happiness like knives dipped in poison. *You're a bastard, Samuel Murphy. A useless, selfish bastard.*

She drained her glass and carefully laid it on the bar. 'So, all that talk about making our own lives, doing all you can to carry out your friend's plans for you, are finished because of your sister's pregnancy? Doesn't your mother understand that you have survived what I think will be one of the worst nautical disasters the world will ever see?'

'*You* don't understand.'

'Don't insult me.'

He winced at the sharpness of her tone, the fire in her voice.

She leaned closer to him, her cheeks red and her eyes angry. 'You have no idea who I am, Samuel, no idea at all. You don't know what I've endured, and the things I've triumphed. If I stay here, I risk hurtling back to the poverty I once knew, the loneliness and days of being so unsure of myself that it was sometimes hard to drag myself out of bed. I was raped. Raped by a man I should've been able to trust. Raped, used and discarded. Yet, here I am, in New York, sitting beside one of the most amazing men I've ever met and drinking sweet white wine. If you, or anyone else, thinks they can extinguish the certainty, the absolute euphoria, I felt in that store today, you are sadly mistaken. I am still undecided if I will stay here or return to Pennington's, but I will take these two weeks and wring every last drop of happiness out of them. Then, and only then, will I decide what I want to do next.'

His heart beat fast.

She was raped? His Amelia? Some bastard had hurt her, violated her . . .

Anger turned his vision red, his heart breaking inside his chest as he fought to take his next breath.

He looked deep into her eyes, words to comfort her, to love her, flailing helplessly on his tongue. 'Amelia . . .'

'Don't.' Her eyes blazed with fury, tears teetering on her lashes. 'Don't say anything.' His breaths turned harried as their eyes locked, every person in the room seeming to vanish, the noise surrounding them now eerily muted.

When he'd been rowing away from the *Titanic*, he'd sent up a prayer that he'd be able to get Amelia to safety and see her running towards a new life with abandon. Yet now, all his wants and dreams for this beautiful woman had been replaced with anger and revulsion towards the monster who had attacked and violated her.

He gripped his glass, his shoulders tense. 'Amelia . . .'

'Don't say a word about what happened to me. I only told you to make you understand who I really am. Who the woman is you've been spending time with.'

Sadness squeezed hard around his heart. 'You say that as though that woman is someone to be avoided.'

‘Would you really have treated me so wonderfully all this time if you’d known I’d been raped? Well?’

‘Of course I would.’ He reached out to touch her, but she moved sharply back. ‘I am so angry for you. Furious, in fact. I want to go back home and hunt down the scum who attacked you. This isn’t about me not wanting to be with you now I know — ’

‘Well, whether that’s true or not, I cannot understand why you would listen to your mother, or change your plans for your sister, when you have already looked after them for so many years. Our lives are our own, as are theirs. We are young and without children. Why should we answer to anyone after what we’ve been through? We don’t owe our families our lives, Samuel. We owe them respect and love, but that’s it. You have a job here now. You have to try. We both have to try.’

He looked across the bar. ‘If I don’t go back, I have no idea what will happen to them.’ He turned, sorrow knotting his gut. ‘I promised my father I’d look after Ma and the girls. How can I just forget that?’

She stared at him before inhaling a shaky breath and slowly releasing it. ‘Fine. Then go.’

‘Amelia — ’

But she was already off her stool and marching towards the bar’s doors. Samuel clenched his jaw, every muscle in his body tense. Now what? Did he follow her? Leave her? He couldn’t stay in New York. Yet, deep inside, he knew he couldn’t leave Amelia here on her own either. Especially now he’d seen the deep, deep hurt in her eyes; knew the burden and suffering she’d most likely carried in silence for months, maybe even years. They were set on this path together and his gut told him that they were supposed to end their journeys that way, too.

She'd been raped.

Red-hot anger rose bitter in his throat and he lifted his gaze to the barman. 'Another.'

41

Ruby left Pennington's through its gilded front doors and exited onto the busy street. It was a bright but chilly day and she lifted her hand to shield the sun from her eyes as she looked up and down the length of Milsom Street.

She looked at the faces of the people as they passed, noting the hunch of their shoulders and the strangely slow pace at which they wandered. No one needed any more proof of how the *Titanic*'s sinking had shaken people's happiness and hope.

She breathed deep. Her job was to ensure that whoever passed Pennington's main window felt at least a modicum of joy, even if only for a moment or two. She was determined to create a wedding window so spectacular that people would once again stop in front of Pennington's and stare in awe. People needed something new and beautiful after such a tragedy.

Her heart filled with determination, Ruby walked along the front of the store to the main window. It had been hard opening the curtains to reveal such an unusually empty space, but she needed to consider what she had to work with from outside. Needed to stand in front of the window and envision what the public would see once she'd completed her display.

Lifting her pencil to her lips, she narrowed her eyes.

Instead of having the bride and groom centre stage, she would position them to the side and have the bride wearing as long a train as possible, two young bridesmaids and a family looking on proudly. The backdrop would be a country chapel, fields, blue sky and soft clouds.

She needed to bring a sense of summer; of long days giving way to warm evenings.

Romance. Hope. Possibility.

Feverishly scribbling in her notepad, Ruby poured everything from her imagination onto the page. She stopped and stared again at the window, mentally picturing all she could include from each department. Esther had set the bar high with her effortless ability to advertise as much of Pennington's merchandise as possible within a single display.

Homewares. The toy department. Men and ladieswear. Jewellery. Accessories . . .

Ruby paused. Would Victoria have specific ideas for the Accessories department? Most probably.

Her and Tommy's first night in Victoria's home had been wonderful, and she had no doubt that tonight would be the same. Tommy seemed equally infatuated with Victoria as Ruby, which only reaffirmed Victoria's kindness and amiability. Despite the loss of her husband and her treatment during her childhood, Victoria sparkled with generosity and love, two things that Tommy desperately needed right now.

As anger towards her mother rose like a smouldering ember behind her chest, Ruby strode back towards Pennington's doors, determined her energy in her new project would not be diminished by her concentration drifting in an entirely unwanted direction.

It was near closing time and Pennington's atrium was less busy, so she quickly headed for the door at the back of the main window. Hurrying inside, she pulled the curtains closed, happily humming to herself in the knowledge that the next time she opened them, it would be to reveal the wedding display.

She had just a few short weeks to get everything in place.

The sound of the back door being clicked closed behind her echoed in the small space and Ruby turned.

'How are things coming along?' Victoria smiled. 'I saw you come in from the street and guessed you were thinking about what the display will look like from outside.'

'I was.' Ruby's body tingled with desire as her mind filled with the closeness of Victoria, clad in a white nightdress, as they'd sipped tea in front of the fire last night, the light softly romantic from the two lit lamps on small tables either end of the settee. The yearning to touch her had been torturous.

She tucked some hair behind her ear. 'I know exactly what I want to do, but I worry just how sincere Mr Carter was about allowing me some of his workroom staff to help me. I'm going to need more than one pair of extra hands if I'm to ensure the window is ready by the 1st of June.'

Victoria wandered around the space, the semi-darkness further softening her pretty features and the hue of her red hair. She looked over the floor, towards the curtains and then the ceiling.

Her face was relaxed and happy as she met Ruby's gaze. 'Weddings are so special, aren't they?'

The wistfulness in Victoria's voice aroused a longing in Ruby for a day she would never have. Even if Victoria were to ever return her feelings, two women would never be allowed to marry. Homosexuality was so abhorrent to most of society that men had lost their lives for acting on their passions. She had no doubt there were thousands of men and women all over the world who wished they could feel differently, just as she did almost every day.

'Ruby?'

She blinked and forced a smile. 'Yes, they are very special.'

Victoria frowned and came closer, gently touching Ruby's elbow. 'What is it?'

'Nothing. I'm fine.'

'You had a troubled look on your face a moment ago. You are happy that you and Tommy have come to live with me, aren't you?'

'More than you could possibly know,' Ruby said, trembling under the heat of Victoria's touch, the caress of her beautiful green eyes. 'I've never felt so free. I'm sure Tommy will come to feel the same in time. Right now, he's still thinking about Ma but that won't last long once he understands what living with you means.'

'Which is what? You must tell me if anything is worrying you.'

Ruby dropped her gaze to Victoria's mouth for a hazardous second before meeting her eyes. 'No. Everything is wonderful.'

Victoria's hand continued to linger on Ruby's elbow, her eyes fixed on hers. The atmosphere between them seemed to shift to something . . . more intimate. Ruby watched in fascination as Victoria's gaze darkened with what looked to be longing, her cheeks flushing a light pink, before she abruptly released her.

She smiled brightly and stepped towards the door. 'Are you leaving soon? Only I was going to get away now so I have time to pick up something for dinner. I'll wait for you if you're not going to be too long.'

'Um, no, you go ahead,' Ruby said, feigning interest in her notebook, her heart racing. 'I want to see if I can catch Mr Carter before he leaves.' Her hands turned clammy. Had it really been longing she'd seen in Victoria's gaze? Desire? 'Tell Tommy I'll be home in time for dinner. Is seven o'clock too late?'

'No, that's fine. It will give me time to prepare everything.' Victoria's gaze wandered over Ruby's hair before she turned to the door. 'See you in a while.'

Ruby's feet remained frozen to the floor as the door closed behind Victoria. Every part of her treacherous body told Ruby that something had just happened between her and Victoria. Could she dare to hope that she was beginning to look at Ruby as she never had before? Or was the way Victoria studied her just now nothing more than Ruby imagining things — hoping things — now that they would be spending time in such close proximity?

Ruby crossed her arms and tried to return her focus to her work rather than the nonsensical possibility that Victoria, a woman once married to a man, might come to see her as anything more than a friend.

Closing her eyes, she envisioned the finished wedding display, revelling in the excitement that immediately tumbled in her stomach. Only this time, it wasn't a bride and groom who filled her imagination as they stood resplendent at the side of the window, it was her and Victoria . . .

42

Amelia hadn't spoken to Samuel for two days and the lingering sadness that weighed heavy on her heart refused to abate.

But at least she had seen him . . . even if she had then walked as quickly as possible in the opposite direction.

She couldn't believe she'd shared her shame and humiliation — her rape — with him, and now had no idea how to convince him he couldn't turn his back on a new life at the very first obstacle — his mother and sister. She had been wrong to verbalise her desperation for him to not surrender his dreams by trying to shock him into submission.

Her tactic had been callous. How on earth was he supposed to react to such a vile revelation? Her cheeks burned. How she'd ever face him again, she had no idea.

And now, as she walked through the hotel lobby in search of somewhere for dinner, she was in exactly the same predicament as Samuel. Her obstacle had presented itself this afternoon when she'd received a telegram from Elizabeth voicing her excitement for Amelia to return and infuse her new knowledge about New York's stores into Ruby Taylor's plans for a new wedding display.

The telegram continued to plague Amelia three hours later. Elizabeth was a hard woman to refuse and she had made it clear she was set on Amelia's imminent return. How was she to stay here when she owed all she had to Pennington's? Her selfish excitement now felt like blatant infidelity.

She had been wrong to push Samuel as she had — if she couldn't refuse Elizabeth, her employer, why on earth should Samuel refuse his family? Yet, apology and acquiescence continued to battle on her tongue. Amelia wanted him to remain, wanted him to live the life of his dreams, even if she must return to Bath.

Elizabeth's telegram and Samuel's family had doused the flames that ignited in Amelia at RH Macy's and left behind a mass of ashes; her dreams and Samuel's left grey and dying. They both had commitments neither had the heart or courage to break from. No matter how much they both might wish or dream of a different life, a different future, they were duty bound by promises out of their control.

Amelia couldn't deny their anguish and disappointment, but at least their feelings illustrated them to be loyal and steadfast. Even if their predetermined destinies meant they could not be those things to one another.

The bright lights of Broadway flickered and sparkled in her peripheral vision as she walked, the smells of fried food and spices filling her nostrils, the beeping of motorcar horns and jazz music mixing into an alien city melody. A drumbeat of a life so different than she would ever find in Bath; an excitement she longed to explore now that she'd found it, but it was not to be.

How could she have allowed herself such fantasy? She was nothing more than a girl abandoned by her parents and raised in an orphanage. A servant girl, someone used, violated and discarded. Why would she think herself anything more when all the signs were there that she belonged in servitude and obedience? Every time she tried to better herself, step a little closer towards a brighter future, she was cut down and reminded of her place in this unforgiving world.

She stopped outside a restaurant and stared through the window at the diners enjoying each other's company inside. The restaurant's lighting was low, the wooden tables decorated with pale blue cloth and centrepieces of matching flowers and candles. A musician swept his fingers across the keys of a piano at the back of the room, the bar at one side beautifully lit and stocked with an array of spirits and wines Amelia could not even begin to name.

'It's like an adult's Christmas grotto.'

Startled, she turned. 'Samuel!'

His wonderfully blue eyes settled on hers with an intensity she had started to like far too much. He softly smiled. 'So, you are speaking to me then?'

Heat seared her cheeks and she dragged her gaze from his to look along the street. 'Of course. Why wouldn't I be?'

'Because I've seen you hurrying away from me in the hotel. I also saw you leave your breakfast half-finished when I walked into the hotel dining room yesterday. Not to mention how you now place the 'do not disturb' sign on your door whenever you're in your room.'

All true. She slumped. 'Fine, I've been avoiding you.'

He raised his eyebrows. 'Really?'

The irony in his voice was warranted and Amelia was grateful for it as she laughed and playfully nudged him with her elbow. 'I'm sorry. I was wrong to avoid you after I . . . told you what I did. If you still wish to speak to me, would you like to join me for dinner? Are you hungry?'

He offered her his arm. 'Starving.'

The aromas of basil and spice enveloped them as Samuel led Amelia into the restaurant. She became acutely aware that only couples were seated at the small and intimate tables. No families or single people, just lovers. Self-consciousness rolled through her and Amelia sneaked a glance at Samuel who seemed completely oblivious and unperturbed by their romantic surroundings as he spoke to a waiter.

Once they were seated, their drinks and food ordered, Amelia fiddled with her cutlery as her nervousness returned. She must confess her change of plan about staying to Samuel which was mortifying after she'd behaved so unforgivably towards him. She'd been so brusque. So severely candid. And then just walked away from him, despite having seen his distress and anger after her revelation about her assault.

'So . . . ' He placed his forearms on the table, his fingers close to hers. 'How have the last couple of days been for you? Have you visited any other department stores? Considering my inexcusable reaction when you told me about RH Macy's, I promise I will sit here and listen properly this time.'

She relaxed her shoulders, liking him even more for not berating her behaviour and part in their disagreement. 'I behaved so much worse than you. I'm so sorry.'

'So am I, but no apologies needed.' He squeezed her fingers. 'We were both in an agitated state. Although yours was born of optimism and excitement to begin with.'

She sighed. 'Well, considering how things have changed since we last spoke, my apology is very necessary.'

He frowned. 'What do you mean?'

'I mean — '

'Your drinks, sir, madam.' The waiter placed their glasses on the table with a flourish. 'Your food will be here shortly.'

The waiter retreated and Samuel picked up his glass. 'A toast to us. To survival and friends.'

'Survival and friends.' Amelia clinked her glass to his before sipping the wine. 'You really are a wonderful man, you know. Probably the most wonderful I've ever met.'

Concern immediately shadowed his gaze and she regretted her gushing. No doubt she'd reminded him of the untrustworthy and vile men she'd had the misfortune to meet in the past.

'Amelia — '

'I received a telegram from Elizabeth Pennington today,' she said, slowly placing her glass on the table, not wanting to allow his care for her to distract her from her confession. 'Everything is now changed.'

'But — '

'Please, Samuel, let me say this. I can't think of anything else when I was so pushy with asking you to stay, to honour your friend's memory. I had no right to do that. You see, Elizabeth is desperately looking forward to my return, to seeing me alive and well and listening to my ideas for the store. She begged me to come back to Pennington's on the first available ship and said how excited she was to hear about all I'd seen and done. I just haven't the heart to refuse her. I owe her everything and so . . . ' She took a fortifying sip of wine and forced a smile. 'I, too, will be returning to England. Your adventure is over and so is mine which probably means it will turn out the best for both of us.'

He shook his head, his brow furrowed. 'How can you say that? I have never seen you so animated and happy as when you returned from RH Macy's. You want to stay, Amelia, I know you do.'

She looked at his hand where it still lay so close to hers, uncertainty whispering through her as her remembered joy of the department store, of her time with Samuel, of their kiss, formed an ache around her heart. All that had brought her such happiness was over. It was time to return to the real world.

Throwing caution and her heart to the wind, she took his hand and stared at their joined fingers as he gently brushed her skin with his thumb. Tears pricked her eyes. 'But we still have a week together, so we'll make the most of it.' She met his beautiful gaze. 'I'll never forget you, Samuel. Not ever.'

'Nor I you.' His gaze wandered over her hair and face, his eyes intense on hers. 'I'll be sailing back on the *Adriatic* on the 11th of May. It's the first ship leaving for England.'

She stilled. 'The 11th of May? But that's longer than I've told Elizabeth. I didn't think.'

'Good, because now we'll have longer together.'

He was right. Pennington's would no doubt consume her the moment she stepped through its doors so, if she had a valid reason to stay in New York longer, then she would enjoy every moment.

Their food came and Amelia reluctantly slipped her hand from the warmth of Samuel's.

She picked up her knife and fork. 'So, tell me about

the railroad.'

'Where do I start?' He laughed as he speared some potato. 'The welcome from the other workers isn't the best. I think they would rather work alongside Americans than foreigners, despite the many numbers who work there, but I'm still enjoying it. Anything to do with mechanics and transport and I'm hooked. I'd be lying if I said I didn't resent having to leave this amazing place. I just know I could make something of myself here. I'm as sure of it as I was when my father first took me to the Southampton docks.'

'But you're still determined to return home?'

'Yes, but I'm not sure how long I'll stay there. Your words to me the other night didn't fall on deaf ears. In fact, I'm convinced you were absolutely right.'

Amelia thought he'd never looked more handsome, the low light making his blue eyes brighter and his skin darker. Desire pulled low in her stomach and she quickly looked to her food.

'About what?'

'Families. Duty. We should love and respect our kin, but not surrender our entire lives to them. I'm returning home and I will speak to Ma. This will be a trip to discuss things with her and my sisters, give them the chance to ask questions and, hopefully, I can allay their fears about money and their future wellbeing. I will make it clear Katherine needs to find work and Fiona must either find the father of her child or another way to keep the child fed and warm. I will send what funds I can spare, but it's time my sisters lived in the real world.'

'I'm so happy you've decided to do that.' Amelia smiled, pride filling her heart with excitement for him and what might await him when he eventually returned to New York. 'I have no doubt you'll find your fortune here, Samuel. I believe anyone can.'

'I agree, and that includes you, too.' He laid down his fork and touched her hand, his gaze boring into hers. 'Maybe you should do the same. Come back with me on the *Adriatic*, return to Pennington's, but if it doesn't hold the same power, the same magic, that RH Macy's did for you, come back to New York. With me. What do you say?'

43

Samuel ached from head to toe as he exited Grand Central station after a ten-hour shift, but his heart was already filled with ambition to master the building of railroads and stations. He had already learned so much and was entirely convinced that trains were the biggest advancement in the industrial age so far and there would be no going back from the benefits and advantages locomotives provided throughout the world.

He could practically smell the potential for career advancement every time he struck a hammer to a nail or placed a rivet.

Even though the work was backbreaking, he wanted to be at the heart of it and entirely committed to making his fortune. Nothing came to a man whose actions weren't founded in loyalty. Yet more and more, his family felt lower in his priorities.

Samuel had been over the moon when his new employers had granted him leave, understanding that he must temporarily return home. He would make his mother understand the money he sent home would be more than he'd ever been able to give her before and hoped, with some encouragement and reassurance, she would give him her blessing to pursue his dreams in New York. He would ensure his mother and sisters were all right and they understood that change was necessary for all of them if they were to survive as a family. Not once had his conscience returned to his father's bidding since he'd been in New York. It was as though he was standing right beside his son, urging Samuel forward in his newfound liberty.

He turned down a side street which, if he remembered rightly, led to a shortcut to the hotel. His money was dwindling and sooner or later he would have to find cheaper accommodation than where he and Amelia were staying. The trouble was, he didn't want to be separated from her any longer than his work already demanded. She had two notebooks filled with ideas and plans for Pennington's, her passion for New York still evident, no matter how hard she tried to convince him and herself that she belonged in Bath.

How in God's name he'd managed to land a job on the *Titanic*, survive its sinking and fall in love, he had no bloody idea. But all three had happened and now it was up to him to work out how to show gratitude for each. In his heart of hearts, he believed staying in New York was the first step in showing God, and every single person who'd lost their lives on the *Titanic*, that he would forever remember and respect their sacrifice.

The heavy clomp of running footsteps came from nowhere.

Before Samuel had time to adjust his thinking, two arms like iron bands clamped around his waist and body slammed him to the hard concrete, the punch to his face sending a burst of stars exploding behind his eyes.

'Go the fuck home, you British piece of shit,' a voice growled as low laughter rumbled somewhere in the distance. 'You're not wanted here. Go back to where you come from, preferably aboard a ship with the same destination as the *Titanic*.'

Another rumble of laughter.

'You think we believe the crap you've been spouting about survival. If you were on that ship, you were a turncoat. A man who took a place where a woman or child should've sat. You're a deserter, a coward, and we don't want your sort anywhere near us, Grand Station or New York.'

Anger rose sharply in Samuel's gut as he curled his hands into fists, the wet ground icy-cold along his spine. The man's accusation slashed at his conscience as the reality he'd anticipated began. This was just the start. Once the public understood how many lives had been lost and how many men had survived, the backlash of injustice would be brutal. He'd not said anything to Amelia about how he could be ostracised, judged and condemned because he didn't want to scare her. Didn't want her to see anything other than optimism in their second chance.

Did he get up and fight these men or stay the hell down? As if he had a choice . . .

Taking a deep breath, Samuel rolled to his side and leapt to his feet in one fluid motion, his fists raised. The three men in front of him took a collective step back and the fire in Samuel's heart fully ignited.

'Come on, then. You want me to leave, make me,' he yelled. 'I've got as much right to be here as the rest of you.'

'I don't think so, you yellow-bellied coward.' One of the men strode forward, the whites of his eyes bright in the grime of his dirt-smeared face. 'You come to the station, fill another one of our jobs and spew stories how you survived the *Titanic*. It's a load of bull. Why would someone aboard a ship like that want to work on the railroad? You're not a seaman, you're a labourer. Nothing more, nothing less.'

The man swung a punch, but Samuel ducked and hopped to the side, grateful for life on the Southampton docks and its surrounding pubs. Brawls and fights were an everyday occurrence that a docker and seaman had little chance of entirely avoiding. He might not be the beefiest of men, but Samuel could fight if pushed. Little did his adversaries know, he had Amelia's face tattooed in his mind and over his dead body would he leave this backstreet any other way than on his own two feet.

The other two men came closer, their eyes menacing, the breadth of their shoulders illustrating a life of manual work and hard labour. Samuel was no fool. He didn't have a chance in hell of fighting all three if they decided on a pack mentality. He had to find a way to talk them down if he wanted to walk out of here alive.

Opening the space between them, he took a couple of steps back and held up his hands, ignoring the trickle of warm blood that ran down his cheek where he'd been struck. 'Look, I don't want any trouble. Whether or not you believe I was on the *Titanic*, I was. I was spared because I was ordered to row one of the lifeboats. I'm a sailor and talking about the *Titanic* as though what happened wasn't real isn't right or fair. That ship sunk in just over two hours. From people laughing and enjoying themselves, they saw, heard and endured things that no one on earth ever should. Because I survived, I want to stay here. Stay on solid ground where I can build a life in gratitude. If that isn't good enough for you, I don't know what else to say.'

'You think we really give a shit what you have to say?' the leader sneered. 'You've got no right staying here and taking our jobs. Damn immigrants are taking over the whole country.'

'That's right,' one of the others spoke up, his eyes narrowed. 'The station is going along just fine with *American* workers. The likes of you just swan in and think you can do better than us. Leave right now or we'll make you. Your choice.'

Samuel looked at each man in turn, his heart beating fast as Amelia's smiling face the night she'd returned from RH Macy's flashed in his mind. He wasn't getting out of this street standing. One way or another, he was either going to take a beating or be left for dead. But, by God, wasn't it time he and Amelia stood up to the bullies, the people in this world who thought they had the right to dictate another person's life, another person's decisions?

He stepped forward and raised his fists. 'Then you'd better make me.'

44

The phone in Amelia's hotel room pealed through the silence, startling her from her sleep.

She looked around, disoriented, fumbling for the receiver on her bedside table. 'Hello?'

'Miss Wakefield? This is reception. We have a Mr Murphy here asking to see you. If you'd like to make your way to the side room by the edge of the reception desk as soon as possible. Thank you.'

The line went dead.

Amelia flicked on the lights and picked up her watch. Ten past eleven. She'd thought Samuel was working today and would go straight to bed. Every night he'd returned from Grand Central station completely exhausted.

She quickly threw back the covers and dressed before hurrying from her room. Something must have happened. Sickness unfurled inside her as she bounced from one foot to the other waiting for the lift. At last it arrived, and she travelled the four flights to reception.

A few people milled around, while others nursed late-night drinks in the bar and in the comfortable armchairs by the hotel's front windows. Amelia strode to the reception desk, approached a side door and knocked.

'Come in.'

She entered the room and stopped.

Samuel was being tended by two members of hotel staff, an older man with salt-and-pepper hair and a younger woman with a pretty face and the most wonderful dark hair. Both frowned as they dabbed and wiped at Samuel's face, his skin cut and bruised, dried blood zigzagging down one cheek, his hair matted and dirty. Care for him dried Amelia's throat.

'Samuel? My God, what happened?'

'Amelia . . . ' He tried to smile and then winced, the crack on his bottom lip seeping fresh blood. 'I had some fun and games with a few men from the station.'

'What?' She walked closer and slid onto the vacant seat beside him. 'They beat you?'

'Yeah. They got me pretty bad, but I'll survive. We'll always survive, right?'

She looked into his optimistic eyes, filled with such determination. Despite his swollen and bruised face, he still looked so very handsome.

The man tending him straightened. 'I think that's the best we can do for you, sir. Are you sure I can't call a doctor to check you over?'

'No, thank you.' Samuel reached for his jacket and shrugged it on, grimacing as he pushed his arms into the sleeves. 'I wouldn't mind sitting here awhile longer though, if you don't mind.'

'Not at all. Miss Halliday?'

The pretty young woman who'd been assisting in Samuel's ministrations stood from where she'd been hunched in front of him and stepped back, her gaze glazed with adoration as she took a final sweep of Samuel before heading for the door.

Amelia glared after her, a horrible spike of jealousy jabbing at her chest. Couldn't she see how injured Samuel was? Fancy lusting after him when he was in such a state.

'She's nowhere near as pretty as you, you know.'

She started and turned to find Samuel watching her, amusement in his soft gaze and a smile curving his lips.

'I don't know what you mean,' she said, even as heat warmed her cheeks 'How did this happen? Were you attacked at the station? Didn't anyone help you?'

'I was walking back to the hotel and three blokes jumped me. Seems they have a problem with anyone other than Americans working the railroad. That was the gist of it, anyway.'

'But that's ridiculous. The building will take years. Can't they see that there is more than enough work for a thousand men?'

'No, all they see is a foreigner taking a job from an American. Apparently, they haven't been impressed with me talking about the *Titanic* either.' He closed his eyes and slumped back in his chair.

'Why? What did they say?'

'Nothing that I now suspect won't be echoed by a million others once the true nature of the sinking becomes public knowledge.'

Bitterness coated his words and Amelia gently touched his hand. 'What do you mean? What did they say to you?'

He opened his eyes. 'They made it pretty clear that they weren't sure I was telling the truth about surviving and, if I did, they hated me even more for being a man who escaped.'

Amelia crossed her arms, anger making her tremble. 'Surely, they understand that women and children could not have rowed those boats miles across the ocean to the *Carpathia*? Not everyone will feel that way about the male survivors. They can't possibly judge anything when they weren't there amid the chaos and terror. People will understand that experienced seamen were ordered to see passengers to safety however they could.'

'Maybe, maybe not. What I am sure of, though, is that there will be an investigation of mammoth proportions both here and in England. Everything about the disaster should and will be investigated. Hundreds, maybe thousands, of people will have died, others suffering from hypothermia and God only knows what . . . ' His angry gaze bored into hers. 'And any men among the survivors, including me, will undoubtedly be targeted by the investigators and the press alike. If the fury of the men who attacked me is anything to go by, our return to England is not going to be full of fanfare and thanks to God. Instead, we'll be stepping into a barrage of scrutiny, investigation and judgement.'

Fear that he was right, that Samuel would be subjected to the pressure of public opinion both in New York and England, caused sickness to form deep in Amelia's stomach. She leaned close to him and cupped his jaw. 'I will stand by you and all that you did for me and hundreds of others before we left the ship and afterwards.' She pressed a gentle kiss to his injured mouth. 'I won't leave you to deal with this alone, Samuel. I . . . ' She swallowed. The depth of her growing feelings for him were absolutely terrifying. 'I care about you too much.'

He stared deep into her eyes, his jaw tight and his gaze intense before he reached for her and abruptly covered her mouth with his. The enormity of what they'd survived, what they still had to face, and the uncertainty of their future seemed to amalgamate, and Amelia pulled him closer.

Deeper they kissed, his tongue finding hers as Amelia kissed him with all that was in her heart, her body heating with a desire like she'd never known.

Slowly, they parted, their breaths harried.

He brushed a curl from her temple. 'I'm falling for you, Amelia.'

Words battled on her tongue as her heart burned with love for this extraordinary man. A man who was a hero but could be branded a coward. She ran her hand over his cheek, stared at his beautiful mouth.

'I think I've already fallen for you,' she whispered. 'And I'm not so sure that will be good for either of us.'

He softly smiled, pulled her close and, once again, Amelia surrendered to Samuel's care. To love and hope. They would be leaving New York on the *Adriatic* in two days . . . She prayed the world showed them and every other survivor compassion, because God knew, they would carry the guilt of their every breath for the rest of their lives.

45

Ruby stood in front of the selection of wedding dresses Mrs Woolden, the head of the ladies' department, had selected as possible choices for the new window display.

'Hmm, none of them are really what I'm looking for,' Ruby said, and stood back to look at them from a different angle. 'I want something . . . something . . .'

'With zebra stripes and tassels?'

Ruby laughed. 'Well, no. Not quite.'

Mrs Woolden smiled. 'Why don't we try them on a mannequin? In my experience, wedding dresses never look the same hung as they do worn.'

They walked into the back room and Ruby lifted one of the dresses from its hanger as Mrs Woolden moved a naked mannequin closer. They worked in silence, first trying one and then another. When they'd reached the fifth dress, Ruby's head and arms ached, her frustration mounting.

'I think it's the necklines. I wanted something a little more modern.'

'Modern? I think I have just the thing. Stay here and I'll run along to the stockroom.'

Left alone, Ruby circled the mannequin with a critical eye. Maybe with the right veil and headdress any of these dresses would be suitable . . .

'Good afternoon, Miss Taylor.'

Ruby started, her stomach sinking as Hazel Price sauntered in. 'Miss Price.' She purposefully turned to the mannequin, feigning an adjustment of the long, ivory skirt. 'What can I do for you?'

'I've been sent to find you by Mr Carter. He says you need another pair of hands from the workroom to help with your wedding display and here I am.'

Ruby briefly squeezed her eyes shut. *Damnation*. 'I see.'

'So . . . ' Hazel came to stand beside her. 'It seems we'll be working together for the next couple of weeks. Won't that be fun?'

'Or torture,' Ruby mumbled before turning and planting on a wide smile. 'Well, I'll be sure to thank Mr Carter when I see him. Why don't you go to the design department and speak to one of the machinists? They all know what needs doing so you'll be in good hands.'

'I think it best I wait for you.' Hazel ran her narrowed gaze over the mannequin. 'That dress won't do at all, if that's what you're thinking. It's entirely wrong for a June wedding. Better suited to the autumn, if you ask me.'

'I didn't.'

Hazel turned sharply, her gaze darkening with spite. The atmosphere crackled with tension, the dislike on her nemesis' face undoubtedly mirrored on Ruby's. Living with Victoria and being away from her mother for the last couple of weeks had bolstered Ruby's self-belief immeasurably and her self-confidence had bloomed.

She crossed her arms. 'You will be under my charge, Miss Price. Mine and Miss Pennington's. If you wish to help with this project, then you will do exactly as I ask, when I ask it. Is that clear?'

Ruby's pulse beat so loudly in her ears, she was sure Hazel would hear it.

Slowly, Hazel stepped back, her lips pulled into an ugly sneer, her eyes bright with malice. 'So, it seems sweet little Ruby has picked up some of her lover's bolshiness. I supposed it was to be expected. Although, I must say, I can't imagine any of the staff who have been talking about your grotesque affair will have thought it would happen so soon.'

'Go away, Miss Price. I have no need for you here.' Ruby's heart thundered and, to her shame, tears of anger pricked her eyes. 'You should really be very careful how you speak about people. The world has a way of paying back both good and bad acts towards others.'

'Do you love her?'

'Get out.'

'Do you?' Hazel raised her eyebrows, her eyes glinting with spite. 'Only you do know it's an offense for a woman to be with another that way. Maybe Miss Pennington would be interested to hear the nature of yours and Mrs La — '

'Miss Price.' Mrs Woolden appeared by the back curtain separating the room from the department, her cheeks mottled with anger. 'I suggest you leave right this minute.'

Hazel took another step back and dipped her head, but not before Ruby saw a flash of fear pass through Hazel's eyes. Mrs Woolden was as close to Miss Pennington as any woman could be in the store. She had their employer's respect and ear. If Mrs Woolden disapproved of any of the female staff, Miss Pennington would listen to what she had to say.

Sickness rolled through Ruby as Hazel stalked past her to the curtained partition and disappeared. If Mrs Woolden had heard what Hazel had said, it could be

Ruby's head on the block rather than Hazel's.

The silence that followed heightened Ruby's stretched nerves to breaking. Mrs Woolden stood before her, her gaze unreadable and her lips pursed.

Ruby swallowed. 'I'm so sorry, Mrs Woolden. I told Miss Price to leave several times, but she—'

'Might I give you a piece of advice, Miss Taylor?' Mrs Woolden laid the wedding dress she carried on a chaise longue and started to unzip the protective bag. 'Matters of the heart are complicated and often hurtful. Embarking on a relationship you know will be a source of heartbreak, gossip and judgement is a foolish decision. One that is of an illegal nature even more so. Do you understand?'

Shame bore down on Ruby until she thought she would faint, but she held firm. 'I do.'

'Good. Then let's us hear no more about it.' Mrs Woolden's hands trembled as she lifted the dress and studied it. 'Why don't you go to the bathroom and freshen your face and hands? I'll be here when you get back.'

Mortified, Ruby fled the room and almost ran down the grand staircase, through the atrium to the staff bathrooms. She burst inside and immediately locked herself in a stall and sat down on the closed toilet seat. Her tears came fast and hot, running down her cheeks in rivulets that felt never-ending.

Her heart ached and her mind raced with what Mrs Woolden might do with the information Hazel had so cruelly imparted. Ruby closed her eyes. Oh, to see the disappointment or shock in Miss Pennington's eyes would be more than she could bear.

'Ruby?' There was a sharp rap on the toilet door. 'Are you in there? I saw you running through the store like a madwoman. Has something happened?'

Ruby stilled as Victoria knocked a second time. 'You must go, Victoria. We can't be seen together.'

'Why not?'

'It's Hazel. She . . . she said something about us in front of Mrs Woolden. You need to leave.'

'Open the door. Right now. You should know by now that I won't be hidden from view any more than you should. Open the door.'

Ruby covered her face with her hands before sliding them into her lap and pushing heavily to her feet. The moment she'd opened the door, Victoria pushed her back inside and locked it.

'What are you doing?' Ruby's heart raced as she stood so close to the woman she loved, the woman she wanted. 'We can't stay in here like this. What if someone — '

Victoria's lips crushed Ruby's, her hands on her shoulders pushing her back against the toilet wall. Desire swept through Ruby on an intoxicating wave to pulse deep in her core. She gripped Victoria's waist and pulled her tight to her body, their breasts crushing, their legs linking thigh to thigh. After months and months of wanting this, of wondering what it would be like to kiss Victoria, an almost animalistic lust overcame Ruby as she tangled her tongue with Victoria's, her lips so hungry they ached.

When Victoria stepped abruptly back, her cheeks were red and her eyes alight with an erotic fire that had Ruby reaching for her again.

Victoria smiled and held up her hand. 'No, no more. At least no more for now. I've been wanting to do that for so long, but I just wasn't sure I could.' Tears glistened in her eyes. 'I like you, Ruby. More than like you. I've lived a life that was neither true, nor fulfilling, and as much as I loved my husband, it was women I truly wanted to be with, but I have always been so afraid . . . until you.'

Ruby stared in disbelief, her heart rejoicing yet scared to really believe all she had dreamed of might be reciprocated. 'You want me, too?'

Victoria laughed. 'Look at you. How could anyone not want you?' She smoothed her hands over her hair and the front of her dress. 'Now, tidy yourself up and go back to work. We'll talk tonight after Tommy is asleep. This is our time, Ruby. No one will pull us apart. Do you understand, no one. If that's what you want?'

'It is.' Tears blurred Ruby's vision. 'It really, really is.'

'Good.'

With a final smile, Victoria left the stall and it was only when the bathroom door closed behind her, that Ruby took another breath.

46

Samuel stood on the doorstep of his family home and stared at the brass knocker. His mind whirled with possible scenarios of what would greet him from behind the closed door; of what his mother and sisters would say about his unannounced return.

He purposely hadn't sent word ahead about his return on the *Adriatic*, having no wish to receive his mother's beseeching, Katherine's demands and Fiona's whining in return. Now, all of those things would be unavoidable.

He raised the knocker and let it drop.

Yelling sounded behind the door as his sisters screamed a reason why each shouldn't answer the door. Hanging his head, he closed his eyes and slowly counted to ten until the screaming raised to a crescendo and the door was pulled open.

'Hello, Ma.'

'Samuel . . . ' She pressed her hand to her chest, her blue eyes wide with shock. 'Oh, my darling son. You're back.'

Samuel smiled to hide his immediate concern at the weight his mother had lost and the sadness in her dark blue eyes. 'How are you, Ma?'

His mother gave a dismissive wave of her hand. 'There's no need to talk about me. How are you? Come in, come in.'

She stepped back, her tearful gaze scrutinising his face as Samuel brushed past her into the hallway. The mass of discarded clothes, shoes and God only knew what else strewn around the small space was the first thing that hit him. That, and the screaming of his squabbling sisters in the parlour. He dropped his bag on the floor and slowly took off his jacket before hanging it on the post at the bottom of the stairs.

'I see the cleaner you wanted didn't turn up in my absence,' he said, wryly, looking at the underwear, shoes and discarded scraps of paper lining the staircase. 'Those sisters of mine too busy at their places of work to help you clean up?'

'What you talking about?' His mother planted her hands on her ample hips, her brow furrowed. 'You know I can't afford to employ help. Especially with you disappearing across the water while me and your sisters have had to fend for ourselves these past weeks.'

'Disappearing?' Samuel swiped his hand over his face. 'God, Ma, you do know the *Titanic* sank, don't you? After what I and a thousand others have been through —'

'I don't want to talk about that. It's too upsetting. You survived and there's nothing more to talk about. My nerves can't take any more of it.' She stepped forward and pulled him firmly into her arms, pressing a lingering kiss to his temple. 'Now, go and see your sisters.'

Samuel hugged her and then stepped back, holding her at arm's length, seeing the fear for him clear in her eyes. 'I'm all right, Ma.'

'As I knew you would be.' She brushed a tear from her cheek. 'Into the parlour with you. Go on.'

As he entered the parlour, his sisters' shouts and screams at one another jabbed through his brain like sharpened knife blades.

'Well, that's the sort of homecoming a brother likes

to receive from his beloved sisters.'

They stopped fighting immediately. Each releasing the other's hair before staring at Samuel, their eyes agog and their mouths open. Then they launched themselves at him and he was caught up in a tangle of arms as Katherine and Fiona embraced him.

'Thank God you're back!'

'We're finally saved from starvation!'

Samuel extracted himself from their not-so-loving embrace and pinned his sisters with a glare. 'Is fighting the norm in this house now? For crying out loud, this is not what I wanted to see when I stepped through the damn door. Don't you think the things that have happened over the last few weeks should be enough to pull our minds from petty squabbles?' He dragged his gaze from his sisters' faces to stare around the small, dark parlour, his stomach knotting with revulsion at the sight of the filthy cushions and stained carpet. 'It's a bloody tip in here. Haven't any of you lifted a finger without me here to keep on to you? It's a disgrace.'

Fiona flounced to the settee and sat down, the front of her dress patched and dirty, her hair a mess. She morosely stared at him through narrowed eyes, her arms crossed.

Shaking his head, Samuel turned to Katherine, the older and more responsible of his siblings. 'What in God's name has been going on here?'

She briefly closed her eyes before opening them and planting her hands on her hips, her gaze burning with frustration. 'Well, let's see. Fiona is with child and her bloke is nowhere to be found. Whereas I have been out every single day since you've been gone trying to find some decent work. I come home every night to find *she* — ' she pointed a finger at her sister ' — hasn't done a thing to help Ma about the house and Ma . . .' Her voice softened as she glanced at their mother. 'Ma has been waiting day after day for you to walk up the front path alive and well. Apart from that, *Samuel*, not much.'

Guilt swept over him as he struggled not to crumble under the rare tears glinting in Katherine's eyes. 'I'm sorry.'

The skin at her throat moved as she swallowed before hastily swiping her fingers under her eyes. 'Well, you're back now. Maybe things can get back to normal.'

'Normal?' Samuel sighed and walked to the armchair, lifting some old newspapers from the seat, he sat. 'Nothing will ever be normal again.'

His mother came closer and laid her hand on his shoulder. 'Of course it will. We just need a man about the house, that's all. We're no different than every other woman in this world.'

Amelia filled Samuel's mind. He doubted she needed a man to make a success of her life . . . he certainly doubted she needed him.

How in God's name he'd managed to separate himself from her to come back to this, he had no idea. Well, there was no time like the present to share his intentions with his cherished family.

He looked at his mother. She looked tired and thin, her gaze so sad, it damn near broke his heart. Turning away to look at Fiona, he glared, searching for his inner strength. 'So, how much time have you given to thinking about the *Titanic* and the hundreds who died?' Dragging his gaze from her glare, he glanced at his mother and then Katherine who both seemed suddenly and intensely interested in the grime-covered window. 'I thought as much. You should be ashamed of yourselves. What we went through is a thousand times harder than a bit of hunger and a baby with an absent father and now I'm back, things are going to change because I don't intend staying here very long.'

'What?'

'You have to.'

'We need your wages!'

Their voices raised like nails down a chalkboard, drilling through Samuel's brain. He squeezed his eyes shut. 'Enough!'

Silence fell and he opened his eyes. 'You,' he said, pointing at Fiona, 'are going to leave this house every morning and not come back until you found the man you liked well enough to lie with. Try speaking to him with a little sincerity and love and maybe, just maybe, you can convince him to do the right thing by you. You — ' he faced Katherine ' — will find work wherever you can before the end of next week. No picking and choosing. A job is a job. And you — ' he looked at his mother and softened his voice ' — are going to spend the time cleaning this house while your daughters are out all day. I've never known you let it get this way. I can only assume worry for me was the cause and, for that, I'm sorry.'

Samuel swallowed, trying his best to keep his face impassive and not show his inner turmoil. How the hell was he was supposed to leave them with a baby on the way and his Ma so obviously struggling? Entrapment enveloped him making it hard to breathe, his dreams drifting like floating clouds out of his imagination, evaporating into dust.

He had to remain strong in his words. For his family's sake, even more than his own.

'Nothing will change my mind about returning to New York as soon as possible.' He focused on his mother, ignoring the guilt weighing heavy on his conscience. 'I found work on the railway station while I was there, the money is good and I can regularly send money home, but I'm not staying here. Not anymore. It's time I started living for myself instead of for everyone else in this house.' He looked at his sisters, trying his hardest not to show how much Fiona being with child had affected him. 'I'll see you're all right with money, but I'm not staying. You find the father of your babe and persuade him to take responsibility. If he doesn't . . .'

There was no need for Samuel to finish the sentence, they all knew he wouldn't leave without tracking the coward down himself.

'So, I'll leave you to think on that while I go and get something for our supper. I expect a cleared table and chairs by the time I get back.' He headed for the door. 'Oh, and some clean knives, forks and plates would be appreciated, too.'

Leaving the house, Samuel had a desperate need to see Amelia but, as that wasn't possible, he headed to the centre of Bath and Pennington's. There was little hope of her being at work when they'd only returned that morning, but to be close to her in some way was better than no way at all. He had enough to feel guilty about surviving the *Titanic*, enough to bear knowing all too soon an enquiry would begin into the whys and hows of the disaster and how those escaped managed to do so. The situation at home had only burdened him further.

How could he possibly leave his family in such conditions and circumstances?

He walked the slope of Milsom Street until he stood outside Pennington's. It was indeed a fine store. One of the best in England. Entering the atrium, Samuel stared around in wonder, immediately understanding Amelia's passion for her workplace and the employers who had given her unprecedented opportunity when she had been brought so low by the monster who'd attacked her.

Slowly, he strolled, absorbing the store's atmosphere, the plethora of glittering merchandise and smiling staff and customers. Pennington's magic effortlessly seeped under his skin and, in that moment, Samuel was certain he had little hope of Amelia returning to America with him.

And with that certainty, came the question of what he did next. Did he flee from England's shores as soon as humanly possible? Or stay here, fight for his family . . . and Amelia's love?

47

Ruby lifted her gaze over the edge of the novel she was reading and studied Victoria sitting at the other end of the settee. The woman she loved had never looked more beautiful. The soft lamplight cast an amber glow over the room that turned Victoria's skin iridescent, the flames from the fire flickering over her relaxed features.

Slowly, Victoria raised her eyes and met Ruby's stare. She softly smiled. 'Happy?'

'Very.' Longing rose inside Ruby as she laid her book down on the table next to her. 'You?'

'Yes.'

The atmosphere between them crackled as much as the fire and Ruby's heart beat faster as Victoria also put her book to the side and inched closer. Night after night, they had spent sitting quietly in front of the fire after Tommy was in bed, their conversation easy as they spoke of the store, the weather and everything else but each other.

Their kisses had been snatched and brief, their caresses even more so, and Ruby's impatience to make love to Victoria gathered strength with every evening they were alone.

She touched Victoria's cheek and looked deep into her love's dark hazel eyes. 'You have changed mine and Tommy's lives. You do know that? I have no idea how I'll ever repay you.'

Victoria smiled and eased Ruby's hand from her face before pressing a soft kiss to her palm. 'There's no need to repay me. Having you both here feels right, Ruby. As though you and Tommy living here was what was meant for me all along.' She shook her head, tears seeping into her eyes. 'I was happy enough with John and I would never say or hear a word against him, but . . . ' She briefly closed her eyes. 'It never felt like this. *I* never felt like this.'

Ruby leaned closer and kissed Victoria's smooth lips, her heart aching with an abundance of love and desire that was as fulfilling as it was terrifying. They kissed deeper, Victoria's hand clutching at Ruby's waist and as she gently moved her hand to Victoria's breast. Their tongues tangled, their breaths coming faster as Ruby's body burned with raw longing.

To feel Victoria's naked body against her own would be heavenly; bring her more satisfaction than anything else possibly could . . .

Crack!

Something hard struck the window and Ruby snatched her hands and mouth from Victoria, her gaze shooting to the closed drapes.

'Get out here, Ruby Taylor. I know you're in there!'

Ruby leapt to her feet, her heart thundering as her hands shook. 'My mother.'

'Oh my God.' Victoria stood and clasped Ruby's elbow. 'What shall we do? Do we open the door?'

Her mother continued to screech, igniting Ruby's anger and resentment. She curled her hands into fists. 'I can't leave her to shout on the street. The whole neighbourhood will know what kind of woman I have for a mother. You stay here. I'll be right back.'

She marched to the drawing room door and pulled it open, striding towards the front door with violence and hatred burning hot in her heart. *I'll bloody kill her.*

How dare she come here . . .

'Ruby? Is that Ma?'

Ruby ground to a halt and faced the stairs.

Tommy stood in his pyjamas about halfway down, his hair mussed and his eyes sleepy, his beloved teddy bear dangling by its ear from his fingers.

'It's all right, Tommy.' Victoria brushed past Ruby and hurried up the stairs pulling Tommy into her lap as she sat. 'You stay with me while your sister speaks to your mother. Everything is all right.'

Gratitude mixed with humiliation that Victoria had been dragged into such a situation, spiralling Ruby's resentment deeper into her heart.

Her eyes momentarily locked with Victoria's before Ruby's mother started hammering on the front door.

'Open up! I mean it, Ruby. I'll smash this door down if I have to.'

Barely able to see through the red mist that blurred her vision, Ruby marched to the door, unlocked it and swung it wide open. She glared at her mother before whipping out her hand and flinging her bodily inside.

She slammed the door, her heart racing. 'You should not have come here, Ma.'

Her mother sneered, gin fumes hovering around her on an invisible cloud. 'I've told you before, my girl, I can do what I want, when I want. How do you think it feels to learn your disgusting, filthy daughter is shacked up with another woman? Worse than that, she has the nerve to make her little brother privy to it.'

Ruby glared, not trusting herself to speak the vile words battling on her tongue in front of Victoria. Her pulse beat hard in her ears as she stepped closer to her mother, her pungent smell assaulting her nostrils and turning her stomach. 'You are leaving and will never, ever come back here. Do you hear me?'

A movement from the corner of her eye turned Ruby's head.

Victoria walked slowly down the stairs, still holding Tommy's hand. Her skin was pale, but her face was so set in anger, it looked carved from marble. She suddenly seemed inches taller than she had before. More imposing. More threatening. 'Mrs Taylor . . . '

Her mother visibly flinched and took a step back.

Ruby couldn't contain her satisfaction and smiled. 'Ma, meet Mrs Victoria Lark. My . . . friend.'

Her mother's cheeks mottled as she struggled to recover her composure. She made a pathetic attempt to pull back her shoulders before she lifted her chin. 'You give me my son and I'll leave. I won't be going anywhere without my beautiful Tommy.'

Victoria smiled, her eyes icy-cold. 'Why don't we ask Tommy whether he'd like to leave with you or stay here with us?' With her eyes still on Ruby's mother, Victoria addressed Tommy. 'What would you like to do, my love? Stay here with me and Ruby? Or go with your mother?'

Ruby's heart pounded as she slowly walked forward and looked at her brother, her heart breaking for the predicament his mother was making him face. 'Tommy,' she asked, gently. 'Don't be afraid. Tell Ma what you'd like to do.'

Love for her brother threatened to overwhelm her as tears stung Ruby's eyes. She had never considered that her hatred towards her mother could get any deeper but, in that moment, it sank to the darkest place Ruby could imagine.

Slowly, Tommy looked from Ruby, to Victoria, to his mother. Easing his hand from Victoria's, he stepped forward and held his mother's glare. Ruby's throat dried as she resisted lunging forward and pulling him tight to her so she could hold and protect him.

Then something changed. Something that filled Ruby with pride and love that made her want to weep and punch the air at the same time.

Tommy's face contorted with anger, his brilliant blue eyes flashing with loathing. 'I never want to see you again, Ma. I love Ruby and I've started to love Victoria. You won't make me leave. Not ever. This is my home now. Go away.'

'Why, you — '

The instant their mother lunged for Tommy, Ruby veered in front of her while Victoria took Tommy by the shoulders and pulled him behind her. 'Get out of my house, Mrs Taylor. Now.'

'You heard her, Ma.' Ruby grabbed her mother's arm and hitched it behind her back as she had before and would again. She manhandled her, kicking and screaming towards the door. 'You come back here again, and you won't walk out, you'll be carried out.'

'Take your filthy, tit-loving hands off me!'

Ruby pushed her towards the door as Victoria rushed ahead of her to open it. They stared at each other for a moment before smiling and, together, they shoved her mother out of the door where she landed in a heap on the pavement.

'Good riddance, Ma.' Ruby laughed. 'Have a good life.'

'I'll be back, you good for nothing bit — '

Ruby slammed the door and collapsed against it, her heart thundering but her smile wide.

She looked at Victoria and then Tommy who burst out laughing and the three of them huddled together in an embrace.

Kissing Tommy's hair, Ruby met Victoria's eyes above his head and her heart burst with the knowledge that, from now on, everything would be different. Everything would be perfect.

Always.

48

Amelia sat forward on the settee in Elizabeth's office and clasped her hands together. New York suddenly felt incredibly far away but, now she had returned to Pennington's, she had no wish to be anywhere else but here. She hadn't even gone home first but came straight to the store from the train station.

'So . . .' Elizabeth looked almost pained as she looked intensely at Amelia. 'How are you feeling?'

Despite Amelia knowing it was inevitable her well-being would be the initial topic of conversation, the sinking and her state of mind about everything that had happened was too raw to discuss. Yet, how was she to avoid it forever?

She swallowed and forced a smile. 'As well as I can be . . . I don't suppose you've had news of Mr Weir?'

Deep in her heart, Amelia knew he had gone, but still, she purposefully held onto her hope that Mr Weir would be safe. Elizabeth's silence confirmed he was dead.

'Elizabeth?'

'He's dead, Amelia. I really can't believe it.' Elizabeth's voice quivered. 'I've spoken regularly with his family. They are understandably distraught but coping.'

Amelia stilled as sadness gripped her heart. 'He was married?'

'Yes, with two grown children. You can be forgiven for not knowing. Theoretically, he was married to Pennington's. Mostly to my father, when he was here, then me. I fear that even when Mr Weir was home, his mind was at the store. We shall miss him. He was much changed from how he was when he worked for my father. More human, I suppose.'

Unsure what to say when she hadn't really known Mr Weir very well at all before their trip, Amelia stood and walked to the side of the room where she'd left her bag. Reaching into one of the pockets, she extracted the watch Mr Weir had given her the last time she'd seen him.

Tears blurred her vision and she blinked them back, forcibly lifting her chin as she returned to Elizabeth in the seating area. 'Here. His family should have this. Can you give it to them for me?'

'His watch? He gave this to you?'

Amelia nodded. 'And I gave him a comb from my hair. It . . . was as if he knew.'

'Oh, Amelia.'

'He was very kind to me when we sailed.' Amelia managed a small smile. 'Even if I suspect I stretched his nerves from time to time.'

Elizabeth placed the watch on the low table in front of them. 'Oh?'

'I was very insistent that I experience how things were in each of the class areas. Mr Weir seemed overly concerned that something might happen to me. I thought he had no reason to worry. Now I know I was wrong. If it hadn't been for Samuel . . . '

'Samuel?'

Amelia sighed as her heart filled with longing to see the man she'd fallen for. 'He's a seaman. He rowed me and many others to safety. Not to mention those he helped before we were ordered to leave.'

'My goodness. He sounds the most marvellous of

men.'

Amelia swallowed. 'He is. Yes.'

'Well, when you are ready, however long that might be, I want to hear everything and anything you wish to tell me. It's important that you share as much as you can. The last thing you should do is keep the horror inside. That would be too much for anyone to bear and I don't want you suffering any more than you already are.'

Not wanting to break a promise she could not keep, Amelia changed the subject. 'Let me tell you more about what I learned in New York.' She lifted her notebook from the table and handed it to Elizabeth. 'Everything is in there, but my main feeling throughout my trip was that America is focused on creating an almost maniacal feverishness among its shoppers. The department stores want customers to shop without thinking, to grab what they want and forget about whether or not they really should buy that dress, that parasol, that brooch.'

'Isn't that a little boorish?' Elizabeth frowned, her focus clearly back on work as she glanced over Amelia's notes. 'Don't misunderstand me, I couldn't abide the way my father wanted everything kept at arm's length from the customers but, still, I don't like the idea of people not thinking about their purchasing.' She met Amelia's gaze. 'Wouldn't such a way of shopping almost certainly result in returned items and refunds? Occasionally, that's inevitable, but not considering how to avoid it from happening at all is not good business. No matter New York's retail success.'

'That's just it, I didn't see any evidence of regretful customers or purchases being returned. These customers were happy, Elizabeth. Almost heady with their pleasure and excitement. Pennington's reputation could still be one of elegance and opportunity, but I think we need to adopt ways of building fun, too. I saw jugglers in RH Macy's atrium and a brand new, top-of-the-range motorcar in the atrium of another store. People were agog with excitement.' Amelia smiled, excitement growing inside of her. 'Such things are meant to fuel people's imaginations and encourage them to have a good time as well as shop. The atmosphere was addictive. Isn't that what we want for Pennington's, too? Customers who feel compelled to come back to the store time and time again?'

Elizabeth put Amelia's notebook on the table in front of them, her green eyes amused. 'You really do like this idea, don't you?'

'I do. After . . .' Amelia sighed, sadness clouding her enthusiasm. 'After all the suffering I witnessed during and after the sinking, I know the right thing to do is offer something that will help people grieving to get through this tragedy. Help the world to come to terms with such a devastating catastrophe. If Pennington's can make people laugh and smile for just an hour or two of their day, is that so wrong? Neither you, me or Mr Carter can make people buy what they don't want, but Pennington's could be responsible for making people cast aside their worries and reservations, even for a while.'

Elizabeth nodded, her brow furrowed. 'It's certainly something to think about. Why don't you leave your notes with me and I'll speak to Mr Carter?'

'Of course.' Amelia stood. 'I look forward to hearing his thoughts.'

'Good. Now, please, get yourself home, you must be exhausted. The last thing I expected was to see you the day you returned.'

Amelia picked up her purse and coat. 'I couldn't wait. I suspected you and Mr Carter would want to see my notes and discuss my ideas, so I wanted you to have them as soon as possible.'

They walked to the door and Amelia left the executive floor to take the lift to the ground level. As she walked through the store, she breathed deep, absorbing Pennington's and all it meant to her. Her time in New York had been exhilarating, but now she was back, and she'd seen Elizabeth, she wanted to stay. Stepping back inside Pennington's had been like coming home.

49

Samuel stood in a bleak, beige and brown office at Bath train station and took the station master's offered hand. 'Pleased to meet you, sir.'

'And you, Mr Murphy, and you.' The officer took a seat behind his desk and folded his hands over his ample belly, his bushy brown eyebrows lifted. 'So, you'd like a job at the station. I have to be honest with you, I'm struggling to understand why a seaman of your experience would want to work at a railway station.'

'It's time for a change.'

'From?'

'Life has a way of making a person realise what matters and what doesn't.'

The station master's wily gaze bored into Samuel's, his brow furrowed. 'You weren't caught up in the *Titanic* disaster, were you?'

Samuel shifted in his chair. He hadn't seen or spoken to Amelia in days, their different schedules or catching up with people since their return meaning neither had managed to contact the other. Or, at least, that's what he hoped her explanation would be when he finally came to see her.

And during that separated time, Samuel had mostly been on tenterhooks waiting for news of a *Titanic* investigation. Considering the height of his agitation, the last thing Samuel wanted to do was talk about his experiences with, what he hoped, would be his new boss. He had to take this job. The dreams he'd had in

New York just felt too damn selfish now that he was home.

'I . . . ' He swiped his hand over his face. What choice did he have but watch yet another person's demeanour change when he told them he'd survived the disaster? Unless he avoided the station master's question altogether . . . 'I spent some time in New York, working on the building of Grand Central station. You could say the railway got under my skin.'

The station master frowned. 'New York? Well, that's quite a change from Bath. Can I ask how you ended up there?'

Samuel briefly closed his eyes before opening them again and holding the officer's interested stare. 'All right, I admit. I was on the *Titanic*, sir.'

The station master studied him, a deep sympathy slowly filling his eyes. He stood and came around the desk, his hand outstretched a second time. 'How many did you bring to safety?'

Relief swept through Samuel as he stood and gratefully clasped his hand.

For the first time since he'd been home, someone hadn't immediately leapt to the conclusion he was a coward when they learned of his survival. 'There were thirty-eight women and children in the boat I rowed, sir.'

He nodded, his hand clasped to Samuel's shoulder, his jaw tight. 'I lost my brother on that ship. My uncle, too.'

'I'm sorry to hear that, sir. You have my sincere condolences.'

'No need to apologise, Mr Murphy. I'm sure you did all you could to save as many souls as possible. Heads will roll sooner or later, but it won't be yours.

Rowing that boat across the ocean was a heroic feat. Promise me you'll not forget that.'

Desperate, terrifying screams and cries, followed by the horrible, devastating and momentary silence as the ship sank echoed in Samuel's ears. He looked into the other man's sincere gaze, sickness rolling through him. Samuel stepped back, afraid the trembling that had come and gone in waves for weeks would once again wrack his body.

'I hazard that a small station like Bath isn't going to keep you interested for long,' the station master mused. 'Considering all you have done and seen, I'm not so sure working here is the right thing for you.'

'But I need this job, sir. I have to stay in Bath.'

The station master frowned. 'Take a seat.' He leaned forward in his chair and laced his fingers. 'How long did you spend in New York, son?'

'A few weeks. I travelled back to England on the *Adriatic*, the first ship to come back to England.'

'You didn't want to stay in America? They say Grand Central will be the biggest station ever built. I imagine someone like you, someone with clear bravery and an aptitude for risk, would want to be a part of that.'

'I did, but my circumstances have changed. I have my family to think of.'

'You're married? Have children? They must have been terrified for you when the ship went down.'

'Not a family of my own, sir. I'm talking about my mother and sisters.'

'Ah, I see. Then they must be glad to have you home.' The station master pulled a sheet containing Samuel's past work experience towards him and perused it. 'Here's what I suggest. I'll give you a position on the train running from Bath to Piccadilly. See how you go. You can start your training as a conductor, taking tickets and such like. If you find the job is not for you, I want you to tell me. You're made of better stuff than a career travelling back and forth from Bath to London every day.'

'Thank you, sir.'

The stationmaster stood and waved towards the closed office door. 'I'll see you first thing Monday morning, Mr Murphy,' he said, his grey eyes sombre. 'But keep in mind my door is always open if you should need to speak to me, or you find the job isn't to your liking. You've been given a second chance. It's your duty to ensure it doesn't go to waste.'

'Yes, sir. Thank you.'

Walking from the station, Samuel dared to hope that not everyone would have the preconceived judgement of what the men aboard should or shouldn't have been doing as the *Titanic* began its slow descent into the Atlantic's freezing cold waters. As much as he felt New York was his destiny, for now, Samuel was stuck in England and the outcome of the disaster would undoubtedly be debated and talked about for years to come.

He had no idea how he would learn to live with the speculation and conjecture, but he had no choice than to find a way.

His mother had started to take care of herself and the house, Katherine had found a job at a small milliners and Fiona . . . well, she still had the father of her baby to track down. His niece or nephew was coming in the winter and, one way or another, Samuel would see he or she was properly cared for.

Which meant he wasn't going anywhere any day

soon.

Maybe coming home would turn out to be the mistake of his life, but he'd felt he had no choice. Of course, Amelia had been a big part of that decision, too. She still was.

He walked along the bottom of Milsom Street and stared at Pennington's façade. He longed to see her; longed to apologise for his absence since they'd sailed back to England.

The horror of the *Titanic* sinking, and the lives lost, had affected the whole country in some way or another. His family included. He was pretty certain it would continue to do so for years to come. It certainly would affect him. He looked towards Pennington's again. And it would most definitely affect the woman he hoped would one day be his.

50

Amelia glanced at Ruby as they boarded the train at Bath station and took their seats. The younger woman looked happier than Amelia had ever seen her, and it seemed Amelia's trepidation that Ruby might not welcome her return to the store had been unwarranted. In fact, Ruby had welcomed Amelia with open arms, embracing her input into the wedding display with gratitude and enthusiasm.

Something deep had changed in Ruby, but Amelia wouldn't ask. After all, she knew more than most the sacred privilege of a person's secrets remaining their own.

She pulled her notebook from her purse. 'So, this is our first work trip to London, Ruby. How are you feeling?'

'Wonderful.' Ruby smiled, moving her gaze from the window and the bustling platform beyond. 'I can't believe Miss Pennington allowed us some time away just days before the big reveal. I suspect it was my talking about what Harrods might do if the window was theirs that inspired her.'

'Or my non-stop chatter about RH Macy's in New York,' Amelia laughed. 'I fear, between us, we are making Miss Pennington's head spin.'

Ruby frowned, her blue eyes clouding with concern. 'You don't think I'm getting too big for my boots, do you? I would hate for Miss Pennington to think I have ideas above my station. I am the happiest I've ever been, and I'd hate to do anything that might jeopardise that or make Miss Pennington regret the opportunities she's given me.'

Amelia patted her hand, understanding only too well the fear of losing confidence once it had been gained. 'Miss Pennington's mission is to scour new ideas from everyone around her. That's what Pennington's is all about. She works day and night to create ways to improve the store and the lives of her staff. Never resist being outspoken with her. She wants her staff to talk to her. Really.'

Ruby nodded, her shoulders relaxing. 'I'm glad. You see . . .' Her gaze turned hesitant. 'Without my mother's shadow cast over me day in, day out, I feel like a different person and, with that, my enthusiasm to do well at the store grows and grows.'

Amelia studied her young apprentice. Following a meeting with Mrs Woolden, Elizabeth had pulled Amelia to one side and asked that she keep an eye on Ruby, to watch for any maliciousness towards her by others in the store.

Hazel Price in particular.

Elizabeth hadn't divulged the reason for her concern, so Amelia assumed it had come from Ruby leaving home with her brother. Either that, or the nature of Ruby's relationship with Victoria Lark which Amelia suspected others at the store had been discussing and speculating about for months.

'Well, long may your happiness last.' Amelia smiled. 'Now, I think we'll visit Harrods and maybe Selfridge & Co, and then return to the store early this evening with a clear idea of any finishing touches we'd like to make to the window. I understand Esther is now moving to her husband's country estate in Oxfordshire so, from now on, it's you and me leading the way with the window designs.' After opening her notebook, Amelia took out her pencil. 'Let's use this journey to start thinking a little further ahead, shall we? We'll soon have the Autumn collections to consider and then it will be onto Christmas. Work in the design department is as non-stop as this train.'

Greenery gave way to new, modern buildings as they sped towards London and Amelia was careful to write down Ruby's ideas, encouraging her to expand on them wherever possible, encouraging her to take ownership of who she was and her own unique talents.

Just as they were pulling out of Reading station, a figure appeared at the compartment door.

Amelia looked up and gasped. 'Samuel.'

Her heart raced as she glanced at Ruby before turning to Samuel, noting his station uniform. Her cheeks warmed as she tried to gather her senses, shaken to see him working on the train. Ruby's stare burned into her temple, yet Amelia couldn't drag her gaze from Samuel's. It felt like an age since she'd last seen him and her heart treacherously swelled with futile love for him. He had made it very clear he intended to return to New York. Something she could — or would — no longer do.

'You're working on the trains now?'

His sombre gaze bore into hers, the brilliant blue of his eyes as dazzling as ever. 'Have been for a few days. It's been too long, Amelia. I've missed you.'

The warmth at her cheeks grew hotter and she looked down at her notebook. Had Ruby turned invisible? 'I hope you're well.'

'As can be expected.'

The clipped tone of his voice did nothing to lessen

her embarrassment. Surely he understood that she couldn't speak freely with Ruby sitting next to her?

Ruby rose from her seat. 'Um, Miss Wakefield, I think I might take a walk along the train. The views will be so much lovelier from one of the corridor windows.'

Ruby left the compartment and Samuel slid the door closed behind her.

He immediately sank into the seat next to Amelia. 'I only have a minute or two to talk.' His gaze travelled over her face making her heart beat a little faster. 'I've wanted to come into the store so many times, but I've been running around all over the place. If I'm not working, I'm helping Ma or Fiona . . . '

She slumped her shoulders, her care for him overriding every inch of her good sense. She'd missed him so, so much. 'And you? Are you all right?'

He sighed and gave a wry smile. 'It turns out the big brother in me had no need to worry about one of my sisters, at least.'

'Oh?'

'Katherine has managed to get a job by her own doing and didn't need any interference from me. Now I just have Ma and Fiona to sort out.'

Amelia smiled, pleased that his sister had proven herself capable. 'So, does this mean you're beginning to understand you are not solely responsible for your family? That they are more than competent to contribute to the house and their own wellbeing?'

'With Katherine, yes, but Fiona continues to be a different problem entirely. As for Ma, she'll be all right. Eventually.'

Amelia stared at his mouth, his eyes and hair, her attraction and love towards him as strong as ever, despite the time they'd been apart. Maybe there was a chance he'd decide to stay in England, after all. 'Samuel — '

'I still plan to go back to New York. Back to Grand Central.'

She froze as a sharp pain hitched across her heart.

'I think about New York every day, regardless of my commitments here. I just can't shake the feeling I'm not where I'm supposed to be.'

The urge to ask him to stay, for them to try to build a life in Bath, battled on her tongue and Amelia quickly looked to the window, lest he see her distress. 'I see.'

Sickness coated her throat as her heart broke. Once Samuel left, she would never see him again; she truly believed she'd never love again. How would she ever find a man to measure up to him? To be brave enough, kind enough, strong enough to shoulder all that Samuel knew her to be?

'I really thought I could stay here, work on the railway and look after my family, but I feel like every day is a wasted opportunity. Amelia?' He touched her shoulder. 'Won't you look at me?'

She closed her eyes, gathered her strength and faced him. 'You should go. To New York.'

Hurt flashed in his eyes before he nodded, his gaze steadfastly on hers. 'You really think that?'

'Yes.' She lifted her chin, despising the painful ache around her heart. 'I always encouraged you to follow your dreams and you were happy in America. You didn't leave New York for you, you left for your family and, deep inside, you know they are capable of looking after themselves. It would be wrong for you not to pursue the life you want.'

'And what about you?'

She swallowed and fought to draw as much authority into her words as possible. 'My place is here. Working at Pennington's.'

With each silent second, the more bitter the nausea coating Amelia's throat became. *Go, Samuel. I'm not strong enough for you to look at me that way. Don't you see you're the only man I've ever trusted? The only man I've ever loved?*

Slowly, he stood, and when he looked down at his ticket holder, Amelia noticed his fingers ever so slightly trembled. 'You know, when we were in New York I had every intention of being with you for the rest of my life.'

Tears burned the back of her eyes. 'What?' she whispered.

'I mean it, Amelia. I wanted to be with you forever, but now I see we're never going to be on the same page at the same time. Never going to be ready to reach for our destinies, to fight for what we want and have those two things come together for us at the right time.' His gaze was soft with care and sadness. 'Take care of yourself, won't you?'

He strode to the door and Amelia stood, not sure what to do or say, but not wanting him to leave.

She rushed into the narrow corridor, heedless to Ruby standing a short distance away. 'Samuel!'

He immediately stopped, his back to her as he tilted his gaze to the ceiling.

Holding on to the bars beside her, she walked along the jolting train and placed her hand on his back. Slowly, he turned, his eyes glinting with defeat beneath the electric lights.

She touched his face. 'Don't leave. Stay in Bath. With me. I love you.'

51

The screaming and shouting outside his house hit Samuel before he'd turned the corner into the street. Fiona's high-pitched screech was immediately followed by his mother's deeper pleas for her daughter to come back into the house.

He broke into a run.

Half the neighbourhood stood on their doorsteps watching the spectacle of his family playing out their latest drama in full public view. Samuel swore under his breath as his gaze landed on a young, thickset man in the centre of the commotion. His face was red with exertion, his dark-blond hair awry as he restrained Fiona from physically attacking her mother.

Is he the father of Fiona's unborn babe? Samuel briefly closed his eyes. *God, give me strength . . .*

'Knock it off, Fiona,' Samuel shouted as he came closer. He faced his mother. 'Go inside, Ma. I'll take it from here.'

His mother hesitated, tears glinting in her eyes, before she turned and ambled towards the house.

Samuel looked at his sister and glared. 'You, too.'

'But, Sam — '

'Now, I mean it.' He turned his focus on the stranger. 'You stay right where you are.' He turned around to the spectators circled around him and those watching from the other side of the narrow street. 'Show's over. I suggest you get back to your business.'

His mother and sister stood on the short pathway to their front door, his ma damn near crying and Fiona looking like she wanted nothing more than to wring his neck. Samuel narrowed his eyes. 'Get inside. Now.'

He succeeded in staring Fiona down and she dutifully escorted their mother into the house. The door remained wide open.

He faced the man nursing a red mark on his jaw and nodded. 'Courtesy of my sister, I assume?' He held out his hand, gauging the man's six feet height and shoulders not much narrower. 'Samuel Murphy. You are?'

'Benedict Brown.' He shook Samuel's hand, his brown eyes quietly appraising. 'I came to speak to your sister, but it seems she wants to forget the talking and march me up the aisle.'

Samuel crossed his arms. 'And will you?'

'Will I what?'

'Walk my sister up the aisle . . . or at least the registry office.'

'I don't know.'

'You don't know?' Samuel huffed a laugh. 'You think you've got the privilege of thinking about this now? Don't you think that smacks of locking the gate after the horse has bolted? My sister's carrying your baby. Now, are you going to do the right thing or are we going to have a problem?'

Benedict held Samuel's stare before slumping onto the wall beside them. He ran his hand over his face. 'I carry coal for a living, Mr Murphy. I live with my ma and help support my four younger brothers and sisters. I've got nothing to offer a girl like Fiona. She deserves more than me. Much more. I'd marry her tomorrow if I could, but I haven't a pot to piss in.'

A girl like Fiona? Samuel didn't know whether to laugh or cry. If this man looked at his sister and saw a match made in heaven, there was no way Samuel was going to disillusion him.

He sat beside him on the wall. 'So, what are your options? Have you room at home for my sister to come live with you?'

'I can't see my mother agreeing to that. We're already like sardines and what with the baby coming . . .'

'I see.'

Benedict looked towards the house. 'But I suppose we could make it work if Fiona was willing, but . . . I'm not sure my mother will love her as I do.'

'You love her?'

Benedict grinned, her grey eyes lighting. 'With all my heart.'

Biting back a smile, Samuel sighed. 'Right then, this is what is going to happen. I'll make it my job to sort you out with a cheap suit and Fiona with a cheap dress, we head down to the registry office before she starts showing and then she moves in with you. I don't want your ma going without the earnings you're giving her, and Fiona will help out with your brothers and sisters before and after the baby comes. How does that sound?'

'What's going on?' Fiona's screech came from an upstairs window behind them. 'Don't you chase him off, Sam. We love each other. He'll see me right once he runs the coal yard. Isn't that right, Ben?'

Samuel raised his eyebrow at Benedict. 'That's what you've told her? You'll be running the yard one day?'

The other man shrugged. 'A man can dream, can't he? I love her, Mr Murphy. I just want to make sure she has good reason to love me back.'

Benedict dropped his head as though the prospect of having more than what he had right now was dire. Samuel sympathised with him. At least the man had a dream. That in itself was enough to make Samuel want to help him.

Samuel pushed to his feet. 'Go into the house and make nice with Ma. When I come back, I'm expecting everybody to be in a much happier mood considering you've asked Fiona to marry you. In the meantime, I'll think how we're going to make the rest work.'

Fiona came barrelling through the front door and stood in front of them, her face red with anger. 'Don't you make him leave, Sam. I mean it. You don't get to tell me what to do when you disappeared for weeks, leaving us starving and neglected. You can do whatever you like, when you like, but the rest of us can't so why don't you just go back to America? You're not wanted here.'

'Is that so?' Samuel looked at Benedict. 'You might live to regret it, but you know what you need to do. Go on in the house. I'll be back later.'

Samuel walked along the street and through the town centre, heading for the river.

What in God's name was he supposed to do now that he'd laid down the law to a complete stranger about how his life was going to play out for the next six months? The only thing Samuel *did* know was he couldn't stay here anymore.

His family were draining him of every positive thought, ambition and dream. He would ensure they were fed and warm, the baby, too, but he had to get out before he was brought so far down, he'd never get up again.

Staring into the murky depths of the River Avon,

his guilt and musings of possibility swirled on an eddy inside of him. His love for Amelia was strong and real. The most he'd ever felt for anyone his entire life.

Yet, was love enough reason to live your life in a place that didn't quite fit? Especially when a man knew there was a city thousands of miles away that fed his soul and made him feel as though he could conquer the world.

Amelia's face on the night she'd returned from RH Macy's loomed large in Samuel's mind and he smiled. She'd been so alive. So happy and excited. And she could be again. He hadn't seen that look in her eyes since and he doubted he ever would if he couldn't persuade her that they belonged in America.

She had openly confessed her love for him when they'd been on the train and he'd confirmed his love for her. Yet, neither had said whether they were willing to change their plans — to give up what they believed to be their individual destinies.

He pushed away from the wall at the water's edge and headed for Pennington's. He had to try just one more time to convince her they belonged in America. If he failed, then he would stay here.

With Amelia. The woman he loved with his whole damn heart.

52

It was after hours at Pennington's and Amelia worked alone behind the closed curtain of Pennington's wedding window. She had sent Ruby home when Victoria had come asking when she would be finishing. There was a special bond between the two women, and it cheered Amelia to think of Ruby and her brother having a safe haven to go at the end of each day.

During their trip to London, Ruby had revealed more and more about the terrible relationship she suffered with her mother. The way she was spoken to, disparaged and often struck made Amelia's heart break for her new assistant.

It was clear Ruby knew as much as Amelia that family wasn't always what people had to rely on, but rather friends, lovers and colleagues.

She and Samuel were living, breathing proof of that as much as Ruby and Victoria.

Standing back, Amelia critically eyed the entirety of the display. Tomorrow was the big reveal and her heart was filled with hope that Ruby's very first window would be a success. The design department had outdone themselves with the painting of the country parish scene, the perfect backdrop for the chosen outfits and wedding dress from Pennington's men's and ladies' departments. Each mannequin wore items from Accessories and Jewellery, the children holding toys and a stuffed dog resplendent in matching collar and lead, all of which could be purchased in-store.

Satisfied, Amelia collected up the last of the discarded material, sequins and tissue paper strewn across the floor and put them in a box. She was just about to head for the door when Elizabeth entered.

'I'm so glad I caught you.' Elizabeth smiled as she stood beside Amelia and examined the display. 'It's fantastic. Really.'

'Ruby will no doubt receive the public accolade she deserves tomorrow. I'm so looking forward to it.'

'Yes, me too.' Elizabeth faced her, her gaze sombre. 'Do you have some time to talk?'

Concern immediately knotted Amelia's stomach and she slowly lowered the box to the floor. 'Is everything all right?'

'Come and sit down.'

They sat on two chairs by the door and Amelia smoothed her skirt, annoyed by the slight tremor in her hands. Hadn't she come farther than the shy woman she'd been when she first came to Pennington's? Proven she was so much more than a domestic maid and a target for unscrupulous and violent men? Yet, once again, her insecurity rose despite having a wonderful job, a lovely beau and, more than anything, a second chance at life.

'I've been watching you ever since you returned from America,' Elizabeth said softly.

'Watching me?'

'And, if I'm honest, I'm upset by what I've seen.'

'With regards to my work?' Dread dropped like lead into Amelia's stomach. 'Is it my adjustments to the display? I am more than happy to change anything you — '

Elizabeth put her hand over Amelia's. 'Your work is exemplary. This is me, your friend, worrying about you personally. You seem to be at Pennington's in spirit and deed, but not here as you were before the disaster. I think you need to take some time off. At least, for a while.'

Tears pricked Amelia's eyes and she dropped her gaze to her lap. Elizabeth was a canny businesswoman, but she also had a knack of identifying a person suffering. 'I can't believe what I've been feeling is so clearly written on my face.' Amelia met Elizabeth's gaze. 'You're right, I haven't been the same since the sinking. Not at all. Yet, I'm not sure that I'm sorry for what the experience did for me.'

'What it did for you?' Elizabeth raised her eyebrows. 'Surely, all that tragedy and death has only made you more fearful. I'm quite sure it would have been that way for me.'

'I don't think so. A life-changing experience like that either breaks or makes a person, Elizabeth.'

'And it's made you? Is that what you're saying?'

Amelia nodded, renewed strength making her sit straighter in her seat.

'But you seem so unhappy at times.'

'Oh, I am. At times.' Amelia stared towards the painted church. She owed Elizabeth her honesty. She was the person who had provided a starting point for Amelia to gain confidence and self-belief. However, meeting Samuel, the sinking, and New York had changed her irrevocably. She wanted more, and believed it was her destiny to have it. 'Maybe it's time I shared some things with you. Things from my past.'

'Anything you want to tell me, you can. I won't breathe a word to another soul.'

Amelia exhaled a shaky breath. 'I was abandoned by my parents and lived in an orphanage until I was fourteen. I did well enough, and soon went into service where I stayed until I came here.' She pursed her lips, her stomach knotting with the memory of her rape and the dark abyss she spiralled into afterwards. That, she could not share with Elizabeth. It would remain between her and Samuel. 'And I thought I'd found my place at Pennington's, I really did . . . '

'But?'

'But now everything has changed. The sinking, the things I saw, people dying, drowning . . . and then my survival, has meant nothing can ever be the same again.'

'Of course not.' Elizabeth squeezed her hand, tears glistening in her eyes. 'And neither of us should expect it to be. I'm here for you in whatever way you need me to be. Tell me what you want to do.'

Amelia swiped at a tear as it slipped over her cheek. 'I feel so torn. More torn than I ever have in my life. I met the most wonderful man on the *Titanic*. I told you about him. His name is Samuel and he rowed me and many others to safety. I've fallen in love with him, Elizabeth.'

'Well, that's wonderful.' Elizabeth smiled. 'When can I meet him?'

'Soon, I'm sure, but . . . he's leaving. For New York, and . . . ' Amelia's heart beat a little faster as unexpected certainty gripped her, Samuel's handsome face filling her mind and heart. 'I think I need to go with him.'

Elizabeth's gaze was sombre and considering, the workings of her brain visible in her eyes. She nodded. 'Then that is what you must do. If you feel in your heart you belong in America with Samuel, then you must go. My whole life was planned out for me by a father I despised, but I fought back as hundreds of women have, in so many different ways, before and since. We are given one life, Amelia, but I believe you've been blessed with two. If New York is where you must lead that second life, then go.'

Amelia smiled as she slipped her hand into Elizabeth's. 'I never thought falling in love would be possible for me, but now . . . '

'Now, you've found it.' Elizabeth squeezed Amelia's fingers. 'You must leave as soon as possible. Ruby is doing so well, we'll be fine without you, I'm sure. Now she's . . . settled, and living with Mrs Lark, Ruby has changed for the better and it will be my job to help her in any way I can to live the life she wants. This is *your* time, Amelia, and you must take it.'

The two friends embraced, and Amelia's heart beat fast, every pulse filled with excitement for a life with Samuel and the future that lay ahead of them. Tonight, she would tell him she wanted to leave, too. For them to be together . . . hopefully forever.

She pushed to her feet. 'Well, I think I've done all I can here. I'll be in bright and early in the morning for the unveiling. Ruby deserves to draw back the curtain on her masterpiece, don't you think?'

'I most certainly do.'

Half an hour later Amelia left Pennington's via the staff exit. The last night of May was unseasonably warm and Amelia breathed deep, her coat over her arm, as she strolled past Pennington's entrance.

A figure standing alone at the edge of the store made her slow her steps and then he moved into the glow of the streetlamp.

She released her held breath. 'Mr Evans. Whatever are you doing out here?'

The young salesman from the men's department came closer, his smile wide and his eyes happy. 'I've just been promoted to head of department. I'm standing here in stunned stupor. It seems Mr Carter has more confidence in me than I thought.'

A jolt of shock passed through Amelia, but she managed to keep her face impassive. Poor Mr Weir had barely been gone more than a few weeks. Her heart was saddened by the loss of a man she had only really begun to know on the eve of the tragedy that would take his life.

'Well, congratulations,' she said, before taking a step around him. 'I'll hopefully see you tomorrow when we reveal the main window.'

He touched her arm, halting her. 'Won't you allow me to walk with you? You live on Gay Street, don't you? In shared lodgings with Martha, if I remember correctly?'

'I do.' Amelia studied him, uneasy that he knew where she lived. 'But I'm quite all right getting back on my own. See you in the morning.'

'It's no trouble,' he said, stepping to catch up with her as she walked forward. 'I'm going that way, anyway.'

Amelia drew her lips tightly together, annoyed he clearly was not willing to accept her refusal. She crossed her arms tightly and strode ahead, but he remained beside her.

'So . . .' He cleared his throat. 'Do you have a beau, Miss Wakefield? Only I was talking to Martha and she said — '

'Do you often ask Martha questions about me, Mr Evans?' Amelia demanded, picking up her pace. 'Only I'm not sure I like my personal life being talked about among my work colleagues.'

When no answer came, Amelia turned and her heart skipped.

Mr Evans' amiable smile and friendly eyes had disappeared. Instead, he glared at her, his jaw tight and his gaze intense on hers.

She swallowed and stepped back, forcing a tight smile. 'I think I'll be all right from here. Good night.'

His hand clasped her upper arm and he roughly pushed her into a shop porch, pinning her hard against the window. 'You are always so damn uppity, aren't you? Swanning around, sidling up to Miss Pennington like your shit don't stink. Well, you're no different than me, Martha or any of the other lackeys working at the store.'

His grip tightened on her arms and Amelia's pulse beat hard beneath his fingers. Her mind raced and her heart hammered, her throat so tight she couldn't speak, much less scream. The pain and humiliation, the blood and bruises of her assault and rape flooded her mind, sending her vision white, then red. No! Never again.

With an almighty scream, she whipped her arms free of his grip and pushed her hands firmly into his chest, hurtling him away from her to smash up against the opposite window. It rattled under the impact. He stared at her, his eyes wide with shock.

'Don't you ever lay your hands on me or any other woman, Mr Evans, do you hear me? Or, so help me God, I will hunt you down and kill you with my bare hands. Do you understand?'

He raised his hands in surrender and quickly nodded once, twice, three times.

'Good. Never, ever speak to me again. In fact, don't

you dare to even look at me.'

Shaking, Amelia picked up her dropped purse and walked from the shop porch. Tears coursed down her cheeks as she prayed Mr Evans wasn't following her. She couldn't even summon the courage to turn around, her feet moving forward of their own accord, her nerves jumping.

What had she been thinking by adding herself to Samuel's burdens, to his protection? His entire life had been filled with looking after others and now he was willing to add her to his responsibilities. She was a liability. A temptation to evil men and someone who belonged in the background, out of sight and mind.

Was she a fool to think, even for a moment, that she might have a different life? Might fall in love and be happy? Mr Evans and all the others who'd accosted her over the years clearly saw her as a harlot. Didn't Samuel deserve to be with someone who was so much more than that?

Her tears flowed faster as she hurried towards her lodgings.

53

Samuel walked up the plush carpeted steps of Pennington's grand staircase, and into the ladies' department, hoping to find Amelia. Yesterday, he'd been told by the head of the department that Amelia was off work because she wasn't well and now he was cursing the fact that he'd never been to her home or even asked her address.

If she wasn't back at work today, his worry for her was going to explode. Her work ethic was second to none which meant she had to be suffering badly.

'Excuse me? Mrs Woolden?' He approached the same woman he'd spoken to the day before.

'Oh, hello again.' She smiled, lifting her hands from the gloves she was inspecting. 'Are you looking for Miss Wakefield?'

'I am. Do you know if she is back at work today?'

'I'm afraid not, Mr…?'

'Murphy.' He touched his hat. 'Mr Samuel Murphy.'

'And you are a relation of Miss Wakefield's? A friend?'

He smiled. 'A friend.'

Her eyes narrowed slightly as she appraised him. 'Hmm, well, I suggest you seek out Miss Pennington if you'd like to know more about Miss Wakefield's whereabouts.' She shook her head. 'No, that won't do. Why don't you go to the jewellery department and speak to Miss Kennedy? I believe they share lodgings together and she is more likely to know how Miss

Wakefield is feeling.'

'I'll do that. Thank you.' He touched his hat again and flashed what he hoped was an amiable smile that didn't reveal his need to make haste downstairs. 'You have a wonderful day.'

He strolled from the department but, once he was out of sight of Mrs Woolden, shouldered his way through the crowds of shoppers and back downstairs. The jewellery department was so brightly lit with brooches, necklaces and earrings glinting and shining, that Samuel found it immediately.

He smoothed his hand over his jacket and tried to remain calm. Something was wrong with Amelia. Something serious, and he had to see her. Today. But would a friend of hers just tell him where Amelia lived? He very much doubted it.

He cleared his throat and approached the girl behind the counter. 'Excuse me. Might you point me in the direction of Miss Kennedy?'

'I'm Miss Kennedy, sir.' She smiled, her blue eyes friendly. 'How can I help you?'

'I believe you live with Amelia Wakefield, is that right?'

The girl's demeanour immediately changed, her gaze darkening with caution. 'Can I ask who's asking, sir?'

He held out his hand. 'Samuel Murphy. It's a pleasure to meet you.'

Her eyes widened and then she grinned. 'You're him? The man who saved Amelia and hundreds of others from drowning. Oh, my goodness, it's so nice to meet you.'

Samuel breathed a sigh of relief, a rare heat warming his cheeks. 'I wouldn't say I saved hundreds although

I wish I had.'

She gave a dismissive wave. 'From what Amelia has told me about you, you deserve a medal. Are you wondering why she isn't at work?'

'Yes, I'm worried about her. I was here looking for her yesterday, too.'

'She isn't well at all, Mr Murphy. In fact, she hasn't come out of her bedroom for almost two days. Barely touched the food our landlady left outside her door.'

Dread squeezed hard at Samuel's chest. 'If you give me your address, I'll see if I can persuade her to see me. Something must have happened. I can't imagine she'd miss coming to work over a cold or such like.'

'Me neither.' She frowned. 'And I told her as much through her door this morning, even if she did make it pretty clear she didn't want me bothering her. Here.' She took a pen and paper from beneath the counter and scribbled down the address. 'Take this. Good luck, Mr Murphy.'

Once he'd left Pennington's, Samuel broke into a jog and made his way across town to Amelia's lodgings.

Straightening the lapels on his jacket, he removed his hat and knocked on the front door, concern sitting uncomfortably in his gut.

Footsteps sounded behind the door and then it was pulled open by an older woman wearing an outside coat, her purse beneath her arm. 'Yes?'

'Good afternoon, madam. I am a good friend of Miss Wakefield and wonder if I might give her these.' Samuel held up the bunch of roses he'd bought from a stall in town. 'I understand she isn't well and I'm hoping these will cheer her up.'

She stepped back and smiled. 'I'm guessing you're Mr Murphy?'

Pleased that Amelia had clearly spoken openly about their relationship, Samuel smiled and entered the house. 'I am.'

'Well, why don't you go upstairs and see if you can rouse her to open the door. You'll have better luck than me, I can tell you. Her bedroom is the second on the left.' She looked at him, her eyes flashing with warning. 'I'm going to trust you enough to leave you alone with her, Mr Murphy. I have some errands to run. I'm only breaking the rules because I know what you did on that ship. Don't disappoint me.'

'Yes, ma'am.'

She nodded and walked along the short pathway into the street.

Slowly closing the door, Samuel looked up the narrow staircase, took a deep breath and started up the stairs. He hesitated outside Amelia's door, uncertain how welcome he'd be when she was in bed. He knocked.

'I'm quite all right, Mrs Cambridge. If I need anything, I'll come down.'

'Amelia? It's Samuel.'

'You need to leave,' she said. 'You shouldn't be here.'

'Of course I should, I love you. Open the door, Amelia. Please.'

A few silent seconds passed before the lock clicked and she pulled open the door.

Shock reverberated through Samuel's entire body. In just three short days since he'd seen her, she seemed to have lost weight. Her skin was pale and her eyes too wide in her beautiful face.

'What happened?' He stepped into the room and took her in his arms, tucking her head into his neck and kissing the top of her head. 'Are you sick?' He held her at arm's length and looked deep in her eyes. It wasn't sickness he saw, but fear. 'Amelia? What is it? Did someone hurt you?'

She eased from his arms, walked back to bed and slid under the covers, sitting up against the headboard. 'You need to go.'

He placed the roses on a chest of drawers and sat down on the side of the bed. 'Talk to me. Tell me what happened. Please.'

'I don't think I can.' She squeezed her eyes shut. 'I thought it would be easy enough to tell you we can't be together when I next saw you, but now you're here . . . '

'What do you mean we can't be together? I love you and you love me.' His heart stuttered painfully. 'Don't you?'

Tears glistened in her eyes as she nodded.

'Then . . . ' He took her hand and lifted it to his lips, pressed a kiss to her knuckles. 'Let me help you. Has someone upset you at Pennington's? Somewhere else?'

She ran her gaze over his face, her brown eyes sad and desolate. 'Oh, Samuel. Promise me you won't do anything.'

Caution wound a tight knot in his stomach as he struggled to not clench his fists. 'Tell me, Amelia. Everything will be all right. I promise.'

She exhaled shakily. 'Mr Evans grabbed me on the way home from Pennington's on Tuesday night. He . . . pushed me into a shop doorway.'

Anger ignited and hummed through Samuel's blood. He tightened his grip on her fingers and she pulled away. 'Don't be angry. It will do no good.'

He stood and pushed his hand into his hair, his body trembling. 'He works at Pennington's?'

'Yes, but — '

'I'll bloody kill him.' He snatched his hat from the chest of drawers. 'I'll bloody kill him.'

'Samuel, please, listen to me.'

He stared at her, his love for her making his heart ache and his anger rise to a murderous level.

'Don't you see?' She shook her head, her fingers tightly clenching the edge of the eiderdown. 'This is the way it is for me. Men look at me and see something . . . I don't know what they see, but they attack. Not you, of course, but others. I don't want to be a victim, Samuel. Not anymore, but I just can't go back into Pennington's right now.'

'You don't need to go back.' He shook his head. 'We're going to New York. You'll be with me and I'll keep you safe.'

'I'm not coming.'

He stilled. 'What?'

Her eyes glinted with unshed tears. 'I'm not coming. You need to go without me. Build a life where you have a woman beside you who doesn't invite trouble, who attracts beasts and violence. Please, Samuel, can't you see who I really am? I'm just something to be used and discarded. You won't want to be with me in time and as much as I can't bear the thought of not being with you, it's better we separate now than later.'

He slowly put his hat on the dresser, his mind scrambling for the words to make her understand, make her see how beautiful and mesmerising she was. Walking to the bed, he sat down next to her and took her hand. 'You're beautiful. You have eyes like melted chocolate that light up when you smile and laugh. Your figure must be the envy of a thousand women, but you seem unaware of it.'

'Samuel, please.'

'You are unassuming, kind and warm. But the men you're talking about don't value those things, Amelia. It's the power they want. They use violence because they are too inept, too weak, to spend the time and care they should in the hope a woman might want to be with them. Their failings are not your fault. They are no woman's fault. It's these animals who need to change, to alter their actions and thoughts, not you. I love you. I want to marry you. Please, come to New York with me. Let's get away from here and start again. Just me and you. Always.'

Her gaze travelled back and forth over his face to linger at his lips before she met his eyes. A flash of determination darkened them, colour seeping into her cheeks.

'Do you really believe it is nothing I have done or am doing, that makes me look as though I want male attention?'

He cupped her cheek and looked hard into her eyes. 'You have never done anything wrong, do you hear me? And neither has any other woman who has been attacked or assaulted. I love you with all my heart. So much so, I will stay here, in Bath, if that's what you want.'

A tear rolled over her cheek as she softly smiled. 'I don't want that. I want you . . . and New York.'

Relief flooded through him and Samuel leaned forward, pressed a gentle kiss to her lips. 'I'm glad.'

She pulled back and threw back the covers, her gaze full of love and trust. 'Make love to me, Samuel. Let me feel our love. Please.'

Epilogue

Two weeks later . . .

New York's shores came into view, emerging over the horizon and bathing Amelia in a glow that warmed every inch of her, inside and out. The Statue of Liberty shone beneath the humid, early evening heat, rising through the mist like a woman certain of her destiny. A woman free.

Amelia drew in a long breath and slowly exhaled, absorbing every second of this moment as she and Samuel arrived in America to start their new life.

His arm slipped around her waist and he pulled her close to his body, his physical strength unquestionable, but it was his internal strength, his unbending spirit, that had succinctly captured her heart on her very first sea bound trip.

'Are you happy?'

She turned and looked into his beautiful eyes. 'Very. I've never been happier.'

'Good.' He smiled. 'Me neither.'

Amelia looked across the sparkling water and memories of their lovemaking, the many times she and Samuel had explored and satisfied one another, heart, body and soul over the last fourteen days, washed through her. On her left finger, she wore a diamond and sapphire ring that he'd given her when he proposed marriage, promising to forever keep her safe and cared for.

She'd needed no such promise, just him. Like this,

beside her, strong and proud and ready for their next adventure.

'With Fiona living with Benedict now, and Katherine and Ma going along so much better, I hope we'll be left in relative peace,' Samuel murmured against his ear as he stood behind her and pulled her back against his solid chest. 'We have my savings, your savings and my job. We'll go along quite nicely, I think. Living, working and loving one another.'

'And once I get work at RH Macy's, we'll have my income and yours from Grand Central. We're going to be just fine. I know it.' She turned in the circle of his arms and kissed him, her tongue naturally seeking his as it always did. Slowly, Amelia pulled back. 'I don't think I would have had the courage to take this trip or the one back from New York without you, you know.'

'Yes, you would. You, Amelia Wakefield, are capable of anything you set your mind to.'

'Maybe.'

He kissed the tip of her nose. 'Definitely.'

Fighting the insecurity that continued to ebb and flow inside her, Amelia faced the water again and pulled a small, drawstring bag from her purse. She looked at Samuel as his smile dissolved. He nodded.

With slightly trembling fingers, she pulled open the bag and scooped out a handful of sequins and laid them in Samuel's hand before scooping a second handful. Their eyes locked for a long moment before she quickly faced the water, lest she surrendered to the open wound across her heart for all those that had died on the 15th of April.

Each a lost soul who may, or may not, be recovered from the cold, vast ocean. All people who deserved to never be forgotten. She prayed the *Titanic* was remembered forever. That the next generation and the next were taught of the catastrophe so that such tragedy was never repeated ever again.

She and Samuel held their hands over the railing and together they said, 'For every single one of you.'

The sequins fluttered and shone as they twisted and turned and flew, sprinkling across the water like a thousand silver hearts. Once they had disappeared, Amelia turned to Samuel, tears pricking her eyes. 'Elizabeth said that Mr Weir's wife was so grateful to receive his watch. I wish I could have brought her husband home with us instead.'

He nodded and kissed her forehead. 'I know you do.'

Taking a deep breath, Amelia looked across the water. 'God bless you, Mr Weir.'

Samuel drew her close once more as they sailed towards the dock, closer to where fate awaited them. So much had happened in her and Samuel's life. So much pain, so much disappointment and shame, but the moment Amelia had stepped into Pennington's years before, everything had begun to change.

And now she hoped that change happened for Samuel.

She would miss Bath's finest department store so much. Mostly, because it had given her what it continued to give so many others.

Freedom.

Smiling, Amelia stared at the Statue of Liberty. 'Pennington's is a place everyone in the world should visit at least once,' she said, her eyes squinting under the glare of the sun. 'It has something very special. Something obtainable for anyone who takes the care and dedication to look for it.'

'Magic.'

Surprised that her brilliant, strong, pragmatic Samuel would use such a word, she faced him. 'What?'

He grinned and pulled her tight to his body, her breasts crushing again his hard chest. 'Magic. That's what Pennington's is, no doubt about it. I felt it when I walked into the store alone and I felt it again when I was looking for you. It's a special place, Amelia. It holds the power of possibility. It's given you a new life and given me the love of my life.'

Her heart melted under his loving gaze and astute words. 'It's given me everything.'

Lifting onto her toes, she pressed her lips to his, revelling in the love she had for her future husband and all that awaited them.

Thank you, Pennington's. Thank you so very, very much.

Acknowledgements

My first acknowledgement is to the hard work, patience and never-ending smile of my fabulous new editor, Rhea Kurien. Without her support and expertise, there is every chance I would have given up on the challenge I gave myself to include the tragic sinking of the *Titanic* in this book. I am thrilled that her encouragement inspired me to keep going!

I'd also like to thank the authors of all the amazing non-fiction books, accounts and letters I read while researching this book. Without them, I would not have learned as much as I felt I needed to in order to honour the trauma, love and hope I pray I've managed to convey during the writing of *A Shop Girl At Sea*.

Finally, I'd like to thank all the amazing readers and reviewers who continue to love the Pennington's series and constantly contact me asking when the next book will be released. Love you lots!

Rachel x

We do hope that you have enjoyed reading this large print book.

Did you know that all of our titles are available for purchase?

We publish a wide range of high quality large print books including:
Romances, Mysteries, Classics
General Fiction
Non Fiction and Westerns

Special interest titles available in large print are:
The Little Oxford Dictionary
Music Book, Song Book
Hymn Book, Service Book

Also available from us courtesy of Oxford University Press:
Young Readers' Dictionary
(large print edition)
Young Readers' Thesaurus
(large print edition)

For further information or a free brochure, please contact us at:
Ulverscroft Large Print Books Ltd.,
The Green, Bradgate Road, Anstey,
Leicester, LE7 7FU, England.
Tel: (00 44) **0116 236 4325**
Fax: (00 44) **0116 234 0205**

Other titles published by Ulverscroft:

A SHOP GIRL'S CHRISTMAS

Rachel Brimble

Christmas sees Pennington's at its most glorious, thronged with shoppers, its grand staircase and balcony adorned with holly, mistletoe, tinsel and lights. It should be the happiest time, but dramas are seething beneath the surface. For Cornelia Culford, in charge of jewellery, a divorce hearing looms where she could lose custody of her young sons to her overbearing and unfaithful husband. For Stephen Gower, being head of security at Pennington's is the perfect refuge from his tragic time at Scotland Yard. But then Joseph Carter and Elizabeth Pennington beg him to help solve the murder of Joseph's first wife, now that it seems as if the killer has struck again. For Joseph and Elizabeth, their marriage depends on exorcising the past. Can it ever be laid to rest?

A SHOP GIRL GETS THE VOTE

Rachel Brimble

1911, Bath. Banished from her ancestral home, passionate suffrage campaigner Esther Stanbury works as a window dresser in Pennington's Department Store. She has hopes for women's progression and will do anything to help secure the vote.

Owner of the prestigious Phoenix Hotel, Lawrence Culford has what most would view as a successful life. But Lawrence is harbouring shame, resentment and an anger that threatens his future happiness.

When Esther and Lawrence meet, their mutual understanding of life's challenges unites them, and they are drawn to the possibility of a love that neither thought existed.

With the Coronation of King-Emperor George V looming, the atmosphere in Bath is building to fever pitch, as is the suffragists' determination to secure the vote. Will Esther's rebellious nature lead her to ruin or can Esther and Lawrence overcome their pasts?

A SHOP GIRL IN BATH

Rachel Brimble

Hardworking and whip-smart, Elizabeth Pennington is the rightful heir of Bath's premier department store — but her father, Edward Pennington, believes his daughter lacks the business acumen to run his empire. He is resolute that a man will succeed him.

Determined to break from her father's hold and prove she is worthy of inheriting Pennington's, Elizabeth forms an unlikely alliance with ambitious and charismatic master glove-maker Joseph Carter. They have the same goal: bring Pennington's into a new decade while embracing woman's equality and progression. But, despite their best intentions, it is almost impossible not to mix business and pleasure . . .

Can the two thwart Edward Pennington's plans for the store? Or will Edward prove himself an unshakeable force who will ultimately ruin both Elizabeth and Joseph?